It's a cold war on ice as love and defection breed murder at the Winter Olympics. Who killed world champion skater Dima Kuznetsov, the "playboy of the Eastern world": old or new lovers, hockey right-wingers, jealous rivals, the KGB? Will skating sleuth Lesley Grey discover the murderer before she herself is hunted down?

Death Spiral

Murder at the Winter Olympics

Meredith Phillips

Death Spiral

Murder at the Winter Olympics

A mystery from **Perseverance Press**
Menlo Park, California

Design and cover by Paul Quin.
Typography by John Hammett.

Copyright © 1984 by Meredith Bowen Phillips. Published by

Perseverance Press
P.O. Box 384
Menlo Park, California 94026

Manufactured in the United States of America.

1 2 3 — 86 85 84

Library of Congress Catalog Card Number: 83-62624

ISBN: 0-9602676-1-1

To **Peter**
who is why I am
an Anglophile

Many thanks to the following people who shared information and expertise: Ian Anderson of the United States Figure Skating Association, Bob Paul of the United States Olympic Committee, Kitty Carruthers, Richard Dalley, Patrick Sullivan M.D., and Vladislav Krasnov. Any errors of fact or interpretation in this book are the responsibility of the author, and should not be attributed to any of these people who helped so generously. Thanks also to Karen Frederickson and the staff of the Menlo Park Public Library for years of courteous and efficient research assistance.

The author gratefully acknowledges the thoughtful support and encouragement of the following people who read and commented on various drafts: Richard Bevan, Patty and Patrick Sullivan, Linda and Brodie Lewis, Bill and Bebe Bowen, Mary Ann Seawell, Sandra Schlesinger, Chris Pearson, and Peter Phillips.

It's a cold war on ice as love and defection breed murder
at the Winter Olympics. Who killed world champion
skater Dima Kuznetsov, the "playboy of the Eastern
world": old or new lovers, hockey right-wingers, jealous
rivals, the KGB? Will skating sleuth Lesley Grey discover
the murderer before she herself is hunted down?

Death Spiral

Murder at the Winter Olympics

Olympia is a sacred place.
Anyone who dares to enter it by force of arms
 commits an offense against the Gods.
Equally guilty is he who has it in his power to avenge
 a misdeed and fails to do so.

—from the Olympic truce, eighth century B.C.

Prologue

The arena was cold and quiet. Rays of midafternoon sunlight slanting from the windows near the ceiling refracted and diffused the ice sheet's glitter. Quivering silver spangles danced on the walls.

But in the far corner, the reflections were rosy: an untimely sunset. Face down on the ice, a motionless figure sprawled with limbs splayed awkwardly. A trickle of blood dripped into a spreading puddle. The crimson shimmer tinted the ceiling.

At the door a shadowed shape watched, then slipped out noiselessly. The skating arena grew colder. No rescuer came.

1

The Olympic movement tends to bring together in a radiant union all the qualities which guide mankind to perfection.

—Baron Pierre de Coubertin, founder of the
modern Olympics

Shit, I don't think the medals are anything special; you can't do anything with them. I'd rather get a good warm-up suit—I could use that.

—Eric Heiden, speed skating, five gold medals
at Lake Placid, 1980

Wednesday, February 12, 1 P.M.

I had no premonition of disaster on that first day, nothing but the small nagging worry which had been my companion for weeks. There was no way for me to predict that these Olympics would be the deadliest since Munich.

Afterward, when I looked back, I wondered why I hadn't seen the warning signs on Opening Day, as the carillon of bells pealed through the snowy valley and echoed from the mountains—Squaw Peak, KT-22, Granite Chief. Flags of every color snapped and fluttered in the icy wind, belying the sun's warmth and the azure sky. Scattered around like children's blocks were primary-hued buildings in a jumble of geometric shapes. Once again, the Winter Games had come to Squaw Valley, California.

I squeezed into line behind the Union Jack. Looking around the crowd, I smiled at familiar faces: my coach in front with the officials, friends on the British team, fellow skaters from other countries. As a thousand athletes jostled into place for the opening parade, snow squeaked underfoot and fallen pine needles spiced the champagne air.

A head taller than most of the women, I was able to search the sea of faces fairly easily. I frowned as I scanned the USSR team, a mass of sable and sealskin.

"Hullo, Lesley," said my Olympic Village roommate as she squirmed through the crowd to a place by my side.

"Oh, Angela, have you seen Dima?"

"No, not today," she said, her eyes following my gaze toward the Russians. She grinned. "Looks like the usual mass slaughter on the steppes of Central Asia. Is it true all their furs are borrowed and have to be returned when they get home?"

"Yes, I think so. But wasn't Dima supposed to be their flagbearer? Who's that chap with the flag?"

A gaunt, dark man over six feet tall held the red banner, not the shorter and fairer figure I was seeking. "It's that cross-country skier, what's his name? Ivanov," Angela said.

My forehead creased into a worried grimace as I craned my neck. Angela squeezed my arm in annoyance. "Lesley, you're doing it again! Look, ducks, this is a once-in-a-lifetime experience. You're about to march into the Opening Ceremony of your first Olympics. You've worked toward this for half your life, and you're probably going to win a gold medal in figure skating in eight days' time. *Please* don't spoil it for yourself pining away for your lover! Comrade Dmitri bloody Kuznetsov can look after himself."

I bit my lip, then smiled into her exasperated face. "You're right, as always. Thanks, love." But my thoughts ran monotonously on in the same groove. Where is he? He wouldn't miss an honor like being flagbearer. Something must have happened to him. But what?

The pealing of the bells faded away, and from the loudspeakers trumpeted the opening notes of "Parade of the Olympians," played by the Marine Corps Band in Blyth Arena. Anticipation seemed to crackle in the air like static electricity.

The Greek flagbearer marched through the gate in the ten-foot

Village fence. The next teams followed alphabetically, headed by a girl or boy scout carrying a placard with each country's name.

Gaucho-caped Argentina were succeeded by Australia, then Austria. I began to feel stirred by the long-awaited spectacle, in spite of my worry over Dima and a stubborn feeling I shouldn't be moved by such a pretentious mass ritual. I watched bobbing flags I couldn't quite recognize, along with more familiar ones like Canada, China, the Federal Republic of Germany. Finland's blue cross and France's tricolor diplomatically intervened between the two separate German teams.

As the enormous delegation from the German Democratic Republic marched off, Angela asked, "Which one is that, then? I always get them mixed up."

"That's East Germany," I explained. "If a country's called 'People's' or 'Democratic,' you can always tell it's Communist. Ironic, that."

"Isn't that a goose-step?"

"Just about," I grinned. "Right, we're off."

Six-abreast behind our flagbearer, the British team shuffled through the Village gate past the covered practice rink. The route took us along the "Avenue of the Athletes," lined with snow sculptures of past gold medalists. We turned right between Jean-Claude Killy's and Eugenio Monti's statues to cross the Squaw Creek bridge. Brightly clothed spectators cheered, their applause mitten-muffled. Followed by television cameras, the army of athletes marched.

I passed a TV commentator doing a stand-up, and overheard: "Unlike the 1960 Games, the weather today is clear and sunny. You remember, Jim, the blizzard that year that postponed the Opening Ceremonies and Vice President Nixon's arrival. The snow stopped just as the Greek flagbearer entered Blyth Arena, and everyone said Walt Disney arranged it, along with the rest of the pageantry. . . ."

Past the aerial tramway we marched. The yellow cable car was ascending Emigrant Peak with a load of skiers bound for High Camp. Past the Lodge and the toylike red gondola. Around the hexagonal Spectator Center with its three triangular roofs, which gave watchers a bird's eye view and kids a slide. The throng covered the snowy ground so densely that the two outdoor practice rinks were the only visible patches of white.

"The funny thing about the Olympics," I said to Angela as we waved to the enthusiastic spectators, "is that so many people turn out in the cold to watch sports they usually couldn't care less about."

5

"Right, they only seem to care once every four years, but then they're such fanatics," Angela replied, gesturing to the crowd like the Queen. "Why is that, do you know?"

"I suppose nationalism has reared its ugly head," I said wryly.

The multicolored snake of marchers looped around the oval past the VIP box, dipping each flag to the American Vice President, and lined up near the arena's cable-suspended orange bulk. Today its two-winged south wall was open and the wheeled grandstands swung out, turning the rectangle into a U-shape. From Blyth Arena the audience would be able to see ski race finishes, ski jumping, hockey, and skating. The Nordic ski area was located a few miles down the highway, and the bobsled and luge were to take place in the nearby meadow and foothills of the compact site.

The crowd burst into frenzied cheers as the US team appeared. One hundred and fifty American athletes, in Levi Strauss cowboy uniforms complete down to red bandannas, waved their stetsons in response. As the flagbearer neared the tribune, Angela said mockingly, "*Will* he dip the flag, ladies and gents? No, just an eyes-right."

"They never do, ever since they refused to for Edward VII umpteen years ago. Now, it's actually a law passed by Congress that they can't."

"Well, why should anyone dip the flag, when you come to think about it? He's only the Vice President. Why doesn't their President ever come?"

"They say he's busy with the Pakistan crisis—no time for games."

Although I'd decided to relax and enjoy the show in spite of my worry over Dima's whereabouts, my eyes were drawn again across the oval to the Soviets, who were lining up four-abreast to look like an even larger team. The flagbearer, so definitely not Dima, had carried the Hammer and Sickle the whole distance with one outstretched arm, the silly twit. Dima wouldn't have shown off that way. Where on earth is he? All I bloody need is something more to worry about, after these past weeks when he's been so cool and distant. It's probably just that he's preoccupied with his own problems. Heaven knows he has a right to be.

A new thought struck me. Could they have found out? Oh, God, could they know? Maybe they've withdrawn him from the competition. Maybe he's already on that Aeroflot jet that's been standing by in Reno to whisk away anyone they have even a suspicion of. No, they couldn't know. Don't borrow trouble.

A few boos and one cry of "Go home!" greeted the USSR team, but polite, if lukewarm, applause predominated. The American team took its place next to the Russians, and the march ended with a fanfare of trumpets.

IOC President Baron Manfred von Mutzenbecher moved to the microphone, limping slightly on his gouty foot. Behind him the black cauldrons awaiting their flames flanked the towering steel framework with crests of each of the 35 countries at the Games. In back of the Tower of Nations curved a white wall which bore the laurel-encircled motto *Citius, Altius, Fortius* and, on either end, ice sculptures of a skier and a skater. The Sierra Nevada, marbled in glistening snow and dark evergreens, was a spectacular backdrop.

"Vice President Jeffries, members of the International Olympic Committee, and citizens of Squaw Valley, I welcome you to the XVIth Olympic Winter Games. May all contests be decided in fair spirit here in Squaw Valley, as once in the remote Peloponnesus. And so I say to you all, welcome to Olympia!

"The Olympic Games is mankind's largest gathering for the purposes of health, brotherhood, and athletic competition. Founded 2,768 years ago and revived by Baron Pierre de Coubertin in 1896 . . ."

My eyes wandered again to the Russians, then moved on to the nearby Mongolian team. Their flagbearer wore only a loincloth and a salmon-pink cape in spite of the 50-degree temperature. A fur cap and knee high curly-toed boots finished off his ensemble. I nudged Angela and pointed discreetly.

"Look at the other Mongolians—they're wearing business suits!" I whispered, overcome by giggles.

"I heard they were late, that lot. No one even knew they were coming, and yesterday they just appeared!" Angela muttered back, under the cover of a high school choir's uncertain rendition of the Olympic anthem.

The president of the US Olympic Committee now introduced past medal winners, seated in the boxes. I stood on tiptoe to see the legendary figures: Tenley Albright, Ingemar Stenmark, Janet Lynn, Sheila Young, Rosi Mittermaier, Mike Eruzione, Franz Klammer, Robin Cousins, Aleksandr Zaitsev. The thought of joining this glittering pantheon of Olympic gods raised gooseflesh on my arms, and for a moment I wanted the gold medal so desperately I could taste it—my mouth actually felt metallic.

"Is Irina Rodnina here too?" whispered Angela.

"No, she's back in the USSR. Ever since the Protopopovs' defection, they don't risk married couples both leaving unless they're competitors. Zaitsev's here because he's an ISU official." Everything conspired to remind me of the fate of would-be defectors.

Mutzenbecher called on the Vice President to open the Games, the traditional bit part usually played by the host country's head of state. Jeffries uttered the 13 rather redundant words he'd travelled across the country to say: "I declare open the Squaw Valley Games, celebrating the XVIth Olympic Winter Games." His wife by his side, he acknowledged the applause with an election-year smile.

The cheers abruptly broke off and turned to a confused hum, as a stooping elderly man in a ten-gallon hat shouldered his way to the microphone and took it from the surprised Vice President. We all craned our necks, sensing a disruption in the ceremony's routine. Six middle-aged people in bulky overcoats filed in front of the tribune and turned to face the crowd. There was definitely Something Wrong.

"Excuse me, Mr. Vice President, Mr. IOC President, ladies and gentlemen," he said in a high, cracked voice. "My name is Ulysees S. Whitman, and I represent PLAYFAIR. I'm going to impose on your time to make a brief announcement. Certain countries present here have flagrantly violated, and continue to violate, the sacred laws of the Olympics. I refer to the rules on amateurism. We all know who they are, and I say that they should be expelled and exposed for the cheaters they are!" He shook his fist and his flabby jowls quivered. Boos rang out, mixed with a few cheers and whistles.

The line of graying demonstrators pulled red, white, and blue-bordered picket signs from inside their coats and held them high. Some of the hand-scrawled messages were misspelled, with strange combinations of capital and lowercase letters: PROFESSIONALS OUT OF THE OLYMPICS, RUSSIA OUT OF PAKISTAN, GIVE HONEST AMATEURS A CHANCE. They waved their signs and chanted, "Russia out! Russia out!"

"Mr. Vice President," the old man orated, "these rotten apples must be thrown out of the barrel before their contamination spreads. How can our fine Free World athletes hope to compete fairly with government-supported professionals?"

Mutzenbecher, who had been sitting with one hand over his chagrined face, signalled to the security men flanking the tribune.

"I say, cast them out—" Two Secret Service agents grasped Whitman by the elbows and escorted him away from the microphone down the steps. His mouth still moved soundlessly like a goldfish's.

State police, the California Highway Patrol, swarmed toward the chanting picketers, who lay down in the snow and went limp.

"Shades of the sixties!" I said to Angela incredulously.

"Aren't they a little old for this sort of thing? How'd the old man get up there, anyway?"

"He's one of those eccentric millionaires. He paid for the bob and luge runs, so maybe he was up in the VIP box. That must be why the Secret Service didn't pile on top of him right away."

The Highway Patrol began to carry the protesters away. A white-haired woman, squawking indignantly, hit one patrolman with a sign. To her surprise, she was immediately handcuffed.

While they were being removed, Mutzenbecher apologized to the buzzing crowd and introduced the head of the organizing committee. The San Francisco industrialist took the rostrum to explain to the distracted audience why there were two Olympic torches instead of the usual single one. "In honor of the 1960 Games held here, we are lighting a second flame, as Innsbruck did in 1976. However, for the first time, we're bringing two Olympic flames halfway around the world from two different origins.

"At the sacred grove of the temple of Zeus an olive branch was lit by the sun's rays, and runners carried it from Olympia two hundred miles to Athens. The second was lit, as in 1960, at the cottage fireplace of Sondre Norheim, founder of Nordic skiing, and skiers took the torch one hundred and twenty miles across Norway to Oslo."

My feet began to ache. I shifted my weight and wished the speakers weren't quite so long-winded. I felt my nose going numb in the gathering chill.

"Five days ago in simultaneous ceremonies televised worldwide, laser and satellite transmitted the two flames, one from Athens to Los Angeles, and the second from Oslo to San Francisco. The transmission took one-twentieth of a second, and as Canadian Prime Minister Trudeau remarked in 1976, the ancient Greeks would have thought it an act of the gods."

My thoughts had returned to Dima as if to a sore tooth. Through a fog, I heard: "The two flames have been carried, by fifty runners each, across California with ceremonies along the way like the one televised last night from Donner Pass. Today both flames have arrived here, and in a moment you'll see them, just to the right of the ski jump. Penny Pitou and Betsy Snite, our 1960 Alpine silver medalists, will carry them down the mountain. There they are!"

The crowd murmured as the skiers appeared, each bearing a butane torch high in one hand, and wedeled down the mountain in graceful S-curves. Each torchbearer was the point of an arrowhead of six skiers, American medalists listed by the announcer. The murmur swelled to a deep-throated roar as the skiers stop-christied in sprays of snow on either side of the oval.

"Ladies and gentlemen, our 1960 gold medalists in figure skating, Carol Heiss and David Jenkins, will carry the flames on their last lap."

The white-clad skaters took the torches and glided round opposite sides of the oval to the waiting urns. As the roars crescendoed, they climbed the stairs and ignited the twin flames. The band and chorus crashed into the choral theme from Beethoven's Ninth. *"Freude, schoner Götterfunke!"* rang through the frosty air.

I became even more achingly aware of Dima's absence. He should have been here to share the ceremony with me, even though nationalism would have placed us on opposite sides of the arena. In a mystical way, I felt that the ritual would have united us, almost like a wedding ceremony. Gold medals and Olympic rings would have served as tokens of the matrimonial bands I longed for.

"Rather impressive," I said to Angela, swallowing.

"Yes, considering the rehearsal yesterday. I heard the bandleader say, 'If anyone knows the "Ode to Joy," raise your hand!'"

"Oh, look at the doves—aren't they lovely!" I was moved by the ceremony, and Angela's flippancy now irritated me. I knew that the cynicism was only a cover-up for my friend's profound underlying respect for the Olympics, but I wished Angela would just pack it up.

"Pigeons, love. Cover your head."

Inside the arena, a hundred cages opened simultaneously. Thousands of birds wheeled and fluttered toward the light, then flew off to the west.

"Off they go! Uh oh, that one's heading toward Reno," said Angela. "Oh, my God, look who's going to take the athletes' oath for all of us. The Ice Queen herself, Miss Kimberly Cranford."

The brunette US skating champion grasped the corner of the American flag and recited, almost inaudibly, "In the name of all competitors I promise that we will take part in these Olympic Games, respecting and abiding by the rules which govern them, in the true spirit of sportsmanship, for the glory of sport and the honor of our teams."

"Too bad her mother isn't bound by that oath," Angela whispered.

As the Olympic flag slowly ascended to the strains of *Fanfare for the Common Man*, Angela looked at me in surprise. "Are those tears in your eyes, love? But you said you think all this pomp and circumstance is a load of old rubbish!"

I swallowed and wiped my eyes. "I suppose, deep inside, I don't really. Amazing how one's drawn in, no matter how contrived it is. As you said yourself, we *have* spent half our lives trying to get to the Olympics. And we did it! We're here, and part of it all. Isn't it miraculous?"

Angela squeezed my hand contritely. We smiled at each other and listened to the national anthem and three-gun salute. Thousands of balloons, released by children on skates, rose till they were confetti against the bright blue.

After the IOC president's farewell the athletes marched out, falling into informal groups and chattering in our Babel of languages. Most headed back toward the Village, to change into practice clothes and scatter to the slopes and rinks.

Anxiety and curiosity again bobbed to the surface of my mind. I hurried to catch up with the Soviet team, looking around for Dima's coach or some sympathetic person who might know what had happened to him. I didn't know all the Russian skaters, and had no desire to speak to Nina or Pavel. One never knew who might show up on the Soviet team, aside from a few world champions; injuries and political manipulations constantly changed the roster. But then I spotted a friend, Dima's roommate Nikolai Skachko, who was walking with his wife and skating partner Katya Kulakova. They were wearing their matching medals, the Order of Lenin.

"Nikolai Aleksandrovich," I called, using his patronymic as Dima had taught me to do in addressing Russians. "Where's Dima? Why wasn't he your flagbearer?" I pretended nonchalance, probably unsuccessfully.

"Ah, Lesley. This morning our team leader Nokitov called Dima to meeting. He tell him they decided he's not carrying flag, for good of team. He say too tiring for him. They make Anatoli Mikhailovich Ivanov the flagbearer, say is better. Dima's coach Bogachev telling him he must practice during ceremony."

"Oh, I see," I breathed in relief. "What a shame! Was Dima angry?"

"Sure. He throw a few things in our room. Then he calm down. He say he don't care, he marched in last Olympics at Calgary—bloody

11

bore. He say he need to work on figures, also his quadruple toe loop keep turning to triple."

"Why are they disciplining him?"

"Who knows?" put in Katya. "Maybe they think he's prima donna, gets too many attentions. They are always saying he acts like superstar and should consider more the collective effort of the team."

"Probably is too much vodka, parties, break training," said Nikolai, shaking his head disparagingly. "He never come back to our room before dawn."

Katya poked him in the ribs and frowned. "Kolya, don't say foolish things," she said sharply.

"Lesley knows this already. Or maybe they are having other reasons we don't know. Sorry, Lesley."

"It's okay. *Do svidanya.*" I looked round for Angela, but she was talking to her ice dancing partner, so I walked on alone, my steps lightened by relief. I thought with amusement that Dima had everyone fooled with his playboy act, even his roommate. The world suddenly looked brighter. Two kids swordfighting with icicles brought a smile to my face.

Autograph-seekers stopped me a few times, but here in the US I was overshadowed by Kim Cranford, though the British press hounded me at home in baying packs. Kim stood surrounded by fans and reporters outside the Squaw Valley Inn. How these Americans idolize their Olympic athletes, I thought—once every four years, anyway. Thank God, I don't have to deal with pressure like that this time, everyone counting on the golden girl to win. Not worth the home-field advantage. And it's especially heavy for American skaters, I reflected, because it's the only winter sport the US excels in.

I threaded my way through more picketers from PLAYFAIR, and other political groups as well, with their own axes to grind: READMIT TAIWAN. BOYCOTT SOUTH AFRICAN RUGBY.

"*Bonjour*, Lesley. *Comment ça va?*" Jean-Marc Caron greeted me. I saw his sister Danièle, nicknamed Dany, talking to the American men's champion Matt Galbraith. As we exchanged skaters' small talk, I realized I'd never seen the twin French pair skaters apart, except in the Village dormitories where men and women were housed separately. (That was why Nikolai was Dima's roommate in Placid, while his wife was in St. Moritz, the women's building. It was off-limits to men upstairs, though women could enter the three men's dormitories.) The Caron twins had shocked straight-laced American skating officials with their insistence on sharing the same dressing room, as they did in Europe. Something about them put me off, and I wondered, not for the first time, exactly what it was. Probably their arrogance, chauvinism, and total absorption in each other.

"Hey Jean-Marc, how's it goin', man? Hi, Les. Where's your little friend?" Matt Galbraith joined us, and I stared at the American skater's sardonic, auburn-bearded face in annoyance.

"If you mean Dima, that's what I'm on my way to find out," I said coldly. "And you're not to call me Les." Little friend, indeed! I didn't know which I resented most: his snide implication that Dima was always with me, or that he wasn't with me when he should be, or that he was several inches shorter than Matt and in fact just matched my own height of five feet nine. Cheeky beggar, I thought. Why is he always so abrasive?

The Carons chattered about schedules—"Do you know when they expect us to practice? Two till four o'clock in the morning! *Sacrebleu!*" —and their parade uniforms—"Not at all chic, these stripes"—as we sauntered across the bridge toward the Village.

"Matt, you must explain why the American President never condescends to open the Olympics," said Dany indignantly. "De Gaulle was at Grenoble in 1968, and in every other country the head of state always attends. It's an insult to the athletes!"

"I don't know why," Matt answered, "but it's true that he always seems to send the Vice President. Either he's busy campaigning or he seems to think the crisis of the moment is more important. Let's see, Carter sent Mondale, Eisenhower sent Nixon, and even back in 1932, New York Governor Franklin Roosevelt stood in for President Hoover. Or should I say, sat in?"

"Oh, Matt, that's sick," I said with distaste. I stopped at the door to the practice rink, outside the Village fence. "Go on ahead, I'll just see if Dima's still practicing."

The others looked at me curiously. "Hmm. Now, is he really that much of a perfectionist, or has he been a naughty boy?" Matt asked with a smirk. As I opened the door, they crowded after me into the dim arena.

I noticed the pink reflections on the far wall first, and wondered in confusion if it were sunset yet. Then I saw him, a motionless figure sprawled on the ice. One eye in the dead-white profile stared sightlessly into a crimson puddle of blood.

13

Thus, in a pageant show, a plot is made,
And peace itself is war in masquerade.
—Dryden

"**M**on Dieu!"

"Oh, God, it's Dima!"

"Run for a doctor, Dany! Jean-Marc and I will get him off the ice," Matt said, seeing that I was standing frozen. The door banged behind Dany's running figure. Matt yanked off his cowboy bandanna and pressed it against Dima's forehead, which still oozed blood.

"Is he dead?" I asked in a trembling voice. Falls are common in skating, but I'd never seen such a pool of blood as the one around Dima, and he was so frighteningly still. I felt as if I might faint. My limbs were numb and my head light, full of buzzing echoes.

15

"No, I can just feel a pulse. Unconscious, though. Jean-Marc, you take his legs and I'll take his arms. Lesley, you support his head."

"Should we not leave him?" Jean-Marc argued. "There might be broken bones, even his spine."

"I don't think so. Skaters bounce like rubber. We should have kept your sister here for first aid—she's a medical student, isn't she?"

We picked him up gently and eased him through the gate in the barrier onto the rubber flooring. I cradled his head in my lap and stroked the fair hair, all matted with blood. The American took off his sheepskin jacket and tucked it around Dima's unconscious form.

"Oh, Matt, he's so cold!" I cried frantically. "And all that blood!"

"Of course he's cold, you silly girl," Matt snapped. "He's been lying on the ice for God knows how long. Don't you know a scalp wound always bleeds like a stuck pig? He'll be all right. You'll be more help if you don't have hysterics."

"But what if he's in shock, damn it?" I glared at him, then made an effort to pull myself together. "Okay, steady on, Lesley. Let's see— treatment for shock. Warmth, what else? Put his feet up. Pull that chair over, Jean-Marc." As I propped Dima's feet on the seat of the folding chair, his right skate blade wobbled. I automatically noted from the large toe pick and heavy boot that it was for freeskating, not figures. I quickly looked at the sole where the toe- and heelplates were screwed on.

"Look! Some of the screws are loose, and one's sheared right off! Here's one bent sideways." At a touch, it fell out into my hand. The two men examined the underside of the boot.

"Is that his landing foot?" Matt asked. "What jump was he practicing?"

"Nikolai said he was going to work on the quadruple toe loop. Yes, the right's his landing foot." I walked onto the ice and looked at the deep rut the toepick had made, then at the wooden barrier. "But he would've been skating backward toward the boards when he landed; could he have hit his head on them? Yes, here's some blood—and his head dented the wood!" I laughed shrilly, then forced myself to stop. I didn't want Matt to accuse me again of hysteria.

"You can't tell which direction he was facing when he fell," Matt said. "It could've been the middle of a revolution, if the screws gave way when he jumped off that foot."

Jean-Marc unlaced Dima's boot and glanced around. "There is his

16

skatebag, I will put them inside. He would not want to lose them if they can be repaired."

"Don't worry, the Politburo will buy him a new pair," said Matt sarcastically.

I took Dima's gloves off and held his cold hands, unable to think of anything else to do. I was still numb with shock, but knew now I wouldn't faint. I gazed round the rink, seeing from the ice nearer the door that Dima had first been practicing figures: doing his patch, in skaters' jargon. The brackets and counters, complicated variations of the figure 8, were heavily inscribed on the ice in several places. Dima's red warm-up jacket with its white cccp was draped over the barrier near the figures, and I pointed it out to Jean-Marc. As he put it in the bag, I asked, "Are his figure skates inside?"

"*Mais oui*, all dried off with their guards on."

I stared blankly at the snailshell spirals and tracings while I rubbed Dima's frigid hands between mine and tried to reconstruct what had happened from the hieroglyphics on the ice. Say he'd patched for an hour, then he must've just begun his freestyle practice. Around the edge of the ice the marks looked like he'd done some power-stroking laps, and a few jumps and spins to warm up. Something in the center of the ice struck me as strange, out of place. Had he been alone here? Dima stirred and moaned faintly, and my attention snapped back to him.

"*Ici, madame. Et voilà.*" Dany hurried in with Dr. Sologubova, followed by two paramedics. The matronly Russian doctor quickly checked Dima's heartbeat, pulled up his eyelids, and examined the head wound.

She leaned over and shouted in his ear: "Dima! Dima!" He groaned again. "Open your eyes!" He looked around blankly. "Do you know who I am?"

"Doctor. Dr. Sologubova. What happened?"

"You tell us, my friend."

"Don't know."

"How long he has been here?" she asked us.

"We don't know," I said. "We just found him."

"Did you move him off the ice? A fractured neck is the main concern." Jean-Marc stared smugly at Matt.

"We steadied his head," Matt explained, "and kept his neck in the same position. I was worried about hypothermia or frostbite."

17

"Frostbite of his face is possible—that's the only part of his skin that would have touched the ice. I don't think we have to worry about hypothermia, it's not that cold in here." As she spoke, the doctor gently lifted each arm and leg, then pressed on his collarbone and pelvis. "He doesn't seem to have any fractures, and his reflexes are normal." She immobilized his neck in a whiplash collar. "Dima, do you know where you are?"

"Practice rink."

"Who are these people?" she tested him.

He smiled weakly at me and said, "Hello, *deushka*." His eyes flickered toward the others. "Dany, Jean-Marc. Hey, Matt, don't count me out yet on that gold medal."

The doctor supervised her assistants as they rolled him onto the stretcher. When they had carried him out the door, I asked, "Can you tell yet if he'll be all right?" I clasped my hands together till the knuckles whitened.

"I have to do more tests, of course. A complete neurological exam for brain damage; head and neck X rays. I'll look for subdural hematoma—that's bleeding inside the brain." Her voice trailed off into a mutter, then she suddenly smiled, lightening the impact of her ominous words. "I hope I don't have to shave off any of that beautiful golden hair to stitch the cut."

"Oh, Doctor, will he be well enough to compete?" I asked, my voice wobbling.

"Too early to say, but he's a tough little bird. When does the men's competition begin? Six days? Well, we shall see." Her eyes twinkled. "If the vodka's left him with any liver function, he'll recover all right, barring complications. A day or two for observation and rest, then back on skates, yes?"

"Can't I come to hospital with him?" I pleaded.

"*Nyet*, you be in the way. Come tonight if you wish, only briefly."

The doctor climbed into the back of the ambulance and pulled the doors closed. We watched it drive away toward the tiny Quonset hut hospital at the back of the Village. I'd been there myself only once, to receive the ludicrous "Certificate of Femininity" issued after an examination of the chromosomes of cells scraped from the inside of the mouth.

"Where's Fyodor?" Matt suddenly asked. "I thought he never left Dima's side." The hulking KGB man was listed on the official roster as a trainer, but he was really a bodyguard and unofficial shadow—more

18

to protect Dima from thoughts of defection than from any outside threat. The Russian slang described his function accurately: he was a *mamka,* a nanny or babysitter.

"He is Dima's interpreter, *n'est-ce pas?*" Dany asked.

"Interpreter, my ass!" Matt snorted. "Dima speaks English better than Fyodor does."

"*Eh bien,* don't look so worried, Lesley. It does not seem serious. He will be all right soon." That's easy for you to say, I thought in annoyance, as I thanked them and replied distantly to their offhand "*à bientôt.*" The French pair walked off arm-in-arm, pausing at the gatehouse to show their credentials and skatebags to the Pinkerton guard, and passed through the metal detector.

"They look like Shields and Yarnell, the mime team, don't they?" said Matt, staring after them. "With that straight black hair and those unisex haircuts, I always have to look twice to see which is which unless Dany has a skirt on."

"Right. Well, thanks for your help, Matt."

"No sweat. Say, you want to have a cup of coffee or a drink?"

"Oh, I don't know. I don't think so."

"Come on, you could probably use a drink after that. Besides, there's something I want to ask you."

"All right," I agreed, vaguely curious. "The Five Circles bar?" We began to walk toward the day lodge, Olympic House.

"You'd better take off your coat if you don't want to attract attention. It has bloodstains all over it."

"Oh, dear." I looked down at my white maxi-coat, remembering with a pang Dima's head cradled in my lap. I took the coat off and draped it over my arm, retying the wool Union Jack-patterned scarf around my neck. My red jersey and blue stretchpants were warm enough for the short walk.

We hung our coats on wall hooks and found a table in the crowded bar. "What do you want?" Matt asked as the waiter approached. "Campari and soda? I'll have an Anchor Steam."

When the waiter had gone, he said, "It's a good thing they don't check ID's, at least for age, during the Olympics. I'm twenty-four, but twenty-year-olds usually can't drink in California."

"Oh, right, I forgot. I'm still used to pubs."

"Even after living for a year in Colorado?"

"Actually, I don't drink much at all, so I don't go to many bars. What did you want to ask me?"

He began to tear a cocktail napkin carefully into strips, then said in a low voice, "Do you think what happened to Kuznetsov just now was an accident?"

My eyes widened. "My God. I don't know, I haven't had time to think. You mean sabotage or something?"

"It's not impossible, is it?"

"Someone sneaked in with a screwdriver while he was engrossed in his paragraph brackets?" I asked skeptically. "What utter rot. The force of the quad was just too much for the screws."

"Bullshit. I bet he checked them automatically every practice, just like I do. I have a quadruple jump too, and my blades are holding up okay."

"Well, the chances of causing an injury by doing something like that must be rather slim. As you said yourself, skaters usually bounce."

The waiter set the drinks down. "That'll be five dollars."

Matt slapped his pockets. "Haven't a cent. Do you have any money?"

"No, sorry," I said. Typical, I thought.

"We'll catch you later, okay?" Matt said. The waiter looked dubious. "Look, we're competitors, we're not going to skip town. We'll hock our gold medals to make sure you get paid."

I took a long swallow and began to relax as the Campari's warmth flooded through me. Once again pushing down my anxiety over Dima's injury and the deeper, colder fear beneath it, I watched the ebb and flow of people through the crowded room. Matt moodily stared into his beer glass, picking it up and putting it down to make an Olympic pattern of five wet rings.

After a while, I said, "Well, if it were sabotage, who did it? And why?"

"Who knows? Maybe one of those anti-Communist zealots we saw at the Opening Ceremony. Or maybe, on the other hand, the KGB. I find Fyodor's absence a little suspicious."

"That's absurd, he's here to protect Dima."

"Not doing too well, is he? I wouldn't rule out a KGB plot. And probably a few women have it in for the Warren Beatty of the skating world, as well. How about Nina Aleksandrova?" He scrutinized my face intently.

"What about her?" I said noncommittally. A picture of my Russian rival floated through my mind: cold, haughty, and graceful, wearing her world champion's gold medal.

"Come on, you know she and Dima were lovers."

"Past tense."

"Dima may have moved on to plowing—if you'll pardon the expression—new pastures, but I think she's still hot for him." My lips tightened as I bit back a sharp retort. He went on, "And I think she could be very jealous, and very vindictive."

I was about to tell him it was utter rubbish when I heard, "Hi, Matt. And Lesley Grey—the very person I've been looking for!" I glanced up and saw an attractive, silver-haired man with an orange journalist's credential hanging around the neck of his black parka.

"Hullo, Josh," I said, shaking his hand warmly. "How've you been? I haven't seen you since last year's Worlds, but I read your column faithfully."

"I've kept up with you, my dear, you've been making quite a splash in the skating world. A meteoric rise in fact, to mix metaphors. Could we make an appointment for an interview? How about tomorrow at two? Fine, let's meet at the coffee bar then. So long."

I watched him walk out, greeting people along the way. Everyone seemed to know him. I put on a blasé front, but beneath it I was thrilled by the legendary *New York Times* sportswriter's interest. He was a star-maker.

"He's okay," Matt announced. "He won't do a hatchet job on you. He did a nice piece about me during Nationals."

"Glad you approve," I said shortly. "If that's all you had to tell me, I really must go now. I want to have a quick meal and visit Dima in hospital."

"I'm trying to do you a good turn," he said in an injured tone. "Watch out for Nina Aleksandrova. I don't think she'd stop at anything. She's really hung up on the guy."

"Why do you think so?" I asked reluctantly.

"I've seen the way she looks at him. And at you—if looks could kill, you'd be leaving here in a body bag."

"Don't be ridiculous," I snapped.

"Last year, during the skating tour after Worlds, I usually had the hotel room next to Kuznetsov's. One time—" He began to laugh in a leering sort of way. "One time, a friend of his was knocking on the other wall to warn him the chaperone was coming. You probably know his bed check routine by now!" Matt chortled. "And he must have been humping Nina up against the wall, because they were banging away so hard they couldn't even hear the knocking! From her

21

moans and screams, it was standing-O time. And I don't mean ovation."

I furiously pushed back my chair, hitting a passing skier. "I didn't come here to listen to filthy stories!" I hissed in an angry whisper. "Don't do me any more favors."

"Say, is he really that good?" Matt sprawled back in his chair, still smirking. "Hey, wait a minute—"

I snatched my coat and stalked out the door. Striding toward the Village, I let the frosty air cool my hot cheeks. I tried never to think about Dima making love to another woman, and Matt's description had been so uncomfortably graphic. At least, I knew he had no interest in Nina any longer. But was she really still carrying a torch?

I slowed my pace, half-noticing a figure in a black coat some way behind me, who also slowed down. We were momentarily the only people in the icy landscape; dinner must have begun.

The sun had dropped behind Squaw Peak, and the western faces of the snowy mountains blushed rosily against the darkening sky. I shivered. The alpenglow looked so much like the reflections of Dima's blood on the walls and ceiling of the ice rink. The doctor's words came back: 'Subdural hematoma'—what was that? It sounded dreadful. I'd better find out more about it.

I passed through the gate and turned toward the Athletes' Center, joining the stream of people headed for dinner. When I glanced back, the person in black had been absorbed by the crowd.

At the cloakroom outside the cafeteria, I checked my coat and stuffed my scarf and gloves into the patch pockets. Paper crackled inside one of them; I didn't remember putting anything there. I pulled out a folded note. It read: WHY DON'T YOU GO BACK TO RUSSIA WITH YOUR COMMIE BOYFRIEND? WE DON'T WANT TRAITORS HERE.

Crumpling it in disgust and dropping it into a trashbasket, I joined the line outside the cafeteria door. I scanned the four-language menu board and signed in exasperation. It looked as if Matt Galbraith and his teammates had been at it again. They thought it great fun to scramble the letters of the English and French language dishes—and maybe the Russian and Japanese, who could tell?—to spell their own humorous versions. Tonight the menu's theme was "American Night"; the soups were listed as Scream of Tomato and Mashroom Soap. Cold Buffet became Cold Muffet, and Roasted Chicken Livers had turned into Raped Chicken Lovers. Also on the menu were Roast Turk with Cranberry Belly, and Donner Surprise.

I'd known Matt was cynical and cocky; he seemed to be rude and childish as well. I'd never liked his constant stream of sarcastic wise-cracks and usually tried to avoid him. He had all the qualities I disliked most in Americans. And how could he say such crude, hurtful things to me? He must know I'm in love with Dima. Still, to be fair, he had been concerned after the accident, and had done all he could when I was catatonic with shock. He was a good skater too, a lyrical stylist, though he lacked the robust athleticism of Dima's virile performances. I couldn't really detest skaters as accomplished as Matt or the Caron twins, even though I found them unpleasant off the ice.

Skirting a rowdy table of American hockey players, I carried my tray over to a group of figure skaters although the Carons were among them. Like most competitors, I socialized not with my countrymen, but within my own sport. Many of us had been acquainted for years and saw each other regularly at competitions. Familiar faces seemed to mean more than chances to broaden friendships. After all, I had more in common with even a Chinese skater than with a British luger or ski jumper.

Jean-Marc was complaining about American food. "When we were on the US tour after Worlds last year, we were offered virtually nothing but *le fast-food*. McDonald's, Big Boy, Denny's, Howard Johnson's everywhere. It took weeks back in Paris afterward to restore our palates. I felt unwell for the entire tour. My liver was affected. I was constipated, and I had a sore throat that lasted a month."

"I gained four kilos," chirped Dany. "You could hardly lift me, could you, *chéri*? Your throat infection probably lingered so long because of the poor nutrition here. Americans eat too many processed foods—refined flour, preservatives, no fiber, too much sugar. With the American cuisine, one must drink a large quantity of milk to get proper nourishment; *mais alors*, we don't like milk." She sipped the burgundy the French team had imported by the case, not trusting Californian wine.

"There is no cuisine," said Jean-Marc scornfully, "unless *le sandwich de beurre d'arachide*, the peanut butter, is considered a cuisine."

"Steady on, Dany," said Nigel Dodson, Angela's ice dancing partner. He raised his voice over the hockey players' din. "Since you've learned so much about nutrition in medical school, you must know that the average French diet is a bit lacking—from that standpoint, anyway. Coffee and croissants for breakfast; the American breakfast of fruit and cereal is better for you by half."

"And French lunches are so heavy," I added, "with too many sauces and sweets." The French must be kept in their place.

"*Bien sûr,* but we have the fresh fruits and vegetables, always what is in season. Our soup is marvelous—soup to Americans means opening a tin. And our portions are moderate. How much food do restaurants here throw away each day? It's a scandal!"

There was a thump. A hard roll hit the top of Dany's head and fell into her lap. She looked around, astonished. The boisterous hockey players were having a food fight. The captain, Bruno Novak, shook up a can of Coke and sprayed his teammates. Vinnie Luciano, the goalie, pelted the wing with mashed potatoes.

"At last," said Jean-Marc with disdain, "the proper use for American food."

Jell-O, spaghetti, and cole slaw began to fly as the combat escalated. People nearby ducked and moved away. Nigel picked up the roll that had hit Dany and walked over to Bruno.

"I think this belongs to you, old man. It hit an innocent bystander." A piece of lemon meringue pie caught him squarely in the face.

"Oh, excuse me, old man, you're a figure skater, aren't you?" mocked Novak, imitating Nigel's accent. "Or are you one of those bisexual biathletes? I guess we're too rough for you genteel fellows. A thousand pardons."

I left them to it, and headed like a homing pigeon toward the little hospital at the back of the Village. Outside Dima's room, Fyodor stood sentry.

I greeted him. "What happened today? Why weren't you there?"

A vodka-scented stream of Russian was his reply. Since his English was usually adequate for simple conversations, he apparently didn't want to talk to me. He turned his back rudely and didn't prevent me from entering the room.

Propped up on pillows with a white bandage rakishly encircling his head, Dima grinned at me, making my heart leap.

"I'm not dead yet, so don't look so worried, *deushka.*" I kissed him lingeringly, and handed him some grapes cadged from dinner.

"I have to worry, it's my nature. What happened, darling?" I pulled a chair close to the bed.

"How do I know? The last thing I remember is tracing those damn paragraph brackets for about the thirtieth time."

"Who else was there?"

"No one," he said.

"Are you sure? I somehow had the impression that someone else had been practicing."

"I don't think so."

"You don't recall doing any jumps?"

"No, I don't even remember putting on my freestyle skates. But I must have done, because no one could give his head a bump like this doing figures."

"But they *were* on," I said, puzzled. "And about four of the screws were either loose or bent—one sheared right off. You must have got a bit careless about checking them. And your figure skates were in your bag, dried off, with the guards on."

Dima frowned and tried to rub his forehead, but it was covered with bandages so he massaged the bridge of his Roman nose instead. "Shit, my head hurts, more than any hangover I ever had. Is worse when I try to think. And I've caught a cold or the Olympic flu. Give me a handkerchief."

"You must have concussion, that's why you can't remember. But where was Fyodor while you were practicing?"

"I said he could watch Ceremonies, he'd see lots of pretty girls in tight sweaters."

"Have you had X rays and things?"

"Yes, everything looks okay, the doctor said."

"I'll let you sleep now, darling. She said I shouldn't stay long. Did she tell you when you can get up?"

"*Nyet*, the old *babushka* won't say. But I get up when I'm ready, don't worry."

I kissed his beloved cheek, again its normal rosy tan instead of the blanched whiteness that had frightened me so, and left him, feeling much happier.

Freeskating practice was scheduled for 8:00, so I went back to my dormitory, St. Moritz, to change clothes and collect my skates. The flat-roofed block, adorned with hanging stalactites of ice, seemed like home after two weeks there. In the crowded lounge, a guitarist competed with rock blaring from the radio. An Italian journalist was trying to interview a skier from the Italian Tyrol who spoke only German. I waved to Angela, who was beading a costume while talking shop with a Hungarian ice dancer. A camera flashed, and I saw the back of a sleek dark head and heard a babble of French. Apparently Dany Caron was being interviewed by a crew of reporters and photographers from *Paris Match*.

I climbed the two flights of stairs and opened the fire-door onto my corridor. Kim Cranford, nude except for a towel around her head, walked out of her room next to mine toward the bathroom. She loved to walk about starkers, showing herself off. A brunette in tricolor-striped French team warm-ups went into a room down the hall. That's odd, I thought, didn't I just see Dany? It must have been Jean-Marc downstairs. They truly are clones.

I opened my door and gasped. The floor was strewn with our belongings. The open closet door gaped at empty drawers, with clothes covering the room in tumbled heaps. The razor-sharp blades of Angela's dance skates had torn a jagged rent in her costume. Cosmetics and the contents of the medicine cupboard were all over the place; books and papers were scattered as if by a hurricane. I stood still for a moment, trying to take it in, then ran back down to the lounge to tell my roommate.

"Bloody hell!" Angela jumped up, and her box of beads overturned and scattered under the feet of the journalists who were saying *au revoir* with handshakes and kisses on both of Dany's cheeks.

"We'd better tell the security guard." We dodged round the group and ran to the desk which guarded the living quarters from men and outsiders.

The middle-aged guard shook her head sadly at the carnage. "We've had some other vandalism before, I'm sorry to say. What a shame! All I can tell you is that no one has been allowed upstairs who doesn't live here. No officials or reporters, and of course no men at all. Awful to think it's one of the girls doing this. Is any money missing?"

Mine wasn't, but Angela thought some of her traveler's cheques might have been pinched. She offered to clear up the mess so I wouldn't miss my practice. I agreed guiltily, grabbed my skatebag, and hurried through the Village gate past the practice rink.

I tried to replace its inevitable reminder of the unconscious figure of the afternoon with the more robust one I'd seen a while ago in hospital. At least, now I have some brand-new worries to take my mind off the old ones, I reflected wryly, as I picked my way through the crowd leaving the hockey match and the chanting parade of PLAYFAIR pickets. It's surprising how violated one feels when one's possessions have been rifled. I was beginning to wonder if there were a systematic campaign on to harass the athletes.

But skating worked its magic as always, and I was soon totally absorbed, body and mind, in its exacting and exalting discipline. Swooping, slashing, gliding, and swirling, I was oblivious to time as an hour flew by. My concentration was so complete that I didn't even hear the Zamboni ice-resurfacing machine till it was grinding its way along the ice toward me.

Sitting down in the front row of the stands to wipe her perspiring face was Nina Aleksandrova. I took the seat next to her.

"Did you hear about Dima's accident today?" I asked.

"*Da,*" the Russian said flatly.

"How could such a thing have happened?"

"How should I know?" she replied in an insolent tone, adjusting a hairpin in her French-braided blonde hair.

"I rather thought you might."

"*Nyet.* Dmitri Pyotrovich means nothing to me, less than this bit of dust." She flicked a speck of dandruff from her shoulder. "But why don't you ask Kim?" she said with malice in her voice, flashing her hazel eyes upward.

"Kim Cranford? Why?" I turned to look at Kim ten rows above. Her curly dark head was bent in an earnest conference with her coach. Zack Higgins, bundled up in his usual black leather coat and gloves, gave me an impassive stare, then leaned solicitously toward Kim. When I turned back, Nina was gone.

I spent another hour on my serpentine footwork and triple lutz combination, then collected my gear. I strolled out of the arena toward the Village, my boots crunching in the snow, and gazed at the moonlight on the quiet hills. But as I rounded the back corner of the arena, the stillness of the scene was shattered by rowdy catcalls and drunken laughter. A dozen or so jostling people by the floodlit Tower of Nations were looking up and pointing at a tiny figure inching toward the top of a flagpole.

I supposed this must be the traditional Olympic prank of stealing a souvenir flag. I walked around the oval toward the group. Encouraged by his friends' yells, the man had almost reached the top. Leaning quite far out, he yanked at the Olympic flag to pull it from its moorings. He hoisted himself a bit higher, then seemed to slip. He made a desperate grab at the flapping flag, as if it could support him. Suddenly, he lost his grip and fell like a stone. Everyone froze. In the instant hush, his head hit the concrete base with a sickening thud. Someone screamed piercingly.

The scene lurched back into life as the crowd scattered. Some people knelt around the body, and others ran for help. A hulking figure cannoned into me, knocking me down. He muttered something that sounded like Russian, then ran off, followed by half a dozen others.

I was sprawled on the freezing ground near the horribly injured man. He was Vinnie Luciano, the hockey player who'd been throwing food at dinner. His blue USA parka was darkened with the blood that poured from his head. Through my nauseated haze, it seemed squashed like a cantaloupe.

The Olympics do more good among nations than anything I know of.

—Bob Mathias, decathlon, two gold medals at
London, 1948, and Helsinki, 1952

It was a banality some time before I was born that the Olympic Games do about as much to induce good feeling in the world as summit conferences or world wars.

—William F. Buckley, Jr.

The next morning I awoke from a dream of Dima. We had been making love. It had seemed so real that I was still tingling with excitement. I stretched voluptuously, trying to remember where we'd been, which bed: the feather mattress in the Moscow flat, the ornate hotel bed in Paris, or the squeaky iron cot in Dima's Olympic Village room.

No, it was the Pullman berth, and no wonder. We'd spent the whole of the 24-hour trip on the California Zephyr from Denver to Truckee in my tiny compartment, missing all the gorgeous mountain scenery and emerging only for meals to the ribald jeers of his teammates in the dining car. I hugged the memory to me for a few more minutes of langorous delight: the rhythmic vibration of the wheels echoing our own passionate rhythm in the violet glow of the night light, the little room enclosing us in our world of love.

It hadn't been so right again ever since we'd arrived at Squaw Valley. He'd been distant and short-tempered. In fact, we hadn't made love for a week, had hardly been alone together. Sometimes I wondered if the wild, sweet yearning I felt for him was worth the heartaches, but whenever we made love, I knew it was.

I pushed back the down-filled quilt and tiptoed past my sleeping roommate through the dimly lit room, now set to rights again. The Olympic posters on the wall (SAPPORO 1972 and MOCKBA 1980) were barely visible, and the bright yellow and green furniture still looked gray in the half-light. The doorknob zapped me with the usual static electricity shock.

Surely it'll come right again, I thought, walking down the hall to the communal bathroom. We'll get through this bad patch after the Olympics when the pressure's off. It's better, really, not to see each other much while we're under such stress, both concentrating so desperately on winning.

If he defects . . . no, *when* he defects, the gold medal will be the prize he brings the West. The idea still gives me chills, even after two months of thinking about it. He *must* win the gold so his defection will be an even bigger blow to the Soviet Union. And *I* have to win so I can make stacks of money and pay off my crushing debts. And we both have to win because we are competitors, after all, and for years the medal has been on the horizon like a great golden sun, eclipsing everything else.

I closed the door of the bath cubicle, turned on the taps, then brushed my long dark hair hard, to banish scary thoughts. I twisted it to the top of my head in a straggly version of my usual skater's knot. As I looked in the mirror, I wondered why people say I'm beautiful. I think so only when my complexion is flushed like a peach from skating or love-making, my eyes big and emerald green. I have the kind of face that shows up well across an arena, like Peggy Fleming's, or on a giant cinema screen, like Jill Clayburgh's. But close up, I think my features are too large. At least my coloring is good, and my body, with long slim legs and firm breasts.

Soaping myself, I mused that I must be incurably English to bathe still and not shower, American-style. The building had only one bathtub per floor of fifty women, and lavatories and showers were dormitory-style. Kim Cranford had snapped that the Eastern bloc athletes would feel right at home, not being used to private plumbing. But I seldom had any competition for the bath in the morning, although after skiing it was more in demand. Fortunately, the Alpine skiers were all down on the ground floor—first floor, I reminded myself—so their noisy boots wouldn't disturb everyone.

I heard running footsteps and a banging door. Someone had made it into the toilet cubicle just in time to lose her breakfast. This wasn't the first time I'd heard that; it happened regularly during my early morning baths. I wondered if this woman I'd never seen was having morning sickness. Pregnancy scares are common among athletes in sports strenuous enough to cause amenorrhea, no periods, because of low body fat levels. The team doctor told me that almost half of all skaters, gymnasts, dancers, and runners have this condition. Birth control pills are the only way to peace of mind, since one is still fertile. I reminded myself to take my pill, then toweled off and rubbed lotion into my skin against the dryness of the air.

Dressed in my red team warm-up suit and Nikes, I descended the stairs and emerged from St. Moritz into the frosty air. The sound of snowcats came from Squaw Peak. Herringbone formations of soldiers were packing the overnight snowfall, followed by the blue snowsuited "clones" with brooms and shovels. Shivering, I jogged carefully down the icy path past Garmisch and Cortina to the dining hall, each breath burning my lungs. Unbelievably, someone was swimming laps in the outdoor pool—heated, of course, but what would getting out be like?

Really, I wondered, why does figure skating have to be a winter sport anyway? Competitions have been indoors ever since 1967, and they could be held in July as easily as in February. Considering the fact that I hate snow, cold, and icy mountains, it's rather surprising I'm here at all. The ice rinks are cold enough without sub-zero temperatures outside. At least the latest energy crisis has cured the Americans of heating their buildings to boiling-hot, so you don't sweat indoors in winter clothes anymore. As I entered the cafeteria, I smiled to myself at the memory of Auntie Mavis insisting on "wool next to the skin" every winter. An Italian with a *Club di Bob* emblem on his jacket broke off the aria he was singing to smile back and whistle lasciviously at me.

It was still well before 7:00, so I could breakfast alone as I preferred. Only a few athletes were scattered around the large wood and stone-panelled room under the flags, most of them reading *The Daily Olym-*

pian. I carried my tray of kippers and toast with marmalade (thoughtfully provided for the British team) to a table by the full-length window with a view of the mountains. When only my pot of tea remained, I found a *New York Times* on the newspaper rack (DEMONSTRATION MARS OPENING CEREMONIES) and turned to Josh McDonnell's column. Over the years it had evolved into a sports essay, leaving daily coverage to less senior reporters. The headline was:

Plus Ca Change . . .
By Josh McDonnell

Squaw Valley, CA, Feb. 12——"The more things change, the more they remain the same." Comparisons are inevitable between the 1960 Winter Olympics and the Games beginning today. Stories filed from Squaw Valley recently have been dominated by boycotts, court suits, political and environmental protest, construction injuries and cost overruns, price gouging, transportation problems, ski lift safety concerns, and the like.

Those who yearn for constancy in an inconstant world can be assured that some things never change. "Disputes and Confusion Embroil Winter Games Two Days Before Start," read a headline in this newspaper dated Feb. 17, 1960. A rival journal used this lead: "The dissension-packed eighth Winter Olympic Games will open tomorrow with Nationalist China and India still on the sidelines."

Disputes? Dissension? Did they go in for that way back in 1960, with Ike in the White House and the 50th star just added to the flag? We remember the first Squaw Valley Games fondly as the most peaceful, harmonious, cozy Olympics ever—and the last ones on a human scale. Those Games also pioneered the first artificial skating ice, the first use of computers for scoring, and the first Winter Olympic Village.

Most people have forgotten that the place was known as Squawk Valley for the five years of preparation preceding 1960. The feuders included local property owners whose lands were condemned, the California Legislature, the IOC, the bobsledding federation, the Forest Service, and the State Department. So much ire was in the air that Walt Disney, who organized the pageantry, suggested a man-made avalanche to bury the squabblers.

But what was all the ruckus about? I wasn't here; I was then still a copyboy, so I recently delved through microfilm and yellowing stacks of old newspapers. The trivia thus unearthed yields strong suspicions of journalistic overkill.

The sidelined Indian team mentioned in the article consisted of a single Denver University skier with a Polish name; he was ineligible because India was not a member of FIS, the skiing federation. Nationalist China likewise fielded a one-man team; he was denied entrance for reasons all too familiar by now. The IOC compensated the Formosan and the Polish-Indian for their disqualifications by making them official forerunners on the ski courses.

Other disputes: the East and West Germans were bickering. (Till 1968 they were a single team, half of which did not speak to the other half.) CBS-TV called the Japanese team "Japs" on the air, later apologized.

The State Department spokesman who called East German journalists "Commie agents in stretchpants" did not apologize. The hockey players and figure skaters argued about who had more ice time. The parking regulations were unpopular.

On Opening Day, there was only one attendant to collect parking fees, and he took half an hour to change a $50 bill while two miles of cars waited. The prices were too high: $5 for a lift ticket, 15¢ for coffee, 40¢ for a gallon of gas. (Read it and weep.)

Blyth Arena was so cold that shivering concessionaires had to put the coffee cream *in* the refrigerator to thaw it. Nevertheless, the sun melted the ice surface to slush. The organizers fixed that problem with a rope curtain that blocked the view of the ski jump. (The arena was renovated after the roof collapsed in 1983, and enclosed with a two-part glass window that permits the opening of the south wall.)

The speed skating timing devices were inadequate, the speed skating officials were inept, the Swedish cross-country skiers got lost in the woods, and a figure skater's (musical accompaniment) record was warped. Customs held up foreign athletes too long at the airports.

Big deal, huh?

To put the present and past Squaw Valley Games into perspective, most Olympics get a bad press at the time. Perhaps journalists make mountains from molehills of pettiness because TV's instant communication has made their reporting of medal winners and world records obsolete, and they have to write *something* interesting for you to read at breakfast the next day. Every Winter Olympics has suffered problems of cost, organization, transportation, and weather that are generally forgotten in a year or two, just as labor pains are said to be dimmed in memory before the next birth.

With our recollections of the genuine disasters of Mexico, Moscow, and especially Munich, why should I waste space writing about these trivial squabbles? With our hindsight vision of the perennial controversy and occasional tragedy that have engulfed the Games in ensuing Olympiads, why should you spend time reading this?

It never hurts to remember how we were before we lost our innocence. The Olympic Games in 1960 were still primarily an arena for athletic competition, not a political arena. And that it shouldn't be, regardless of the very real sufferings of American blacks or Afghan tribesmen or Palestinian refugees.

As Teddy Roosevelt said of the Presidency, the Olympics make "a bully pulpit," but this is not the place to right the world's wrongs.

More tomorrow.

"Hullo, Lesley." Angela, Nigel, and some other British teammates slid their trays onto the table.

"Have you all heard about the hockey player who fell from the flag-pole?" asked bobsledder Trevor Smith-Garnell, shoveling into his porridge.

"I saw it," I said with a shudder. "It was horrible."

"He's at hospital in Reno, in coma with a fractured skull and lots of broken bones," he went on ghoulishly.

"Fancy playing capture the flag at his age! Why didn't he just lower it instead of climbing the flagpole?" Angela asked.

"No sport in that," Trevor explained. "Anyway, the pulleys are pad-locked. Have you never looked at them?"

"No, it never occurred to me to pinch one. Boys will be boys—per-ennially," she said, raising her eyebrows sarcastically.

"Will they stop competition?" asked Gillian Herring, the British number two skater.

"Good Lord, no. Not even if he dies," said Nigel. "It's happened be-fore. Athletes dying during the Olympics, I mean, other than at Munich. A Brit, who I think was a luger, and an Aussie skier, both in 1964."

"The show must go on," Angela said.

"By the way, thanks so much for tidying our room, Angie," I said. "Was anything missing?"

"Yes—twenty pounds and, funnily enough, my bottle of codeine tablets. If you had any, they're gone too."

"What happened?" Trevor asked.

"You tell them, Angie. I'm going to be late." My wristwatch read 7:28, so I grabbed my skatebag and hurried to the gate. I was held up briefly at the guardhouse by the East German biathlon team checking out their rifle bolts, which had to be surrendered on entering the Village.

Today's practice was a patch session in the small practice rink, so I shared the layout ice with seven other women. As I sat on a bench to lace my figure skates I watched Nina Aleksandrova, the reigning world champion, squinting at her tracings through horn-rimmed glasses. Her delicate features were wrinkled into a mask of concentration. Our beefy West German rival, Putzi Meier, was already hard at her paragraph loops. Only her methodical Teutonic superiority in the school figures had allowed her to beat me at Europeans last month. Paula Emery's coaching in school figures was responsible for my swift rise through the world ranks, from 25th to 3rd place in two years. Putzi and I had a great deal riding on these compulsories.

"You have patch number four, Miss Grey," said a volunteer from the local skating club which was coordinating the practices. "By the way, if it's no trouble, could I have your autograph for my little girl?"

After I had mechanically glided through countless repetitions of the counters and then the brackets, I noticed the 20-by-40-foot patch next to mine was no longer vacant. Kim Cranford, in pink Polar Sport warm-ups bedecked with St. Christopher's medal, shamrock, figure test skate pins, and other good luck charms, was about to begin. We smiled briefly at each other, then resumed full concentration, circling and passing like small planets on separate orbits. Kim's coach Zack Higgins sat down nearby, silent and impassive as always behind his lavender-tinted aviator glasses.

I felt myself being watched and looked up at the next change of foot, expecting to see Paula. But it was Kim's mother Elizabeth Cranford who was scrutinizing my loops. After a good long stare, she clutched her fur coat around herself and moved down the barrier to watch Putzi and Nina. Really, I thought, these skating mothers are a bit much. Ten years of shivering in rinks to spy on her daughter's rivals and she's still at it.

"Morning, Lesley." Paula flopped onto the bench. "God, the traffic! It took me one full hour to drive seven miles from Tahoe City. Crawl, lurch, and fume." The coach ran her fingers through her silver-frosted hair in a characteristic gesture of irritation.

"Well, the men's downhill must be rather a draw."

"Okay, let's look at 'em." Paula walked onto the ice and I took her place on the bench. She studied the figures through her half-glasses, checking their alignment, pacing off their length, brushing snow from the turns.

"Brackets okay. Counters not very good, Lesley." She lowered her voice and looked around to make sure Mrs. Cranford and Higgins were out of earshot. "I'd give this one a 3.0. To paraphrase that hockey coach at Lake Placid, your counters are worse every day, and right now they're like next month. There should be only one tracing here, and I see three."

"I know, neatness counts!" I said with a grimace.

"Do it for me now on clean ice." She watched. "Your weight isn't over your hip at the turn, and it's giving you a double change of edge. Again. Better.

"Now, the loops. This one is off-axis and too small. You're breaking out of the first lobe too early, anticipating the change of edge. Do it again. Good. Now, you know you've got to place at least 5th in the compulsories to have a mathematical chance at the gold medal. You'll be coming from behind in the freestyle, as the best freeskaters always have to do. But let's not give away any more than we have to on the figures. Okay, it's ten o'clock, time for elevenses. Let's go have coffee."

She watched me tie my shoes, abstractedly running her fingers through her hair. I wondered what was on her mind; plainly, it was more than loops and brackets.

"Let's go up in the tram to the Granite Chief Restaurant," Paula suggested. "I'd like to get away from all these coaches and mothers."

As we walked toward the blockhouse-like cable car terminal, I could hear faint yips and howls from the downhill course. "Probably the Austrian railbirds supporting their team," the coach said. "Hear the cowbells?"

"They sound like a pack of hyenas."

Paula stuck to small talk and gossip during the 20-minute ride. I was glad to have her there to take my mind off the tram's nerve-wracking height and swaying. Don't be such a baby, I scolded myself.

"Have you seen the compulsory figures judges' list?" Paula asked. "Some wise guy programmed the computer to print out a thousand copies with the names Byron White, William Rehnquist, Sandra O'Connor, John Paul Stevens. . . ."

"That's the US Supreme Court!" I laughed.

"Right, Warren Burger and the Supremes. And the pairs list included some extra pairs, like Lois Lane and Clark Kent of Yugoslavia."

"It was probably Matt Galbraith. He's a famous practical joker, the silly ass."

"Whoever it was, it looks like he's figured out how to get access to the computer codes, and I hear the IOC's worried. If he wanted to, he could manipulate the results."

"Wouldn't it be obvious?" I asked.

"Not necessarily, apparently it can be done very subtly. Oh, and did you hear about the PLAYFAIR sit-in at the hockey match last night? About fifty people were sitting on the ice in Blyth trying to prevent the game between Russia and Finland. The Highway Patrol had to drag them off again, one by one—just like the sixties."

"Except for their ages and their politics."

"The match started an hour late. They say they're going to disrupt every competition with Russians in it," said the coach.

"What a bore."

When we were sitting with our coffee on the deck outside the striking modern restaurant, Paula said, "We're going to have to make a small change in the short program."

"Oh, why?"

"You've been going into the double axel from a Bauer spread eagle for better choreography. Well, Kim's coach Zack Higgins has been telling some of the judges that it's an illegal move because it's not one of the required seven."

"Oh, for God's sake!" I laughed in exasperation.

"He's a real operator, all right, and a psych-out artist too. Notice how he won't let Kim practice anything difficult when there are judges around?"

"So I should just go right into the axel after the serpentine step sequence, and forget the Bauer?"

"Yes, but not in practice. Let's not let him know we know, or he'll think up still another dirty trick. Now, tell me about what happened to Dima yesterday."

After my account, she drank her coffee in silence for a minute, then asked, "Why are you so sure it was an accident?"

"You too? That's what Matt thought!" I said uneasily.

"He's not stupid, even if he is a bit outrageous."

"Well, I think it's rather unlikely. Most skating falls do no harm at all."

"I know, I've had my share. Loose and cracked blades too. They don't usually do much damage; what does is foreign objects on the ice. Hairpins, flower petals, chewing gum, that sort of thing. Or ruts in the ice. Did you look for anything like that?"

"Even if someone had put something there," I objected, "what would the chances be of his skating over that exact spot?"

"Pretty good, I'd say, if you'd watched him practice his program and knew when he was skating backwards and where he jumped. Or, here's another possibility: Dorothy Hamill once had a bad accident when she skated full-tilt into a rope strung across a dimly-lit arena. A thin wire, which could be removed afterward, would have the same effect. All right, smile at me. But look at it this way: who would want to harm him?"

"Why, I don't know," I said, ignoring icy fingers of apprehension creeping down my spine. I couldn't afford to worry over this sort of idle speculation—I had enough real worries of my own.

The coach lowered her voice. "You've told me he's thinking of defecting if he wins. And I think he'd better. Sooner or later they'll have to suppress him, he's too much of a free spirit to fit into the Soviet sports machine. But we're talking high stakes now," she said in an emphatic whisper. "If he does defect here, it would be horrendously humiliating to the Russians. It's never happened to them quite that way before. Either the defectors are small fry no one's heard of, or if they're gold medalists, they do it quietly ten years later like the Protopopovs did. But *during* the Olympics, with all the media here, the whole world watching! Right after supposedly proving the superiority of their system, to have their biggest star spit in their faces like that—see what I mean? It would be bigger than Nureyev and Baryshnikov and all those other ballet stars rolled into one. And Dima *is* a star, with all those teen-agers screaming his name every time he competes. He's one of the few skaters that people who aren't fans have heard of."

"I see what you mean. But I'm sure the Russians don't know his plans." A chill shook me. What if they did?

"I wouldn't be so sure," Paula said ominously. "You've gotten used to Fyodor and you think he's a big teddy bear, kind of a figure of fun. But he *is* KGB, after all, and I don't think bumblers last long there. Think of how many defection *attempts* there must have been that no one's ever heard of. And no one's ever heard of the people again, either."

"But Dima hasn't told anyone but me, because I have to organize a lawyer and then a press conference, after he's smuggled out of the Village to a safe place. So, of course Fyodor isn't there when we talk about it. He isn't suspicious of me, truly," I assured her. "Dima tells him we're going to get married, and I'm going to defect to the Soviet Union."

"So *that's* why he accepts your being there all the time, and Dima gets to go places that the other Russians don't. I've often wondered why he has so much freedom."

"Dima strings Fyodor along, telling him I haven't quite made up my mind yet so he should treat me well, but I'm basically *nasha*. That means 'one of us, on our side.' Fyodor takes me for granted."

"Well, maybe."

"Oh, that reminds me." I told Paula about the happenings of the night before, including the anonymous note. "Someone besides Fyodor must think I'm going to defect to Russia." I laughed ironically.

"Did you keep the note?"

"Of course not, I chucked it out. It's no good taking any notice of that sort of thing."

"I suppose it was from some right-winger, probably one of those PLAYFAIR creeps. How could it have gotten into your pocket?"

"I had a drink with Matt at the Five Circles, and my coat, covered with bloodstains, was hanging up behind me. People were streaming in and out the whole time."

"I think you should tell the police about the note, and about your room being torn apart." Her brow was wrinkled in a worried frown. "There might be some connection with what happened to Dima."

"Don't be ridiculous," I scoffed.

"Well, I think the KGB was most likely responsible for the fall, anyway. Did you and Dima ever discuss his defecting when you were in Moscow?" Paula asked. "You can be sure the Rossiya Hotel has a bug in every room; videotape cameras too, they tell me. And I'll bet the apartment of a VIP like Dima is also bugged."

"No, we were careful in those places. Even the restaurant tables there are wired for sound. A friend of his lent us his flat, someone very unimportant. He was sure it was okay. The officials wouldn't even have let him come here if they were suspicious—he was thoroughly vetted."

"Do you want some more coffee?" Paula asked.

When she had returned with refills, she went back to worrying the topic like a terrier with a sock. "What country is he defecting *to?* I know he's quite an Anglophile. Does he still want to live in England?"

"Not so much, I'm afraid, since I've told him about a competitive skater's problems there. He's leaning toward the US now."

"You mean he wants to go on competing?" she asked, astonished. "I assumed he'd turn pro and join an ice show."

39

"He's very 'Soviet' about that, he says he'll never sell his body and soul to 'skating merchants.' And he's dead keen on competition; I sometimes think it's *the* most important thing to him," I said ruefully. "He wants to defect now because he's afraid the sports officials will force him to quit competing and become a coach after the Olympics. They want to make room for younger blood, like Pavel Marchevsky. That's why the Protopopovs defected, you know—they weren't allowed to perform for the public any more. And it is terribly unfair to end Dima's career like that, when competition and the limelight is his lifeblood.

"If he were signing a contract with one of the big shows, he could probably have got them to arrange the defection," I went on after a swallow of coffee. "Remember those Czech brothers, hockey players, who were smuggled away from a match by the Canadian pro hockey team? But since Dima's staying amateur, he can't ask help from any organization—the IOC or ISU wouldn't dare get involved."

"Yes, I know," said Paula. She recited in a sing-song: "The IOC doesn't get involved in international matters. The State Department says that's an Immigration matter. The Immigration Department says aliens must go to the nearest office for a permit to stay. What a bunch of buck-passers!" she finished contemptuously.

"And he can't just walk into an Immigration office or a police station and announce he wants political asylum, because Fyodor's always with him when he's outside the Village, and Fyodor would use any means, including force, to prevent him."

"Well, he'd have to, wouldn't he? It's his neck if Dima gets away."

Depressed by the subject because we still didn't have an escape plan, I gazed at the snow-sparkling mountains, dotted with skiers, then at the international crowd enjoying the sunshine on the deck. I couldn't help noticing an amazingly well-endowed brunette in a tight red sweater. In fact, all the nearby men were giving her bold or covert stares. As I watched, her protruding chest, a natural hazard, bumped a man walking by. She smiled and apologized, flirting with her eyelashes. Suddenly, someone caught her by the wrist, and simultaneously grabbed a small dark man, shaking his arm till he dropped a wallet in the snow. While the bystanders gaped, the plainclothesman handcuffed them together, with the help of several Pinkerton guards who swarmed to his aid.

"What's going on?" I asked one of them after he'd spoken into a walkie-talkie radio (or what Dima called a talkie-walkie).

"They're pickpockets. Probably from Colombia, judging by the sound of it." The couple were spitting and swearing in Spanish.

"Why Colombia in particular?"

"The best pickpockets' schools are in Bogotá, and their students are always at big sporting events and international gatherings. You know, like the World Cup, royal weddings, the Oktoberfest, elections of the Pope, and so forth. They really get around. You can usually spot 'em by their M.O.: the woman, who always has big ti—I mean, she's always stacked, bumps into the victim. While he's distracted, her partner picks his pocket."

"Well, I'll be damned!" Paula exclaimed. "Good work." The Pinkertons led the pair away toward the cable car.

"Well, where was I?" Paula resumed. "Oh, yes—if Dima thinks the US government is going to pay his way like the USSR has, he's in for a rude shock. And he can't compete for the US until he becomes a citizen. That takes five years; he couldn't even be in the next Olympics. *And* he'd be a bit old. What is he, twenty-seven?"

"Oleg Protopopov was thirty-six when he won his second gold. Dima did some reading up about eligibility when he was in Denver last month."

I grinned, remembering Dima's account. He and Fyodor would go to the public library and he'd give Fyodor copies of *Playboy* and *Soviet Life* to keep him busy. Then he'd run to the Reader's Guide and look up the ironically-titled topic "Political Asylum and Turncoats." He hated that, and the word "defector" with its negative connotation of a defect. Fyodor's English wasn't up to much so he never caught on, though he probably would have if Dima'd asked for material about citizenship.

"He pretended to be researching his master's thesis," I said.

"I didn't know he's a graduate student."

"That's actually his official profession! It's really a joke—he's at the Central Institute of Physical Culture in Moscow. Tuition-free of course, and his thesis is on 'The History, Organization, and Management of Figure Skating'! Anyway, in his reading he found exceptions to waiting five years to compete for the US. All it takes is getting a Congressman to put through a special bill. It's been done for a Czech skier and a Polish runner and some others. Also, he discovered that Olga Fikatova—remember her, romance at Melbourne?—became a member of the 1960 US Olympic team only three years after she married Hal Connolly."

"I think the situation is different if you're married to a citizen—"

"Quite right, I did get the official material for him later."

Paula took off her glasses and polished them nervously. "—which brings up another point. I wouldn't put it past him to marry Kim Cranford or some other little dimwit just to get eligible more quickly. In fact, I think he'd have to, to compete again in the Olympics for a different country."

I felt my face grow hot. "That's an outrageous thing to say!"

"I hope you're not cherishing sentimental dreams of another Hal-and-Olga Olympic wedding. If you did marry him, do you think he'd allow you a career that might outshine his, even though *you'd* be supporting *him?* No, let me finish. Lesley, dear, I'd do anything not to hurt you, but if someone doesn't speak up soon, *he's* going to hurt you even more. His screwing around is an open secret. Do you know what they call him? The playboy of the Eastern world."

"Yes, I've heard that. It was Vladimir Kovalev's nickname back in the seventies. So what?" I said impatiently.

"That tag didn't come from just drinking and partying, you know. He's a typical Russian consumer—he grabs all the women he can, in case there's a shortage later on. I know of at least four skaters he's slept with just in the past year." She began to twist her hair around her finger again.

"Oh, for God's sake, Paula, that's just a subterfuge. He doesn't sleep with them—at least, not any more. Lately, he's made a point of being seen with a lot of different women, so no one will suspect that he's so involved with me and I'm going to help him defect." I was as sure of this as I was of my own name.

Paula's face remained skeptical. "Well, here's something I don't think you can rationalize away. I've just learned from one of the Russian coaches that Dima has a fiancée in the Soviet Union."

"That's not true either, damn it," I said, exasperated but trying to keep my temper with traditional British control. "It's another cover-up. Russian skaters can't travel to the West without leaving hostages behind. He thought it would be more convincing, that they'd trust him more, if he left a fiancée as a hostage-to-be, besides his family. He never intended to marry her."

"I'm sorry, but I think he's told enough lies to hang himself, at least in my book."

"Your book seems to be *The Story of O* or *Don Juan* or something." I tried to lighten the mood.

"If you analyze what he's told you, it's a maze of contradictions. But that's your problem."

"Quite."

"Don't bother to put on that snippy British tone of voice." Paula's hair was standing on end by now from her nervous rumpling. "I do have a reason for being so inexcusably nosy and interfering. This obsession is seriously affecting your skating. Your figures today showed that; they were much better three months ago. After Europeans, when Dima was in Denver, you hardly practiced at all. You were either on the highway driving up to see him, or when you *were* at the Broadmoor, you two were shacked up in your room. You're losing your concentration and your competitive edge, and you're going to lose not only the gold, but the chance of any medal at all, if you don't snap out of it!"

"You're mistaken." No bloody fear.

"You're an intelligent woman; you should see this for yourself. All I ask is, forget about Dima for the next week. Just one week! Then, if you want to throw your life away being a . . . a doormat for that egotistical jerk with hot pants for anything in a skating skirt, be my guest."

"I suppose your motive is jealousy," I said in my most clipped voice, though I was shaking with rage. "Or maybe you're afraid I'll disgrace you by losing. Then I couldn't pay what I owe you, could I? In either case, what you've said is quite unforgivable." How could Paula, of all people, betray me this way?

"Lesley, for Christ's sake, don't let him come between us," Paula pleaded. "We have a partnership, and it's always worked till now. Believe me, I'd rather not have spoken up, but I wouldn't be a good coach if I let you blow ten years of work right now, when it should all come together." She paused, then added in a vehement burst, "And I wouldn't be a friend if I didn't try to make you see that this man treats people like Kleenex!"

"All right," I said, slightly moved through my anger by her emotion. "I'll try to take it in the spirit you say was meant. But it's my life, and I do know what I'm doing. I wish you'd drop it now."

"What more can I say? If you don't believe me, you don't. Now, then," in a business-like tone, "you're scheduled for short program practice at midnight in Blyth. I'll see you then. Try to get some sleep during the day."

"I was planning to. And it'll be alone, don't worry. Good-bye." Not trusting myself to say any more, I got up and ran toward the tram. I was the last one to squeeze in; the attendant prevented someone in a black coat from jostling in behind me.

As the cable car began its descent, I stared out the window without seeing the rocky slopes far below. I realized later that it was the only time I'd ever ridden it without worrying about another fatal accident like the one in 1978, when the cable had broken loose and sliced into the tram like a cleaver. Still seething, I pressed my hot cheek against the cold glass.

Why can't anyone understand! I thought. Why do they all hate him? Jealousy and spite. He isn't like that! No one knows him like I do. He's *not* calculating and promiscuous. He's vulnerable, he's a little boy. The coldness around my heart melted a bit as I pictured his tousled blond head pillowed on my breast. I remembered Moscow. . . .

Sports will be a weapon in the fight for peace and for the promotion of friendship among all peoples.
—Secretary-General, USSR Olympic Committee

In the Soviet Union, truth spreads only by word of mouth.
—Dora Romadinov, musician, USSR defector

Moscow Skate, the last in the pre-season series of invitational competitions, is held three weeks before Christmas. No snow had yet fallen that year, and it was astonishingly cold, sometimes 30 or 40 degrees below zero. The little band of skaters from eight European countries shivered our way around Moscow on the obligatory tours. Our faces were sandpapered by frost to the color of borscht, and we copied the people on the street, who held their hands in front of their noses to prevent frostbite.

Paradoxical impressions of Moscow whirled around my mind like a kaleidoscope: sparkling and shabby, magnificent and dowdy, efficient

45

and chaotic. The glittering red and gold plushness of the Bolshoi and the audience in shirtsleeves. GUM's thousand shops, splashing fountain, ornate ironwork—and the half-mile-long queues with their *avoski*, "perhaps" bags. Intourist guides pushing foreigners to the heads of the three queues in each store: to select, to pay, and to collect purchases. Change for my rubles in Bulgarian coins from surly clerks.

The *beryozka*, a special shop restricted to foreigners with hard currency, where I bought *matryoshki* wooden nesting dolls for my cousins and a perfume called "Moscow Nights." (Dima told me later that Customs was sure to inspect the innermost doll, a favorite hiding place for smugglers. And he thought the perfume, once called "Svetlana" before the defection of Stalin's daughter, smelled like the Press sisters' old sweatsocks.)

The look of the Metro subway: marble, chandeliers, mosaic murals —and the smell of its elbowing crowds: garlic, sweat, and stale tobacco smoke. Red traffic lights at Spassky Gate changing to green for the Politburo's Chaika and ZIL limousines in their reserved center lanes. Neon signs promoting traffic safety and Communist slogans instead of consumer goods. The sumptuous cathedrals, now "museums"; one in Leningrad was called the Museum of the History of Religion and Atheism. Betting on the horses at the Hippodrome, from which the government took a cut. Detsky Mir, the "Children's World" shop, across the square from KGB headquarters and Lubyanka Prison.

The vastness of the disintegrating Rossiya Hotel, where even the staff got lost along the 10 miles of corridors. The interminable meals there: much of the elaborate menu was unavailable, and the waiter said, "What the hell do I care what you eat?" None of us ventured more than small talk during the five-hour dinner for fear of the notorious bugged tables.

In contrast, the competition in the Olympiisky Sports Complex, decorated by pictures of Masters of Sport, ran as efficiently as the 1980 Olympics. The hall was packed. The Muscovites warmly applauded all the Western athletes, yelling what sounded like "Let's go, Mets!" It turned out to be *"Molodets!"*—Russian for "Attaboy!" Thus encouraged, I placed 2nd in school figures, a personal best, and pulled up to 1st with my short program.

The next day held an Intourist-arranged treat, a skating picnic in Gorky Park hosted by the Russian competitors. During the night, the first snow fell and the drab city was transformed. Legions of kerchiefed *babushki* cleared sidewalks with twig brooms. The temperature rose and the people seemed to cheer up. Even Masha, our dour Intourist guide, made an uncharacteristic joke about Moscow going through two months of pre-menstrual tension before the snow. Suddenly, every hill and open space was dotted with cross-country skiers. Commuters carried their skis and skates to work on the Metro; they were part of the fabric of winter life.

"Now we enter the Gorky Park of Culture and Rest," Masha intoned as our coach passed a roller coaster and a ferris wheel and stopped near the outdoor rink. As we glided gleefully down the frozen paths, we forgot for an afternoon that we were worldclass athletes with the Olympics imminent, and became children again. Music floated from the loudspeakers in the trees. Putzi and I made angels in the snow. French and German pairs collaborated on a snowman.

I started in surprise as Dmitri Kuznetsov skated up behind me and encircled my waist with one arm. I knew him only casually from the previous year's post-Worlds tour and the competition circuit. I'd felt him watching me lately, and was dazzled and unsettled by his interest.

"Come with me, Lesley, they're playing the Skater's Waltz." We crossed hands and stroked rapidly down the path together.

"This is what skating's all about!" I said in exhilaration. "No tatty old rinks smelling of rubber matting and Zamboni exhaust. Just coldness and speed and snowflakes melting on your face. It's easy to forget that in England."

"And here, too, when one trains for the Olympics from morning till night. But I still love to skate even after all these years of competition. It makes me to feel serene and free, a rare feeling in the Soviet Union."

"I understand what you mean, Dmitri, even after a few days."

"Yes, only when skating and making love can one feel free here," he added. "But you ought to call me Dmitri Pyotrovich if you are using my first name."

"What a mouthful! Pyotro—what?"

"It's my patronymic, my father's name. Pyotr is the same as your Peter. There are not so many Russian given names, so we must use the patronymic as well to tell ourselves apart. One year there were five Dmitris in my class at school. Besides, is more proper, *kulturni*. But I'd like it if you'd say my nickname, Dima."

I was acutely aware of his muscular body's nearness as we followed a path that branched off into a birch grove. He changed his arms to dance position and we glided smoothly into a waltz, alternating 3-turns around each other. A jingling troika galloped by.

"Your English is very good, Dima."

"Yes it is, isn't it? I began to study it at quite a young age, and of course I've traveled to the West to compete for ten years now."

"When did you begin skating?"

"I'm not sure—I suppose it was when I was at *detsky sad*, that's kindergarten. Yes, I remember the teacher, an itinerant chap who came once a week with a big sack of second-hand skates on his back. I bought a pair of Spartaks from him for six rubles. But everyone skates here, and skis too."

"You must explain Russia to me, Dima. It reminds me of America in some ways, so big and boisterous and uninhibited. I feel such gaiety here, but such sorrow."

He slid sideways into a hockey stop, but didn't drop his arms. "We *are* like Americans, big-hearted and open. But no—how do you say? —Puritanical ethics, and a secret sadness underneath that Americans never have. Think of our winter, think of our government—we have much to be sad about. I admire you English more than the Americans. You keep everything in proportion, no extremes. I like also your pubs, your tweeds, your Princess Diana. And I like you," he said, tightening his arms around me. "I've been watching you grow up over the last year. You're becoming a marvelous skater. You could be one of the greatest, another Peggy Fleming or Janet Lynn."

"That's high praise from the world champion," I said demurely, my heart beating faster. "Thank you very much indeed."

"But I like more than your skating, Lesley. There is a current that draws us together. Can't you feel it?"

Haunting strains of *Swan Lake* drifted through the bare trees. He turned my hand palm-up and kissed it caressingly, then stared into my eyes. We were exactly the same height. "Your face is like an English rose. And your eyes are green. I thought they were gray."

"Only when I'm wearing green . . ." I murmured, gazing into his blue ones.

"But you're not wearing green today. . . ."

"Or feeling—emotional." I trembled as I waited giddily for him to kiss me.

A snowflake settled on his blond hair, revealing its perfect star shape for the moment before it turned to a drop of water. Our mouths seemed to melt together.

"Mmm, *khorosho*. You feel good. We're going to be so good together, I can always tell."

I clung to him weakly. "We ought to get back. . . . We must stop, Dima. Oh darling. . . ."

"I don't waste time when I'm in love, *deushka*," he said, nuzzling my throat. His lips were hot against my chilled skin.

"Well, you're a fast worker!" I said, amused. "How long have you been in love with me, then?"

"About half an hour. But I knew you for years, and I always liked you. I noticed you long ago."

After 20 minutes and several false starts, we skated slowly back down the path, arms around each other's waists. "Will you come to my flat?" he asked.

"I'm not sure if I should, you know." He certainly didn't waste time.

"No, no, I live with my family. My mother will cook dinner for you. There are not many bachelor pads in Moscow! But I have a friend's flat I can use sometimes. . . ." He kissed me lingeringly again. "I'll see what I can arrange."

We joined the other skaters, who were bunched around a bonfire feasting on *pirozhki*, black bread, smoked cheese, and sardines, and washing it all down with vodka and East German beer. Putzi exclaimed over the *morozhnoye*, the unseasonal ice cream, that she'd just bought from a pushcart vendor. I marveled that they all seemed just the same, when the whole world had changed in half an hour. Nina Aleksandrova glared at me venomously, but I took no notice.

When we had finished eating, Dima drew me aside and said, "Come to dinner tomorrow night. My mother will need a day to prepare for a guest. And I have to make it okay with the Ministry of Sport; is risky to entertain a foreigner without official approval. I pick you up at five at the hotel entrance nearest to St. Basil's—the doorman won't let me inside."

"Why ever not?"

"They don't let Moscow residents inside hotels here without a pass. They say that if you have a home, why should you need a hotel? It's how they try to stop love-making. But we manage anyhow!"

I giggled nervously.

"One thing—" he went on, "wear your hair up, as you would for skating. It's not *kulturni* for a woman to have her hair flowing down on the street."

He gave me a long, hard kiss that left me gasping. "We be together alone soon, *deushka*. The waiting will make it all the better. And then I take your hair down."

49

The next day was occupied with practice for the final freeskating and a fashion show at GUM. (If you liked a dress, you could purchase the pattern and fabric and sew it yourself). At five minutes before 5:00, I turned my room key over to the *dezhurnaya*, the "key lady" on my floor, and walked out of the Rossiya into Dima's embrace.

"Break it up, comrades," shouted a passerby. "This is the street, not your bedroom."

Dima translated this for me. "You see what we must put up with?"

He took my arm and we strolled across the cobblestones of Red Square, past the gaudy onion domes of St. Basil's, pausing at Lenin's tomb to watch the changing of the guard. As the last chime from the Spassky Clock Tower died away, the new guards snapped into parade rest.

Outside GUM, a teen-ager sidled up to us. "You wanna do leetle biz-ness?" he asked in pidgin English, apparently spotting our foreign clothes. "Change money, sell jeans, rock tapes, photo apparat? You want some icons or marijuana from Georgia?"

"No thanks," said Dima.

"You have *zhvatchka*, chewing gum? I buy, I sell."

"Beat it, punk."

I whispered, "Black market?"

"Yes, the *chorni rynok*, we call it."

We passed a group of people reading a six-page newspaper pinned to a notice board. "Why do they read *Pravda* that way?" I asked. "Why don't they buy their own?" Love seemed to make me curious about everything, receptive to all the unfamiliar sights and sounds around me. Dima could tell me all the things I hadn't dared to ask the guide. Anyway, I wanted to learn as much as I could about him and his strange land.

"Because they know it's nothing but lies and propaganda. For instance, the main news headline is RECORD HARVEST IN TURKMENISTAN. Who cares? See how most of them only read the last page? That's the sports page. *Pravda* makes pretty good lavatory paper, though."

"What's the difference between it and *Isvestiya?* I've never known."

"The *Pravdas* are the Party papers and *Isvestiya* is the government paper. Some difference. 'Pravda' means 'truth' and 'isvestiya' means 'news.' There's a joke: there is no news in *Pravda* and no truth in *Isvestiya!*"

"Are jokes like that allowed?"

"They can't forbid everything. Look, there's another good use for *Pravda.*" We stopped by an outdoor market, and watched a customer choose a live fish for dinner. The ruddy-cheeked vendor folded a cone out of newspaper and ladled in some water and the fish. The shopper put his squirming purchase in a green string bag, and we followed him toward the Metro.

The escalator seemed to take us to the center of the earth. The depth of the tube was a military secret, Dima told me, but it seemed much deeper than the London Underground. The fancy stations were designed to distract the passengers from claustrophobia.

During the ride he told me about his family. "My parents' names are Pyotr Ilyich and Nadezhda Viktorovna, and is polite to address them so. I have a younger brother, Sasha, and I had a little sister, but she died as a small child. We're fortunate; we have a flat to ourselves for the last four years, since I won the silver medal in the last Olympics. We used to share the bathroom and kitchen with another family—real slobs they were, too."

"Have you always lived in Moscow?"

"No, we used to live in Novosibirsk in Siberia. When I was eleven, the authorities decided my skating was promising, so they sent me to a special sports boarding school here. It's attached to Club Dynamo, the KGB club. And when I made the Olympic team, they transferred my family here as a reward for handing me over to them as a child. It's very difficult to move to Moscow, you know, one must have a permit, a *propiska.* They want to keep the population stable at eight million. But now my family has *blat.*"

"What's that when it's at home?"

"What's the word? Influence. Not power, but status. Things are better now. My salary is bigger—four hundred rubles a month, for improving my diet only, you understand! And we have a *dacha.*"

"A country house?" I was fascinated by the secret details of the notorious East bloc payoffs to those athletes who brought glory to the state.

"Yes, but it's not quite a stately home, as you use the phrase! It's a shabby log cabin, but at least it's out of the city. We spend our holidays there, or at Black Sea resorts. Also, we are on the waiting list for a Fiat Zhiguli. It takes five years."

"Won't the price be much higher then?"

"We had to pay for it already, ten thousand rubles. Anyway, there's no inflation here, or so they say. To earn the money, I bought cassette recorders at duty-free shops for several years every time I went to the West. Then I resold them for ten times the price in rubles on the black market."

"Is there much of that sort of thing?"

"Of course. The women skaters take orders for bras from their friends before they go abroad, and buy fifty or so. That's a very popular item. This is our stop." We got off and rode up the long escalator.

"What do your parents do?"

"They both work in factories. My father's a machinist, but he continually drinks on the job and gets fired from one plant after another. I'm afraid he's an example of the old saying that progress from socialism to Communism has an intermediate stage, alcoholism," he said ruefully. "My mother has worked in a chemical factory for thirty years, but she's such a good worker that they finally made her a manager. I worry about her, though; I think the chemicals have ruined her health." We trudged along into the biting wind, huddled into our coats.

"When you said she'd need a day to prepare the dinner, I thought she must be a housewife."

"*Nyet*, we have few housewives here, and they are called parasites. Only upperclass men can earn enough to keep their families by themselves. It's a lie that this is a classless society. So—the women are 'liberated,' as you Western women want to be. Liberated to take their children to crèches every day—my little sister died there because they didn't take proper care of her. And they are liberated to stand in shopping queues for hours during and after work, then go home and do all the housework. And the men can drink all day with a clear conscience." His voice had a bitter edge.

We turned into a high-rise building which smelled of cabbage, and entered the elevator. When it stopped, I hung back.

"What's wrong, are you nervous?"

"Yes, of course. Do they speak English?"

"No, only my brother a little, but I translate for you. Just try to eat as much as you can, it will please *Mamochka*."

He ushered me into a room containing a lot of Victorian-era furniture. It seemed to function as sitting room, dining room, and bedroom all in one. A gray-haired man and a towheaded boy of about 10 were watching a snowy hockey match on the tiny black and white television.

52

Dima introduced us, first in Russian, then English. I shook hands and repeated their names. A short woman with faded blonde hair came out of the kitchen, carrying a round loaf of bread on a white cloth. On top of it sat a little silver dish of salt. She smiled at me with Dima's smile and said something in Russian.

"My mother says, 'Welcome to our home.' This is a traditional symbol of hospitality, meaning that even in a house with nothing but bread and salt, the guest is welcome to share."

"Please thank her, and say that I feel very lucky to be here."

"Now, you must cut a slice and dip it in the salt and eat it." They all watched me do so, then applauded, beaming. I handed Dima's mother the bouquet of flowers I had brought, and there were more smiles and nods.

"Please to sit down," Dima said, "and would you like some wine? I noticed at the picnic that you don't care for vodka." He pronounced the word with a *W* instead of a *V.*

I toasted them with one of the few phrases I had learned: "*Mir i druzhba,* peace and friendship." While I sipped the Georgian red wine they said was called *Mukuzani,* I glanced around the tidy room with its potted geraniums, lace curtains at the steamy windows, and divan beds for Dima and Sasha. On the walls hung a picture of Lenin, family photos, and a Samarkand carpet. Nadya, as she asked me to call her, declined my offer to help and returned to the kitchen. Pyotr asked me about the skating competition, then he and Dima had a long, heated exchange. I caught the names of Nina Aleksandrova and Pavel Marchevsky.

"What's he saying?"

Dima glared at his father, who was tossing back his fourth or fifth shot of vodka. "He says Pavel is going to beat me. He's just trying to annoy me. Talk to Sasha, he's studying his second year of English in school."

"Do you want to be a skater too?" I asked the boy.

"*Nyet,* I'm swimmer."

"He'll compete in the next Spartakiad," Dima put in.

"What is that red kerchief around your neck? I've seen a lot of children wearing them."

"Is for Young Pioneers," the boy said haltingly, his face flushed with effort. "Is like your Scouts: we learn about nature, help people, study principles of Communism."

"Oh, yes. Was Dima a Young Pioneer?"

"It is not optional," Dima said drily. "You can't be a member of Komsomol, that's Young People's League, unless you're a Pioneer first, and you can't get anywhere unless you've been in Komsomol. Sashenka, tell Lesley what happened yesterday."

"I am picked to guard memorial of Great Patriotic War."

"How super! How do you do that?"

"I stand at attention in front of statue for two hours each week together with Tanya Ivanova, she's in my class. We carry rifles, but they have no ammunition."

"That must be quite an honor." Good heavens, they train 10-year-olds to be soldiers. I racked my brain for more childish topics of conversation while he told me about the upcoming Winter Festival at the Kremlin, at which Grandfather Frost and the Snow Maiden would give presents and sweets to thousands of children. When I asked if he had any pets, he looked perplexed; Dima explained that hardly anyone had the space or money in Moscow for dogs and cats.

Nadya brought in a plate of caviar and invited us to the loaded table, covered with an embroidered cloth.

"My father insists you drink vodka with the *ikra*, the caviar. Go on, have just one." Dima indicated the chilled bottles standing on the table. "Here's plain Stolichnaya, this one is flavored with peppercorns, and this one with cherries." I smiled and shrugged.

"You might as well begin with plain." He poured small glasses for the four of us and toasted me: "*Za tvoye zdorovie*, to your health."

"Well, when in Russia, do as the Russians do." Dima translated this, and they all smiled as I gulped it down, then laughed as I gasped.

"Take some bread, it absorbs the shock." I quickly tore off a piece of black bread, which quenched the fire somewhat.

"Now, Sasha!" I said jokingly.

"No, I drink *kvas*," he said, showing me his glass of amber liquid. "It's the Russian Coca-Cola, it's made from rye bread."

Nadya passed little cheese tarts called *khachupuri* and loaded toast with Beluga. I asked Dima if caviar were a luxury here.

"Well, that's another way we're privileged. We get to shop in a special store because of my position. It's not the top-grade shop that's only for Party members, but it's better than the state-run shops. The caviar is cheaper there than in the ordinary stores; in fact, they usually wouldn't sell it at all."

He asked Nadya a question and she replied at length. "*Mamochka* says she went into Grocery Store #22 around the corner last week, and the only meat was poor-quality pork, no beef or chicken. And the only *produkty* was cabbage, potatoes, onions, and little green apples with brown spots. There was plenty of vodka, of course. She has heard from her sister in Novosibirsk that the shops there have no milk or meat just now."

"What will the people there do? What about the children?"

He shrugged. "That's life in the Soviet Union. We privileged few get most of what little there is. You saw GUM with its queues and bare shelves; it has a hidden department most people never even see to outfit athletes, dancers, and other delegations when we visit the West. Do you know the word *pokazukha?* I don't know the English word, but it means things like long restaurant menus with no food, merchandise in shop windows one can't buy, model farms and factories only for show to journalists."

Nadya now ladled out a pungent soup, and Dima asked her a question. She laughed and said, "*Borscht!*"

"We have a joke," he explained. "If it's red, it's *borscht.* If it's brown, it's *shchi.* But they are really the same soup, made from cabbage and beetroot."

"Shee?"

"Cabbage soup. With other vegetables as well, and meat if there is any."

"*Shchi da kasha, pishcha nasha,*" Pyotr said thickly and grinned, showing several steel teeth.

"It's a saying: '*Shchi* and *kasha*, that's our food,'" Dima explained. Nadya pointed to the buckwheat porridge: *kasha.* With it she served a pickled vegetable salad, mushrooms in sour cream, and, with obvious pride, tinned peas.

"Save room for *blini*," Dima translated for her. "Traditional dessert. We have *blini* festivals at the spring solstice—they symbolize the sun."

Replete with butter and sour cream, my head spinning from the vodka and wine, I watched Nadya make *tchai* by breaking off a brick of tea. I admired the samovar and the tea glasses with their silver filigree holders.

"*Mamochka* asks if you want lemon or jam in your tea?" He whispered, "Take lemon. She stood in a queue for a long time to get it, and it probably cost her an hour's wage."

"Just for me?"

"Oh no, we cut thin slices, and it will last a week. Sometimes it's the only fresh fruit in the winter, so people think it's worth the extravagance." I reflected that if the average Russian worker could get just one look at an American supermarket, the Soviet government would immediately topple.

Pyotr mumbled something. "My father says I should tell you the old joke about Lenin's height. You've probably heard it. No? Well, a child says, 'Lenin was one meter, seventy centimeters tall.' A Party official says, 'How do you know?' The kid says, 'My father is two meters tall, and he's had Lenin up to here.'"

Nadya looked shocked and scolded them. She thrust a small chalk-board at her husband, who pushed it aside.

"What's that for?" I asked.

"The flat's probably bugged," Dima wrote. "That's how we talk when we don't want them to hear. Or we turn on the taps and talk in the bathroom." He stood up. "Let's go. I take you back now."

"Can't I help with the washing up? No? Well, let me just visit the loo first."

As I washed my hands at the single tap that swiveled between the sink and the bath, I marveled that Americans think British plumbing is primitive. When I turned off the water I heard raised masculine voices from the next room, so I waited a tactful few minutes before emerging.

Nadya and Sasha kissed me, wishing me luck in the freeskating final the next day, and Nadya made a cross with her thumb on my forehead. Pyotr enveloped me in a bear hug, planted a big wet kiss right on my mouth, then leered jovially at his son and slapped him on the back. I didn't need that translated, I thought as we walked to the elevator.

I pulled my camel's hair coat more tightly around me as the arctic wind slapped us. "I wish the British government would outfit *us* for travel, preferably with fur coats."

"It's not far to the Metro, we'll take a short cut through Kazan Station." The vast, spired railway station looked like any of London's, with waiting passengers sprawled on benches, sleeping children, and bored soldiers. The Trans-Siberian Express was about to leave.

"See that girl sitting there," Dima whispered, "the one with the red hair? Check out the bottom of her shoe." I looked at the henna-ed, heavily made-up woman, smoking a *papirosi* with a cardboard holder and swinging her crossed leg. On the sole of her shoe was chalked "10p." Dima said, "Ten rubles, her price."

My jaw dropped. "You're having me on. Surely there aren't prostitutes here!"

"Watch."

A soldier beckoned the woman. They walked out of the station and we followed at a distance. The couple climbed into a taxi, which drove around the corner and stopped on a side street. The driver got out and leaned against the fender with folded arms.

"He's watching for the *militsia*, the police. He gets ten rubles too, and he probably sold the soldier a bottle of vodka." The taxi rocked slightly.

"Good God." I was fascinated.

"Where else can they go in winter? Hotels are off-limits except for KGB *prostitutki* who seduce foreigners to blackmail them. Most flats have a *babushka* guarding the door like the key lady at your hotel, usually KGB stool pigeons. They have the right to open a door if they suspect—panky-hanky, is it? In the summer couples have the parks and houseboats, but the winter's tough. That's just one more way they try to deny us every natural impulse and human need." His voice was bitter again.

"But how do you know all this about the prostitutes?"

"Everyone knows. Don't worry, I don't go to whores. I never needed to." From farther down the street, we heard shouting and saw some running shapes under the blue streetlights. "*Hooliganki.* Come on, let's go."

On the Metro, we sat in silence for a while, watching the passengers. They all looked glum. The young Russians were attractive, but around the age of 30 everyone seemed to grow fat and dour. Perhaps it was then that their dreams finally died.

I stole a look at Dima's handsome Roman profile. I was on fire to be alone with him. I wanted him desperately, in spite of—perhaps because of?—the tawdry episode of the prostitute and his father's leering insinuations.

He turned to me and said prosaically, "Do you think you can beat Nina Aleksandrova tomorrow?"

"I doubt it. The judges would have to be unbelievably impartial for me to have a chance here. I just hope I'll finish ahead of Putzi; that would be a psychological advantage at Europeans. I thought Nina was your girlfriend, by the way."

"No, that's all over."

"How long ago?"

"Since I met you." He swallowed, looking uncharacteristically tentative. "Listen, *milochka.* Sweetheart. Will you come with me tomorrow night after the banquet? I arrange it so we can be together. Please," he implored.

"At your friend's flat?"

"Yes, he will be away, and no one guards the door there. We don't have to go to bed if you don't like, I just want to be alone with you. There's no privacy anywhere, and it's killing me not to be able to touch you." He gazed meltingly into my eyes.

"You too? Oh yes, I'll come. I don't know how I'll be able to wait that long."

As I had anticipated, I was 2nd to Nina in the final standing the next afternoon, and Putzi was 3rd. Dima triumphed easily over Pavel Marchevsky and Hans-Peter Koenig, his only serious challengers. The crowd yelled to him: "My s toboi!" "We're with you!" I was struck by the way all the Russian skaters unself-consciously kissed on the lips, the men as well as the women, to congratulate the winners.

Afterward, I told Angela that I'd see her the next day in time to pack for the flight home, and received an understanding smirk. "Do you think they'll check the rooms tonight?" I asked nervously.

"I doubt they'll bother, a lot of people have already left."

I stuffed a change of clothes into a tote bag and took it with me to the farewell banquet at the Stalinesque-Gothic Ukraina Hotel. It was an amazing spread: seven courses stretched from zakuski, "small bites" (including reindeer tongue and eight varieties of caviar) to dessert, Cuban pineapple and "Siberian omelette" (baked Alaska).

"This must be more food than most Russians see in a month," I remarked to George Ferguson, the International Skating Union official seated at my left. "Are they trying to outdo us capitalists?"

"I don't believe it's ostentation or greed," explained Ferguson, a Canadian who had lived several years in the USSR and seemed to have a philosophical turn of mind. "I think it's their answer to the ancient specter of hunger, the wolf at the door."

"Do we drink vodka with each course?" Apprehensively, I eyed the line of seven small glasses above my place setting. "They'll have to carry me out."

"Ask for mineral water. There'll be a lot of toasting, and you must drink something."

I was sorry I had when I tasted it. It was like drinking liquid detergent, frothy and salty.

"Tell me your impressions of the Soviet Union," Ferguson said as a cold soup called *okroshka*, made from cucumber and game in *kvas* and cream, was served to us on sickle-shaped ice cubes.

As I sipped it, I told him about the black marketeer, the prostitute, and the hooligans I'd seen last night. "Soviet life seems so priggish on the surface, but it seems to be acquiring all the Western vices."

"I can't think of any so-called vices they don't have except domestic pornography; they have to get imported stuff on the black market. There aren't any demonstrations or riots, of course. Not so much violent crime or thievery, but that's getting worse. Notice how everyone has to lock their windscreen wipers inside the car? They'd be stolen, otherwise."

"Could you say that the Russians are adopting Western forms, but not Western values?"

"In a way. You see, Miss Grey, one must live life on two levels here. Every day the average Ivan Ivanovich has to deal with incompetence, graft, goldbricking, absenteeism, epidemic alcoholism. Morale and productivity are unbelievably low. The economy runs mainly by barter, bribery, and fiddling. *Na levo,* 'on the left,' it's called—or the 'second economy.' And the inefficiency! Imagine a society with no such thing as personal checks to pay for what you buy, let alone credit. The city hasn't published a telephone directory in ten years, and Directory Inquiries insults you. It can take hours to make a phone call. Endless queues to buy anything. And a barrage of propaganda that never stops, with political aspects to everything."

"Oh yes, I'm aware of that. Dima told me he fought for two years with the sports officials to skate a program to *The Bells* by Rachmaninoff. He finally lost because they said it's religious music, and the composer defected at the time of the Revolution! The skating association wants him just to repeat the same programs every year."

"That's typical. *Any* actions or decisions get tangled up in the bureaucracy."

The waiter asked us our choices for the main course: spit-roasted chicken, saddle of lamb, or suckling pig.

"What's surprised me most," I went on, "is the inequality in a society that's supposed to be egalitarian."

"Well, the Party says that they're still working toward true Communism, and when it is reached there will be plenty for everyone. But the

Establishment have grabbed all the status and perks, as well as the material goods, and keep the best educations and careers for their children. They're called the *zolotaya molodyozh*, the 'golden youth.'"

I reflected that it sounded as rigid as the British class system, complete with family connections and the old boy network. Elite athletes were probably among the few to be able to break out.

"The ruling class is unbelievably corrupt and parasitic, almost feudal," he said. "No one I know here believes in Communism any more. My Russian friends sneer at the naïve European comrades in places like France and Italy; they're the only idealists left. But I'm afraid we can't expect another revolution. There's still always the fear that anyone might be *stukachi*, KGB informers; that you could be overheard on the telephone, in a restaurant, anywhere. After a while, you stifle yourself—you don't take risks, don't say or even think anything that might be dangerous. People eventually become submissive and robotlike. They say '*nichevo*: never mind, nothing can be done.'" I marveled that Dima had survived with his spirit intact.

"The second level I mentioned is the private one, the inner one," Ferguson continued. "People withdraw from all the hassles and controls and from the weather for most of the year. They form a protective cocoon; anything from the outside world is bad news. They have their families, their friends, their lovers. They treasure and share any small luxuries they're able to obtain. They're keen on sports. They go skiing or picnicking; they drop work to have fun. They'll drink and talk all night as only students do in the West. I think human relationships are warmer here, and people are more hedonistic—they have so little else to give them pleasure."

During the third speech after dinner, when Cuban cigars and Georgian brandy appeared, Dima slipped out. I followed him a few minutes later and met him at the Metro.

The one-room flat was in an old wooden house on a quiet street. I realized that he had probably brought Nina here many times, but I was beyond caring. Dima lit a coal fire and put the Balcony Scene from *Romeo and Juliet* on the phonograph.

I gazed into the fire as he stood behind me, caressing the nape of my neck with his lips, and gently pulled the pins from my hair. My waist-length mane enveloped us both, and he pressed a handful to his mouth. I turned to him and we looked at each other in the firelight for a long moment.

"Nothing will happen if you don't want it to, *deushka*."

"I do want it, Dima." My heart was pounding.

He reached around me and found the zipper of my dress. As he drew it slowly from my shoulders, my skin seemed to glow in the flickering light. I felt his warm breath against me and caressed his tousled hair, then pulled back his head and we drowned in each other's eyes. He pulled me down onto the feather bed as the music soared to fill the room. After a time, he paused.

"Oh, that's so beautiful, don't stop. . . ." I gasped.

"*Lyubov*, my love," he said. "What about a contraceptive? I have Western condoms. Russian ones are terrible, we call them galoshes."

"No, it's all right, I'm on the pill. Please don't stop. God, that's lovely, darling. I'd heard Russian men never bothered with foreplay."

"I read *The Joy of Sex*," he said indistinctly. "I got it on the black market. . . ."

Fire and ice filled my veins. I felt myself falling, dissolving, melting away. I grasped him as if he were a liferaft, and we were swept away together on a tidal wave.

Later, we reclined against the propped-up pillows. The cozy little room, full of flickering firelight, was a haven against the wind howling outside. One of Dima's arms encircled me and the other reached for a glass of brandy. "And I thought Englishwomen were supposed to be cold," he said sleepily.

"I suppose a few of them are, poor things," I said, nestling closer to him. "Like anywhere."

"Not this one. You're my first Englishwoman." He took a swig of brandy and lit a black-market Marlboro, pinching it between his thumb and forefinger.

"Whose flat is this? I'm grateful to him."

"The brother of a school friend who died last year."

"Oh, how?"

"He was a Jew who'd tried for a long time to emigrate to Israel with his wife and child. They were fired from their jobs of course, attacked in the street, and hounded for years. It was plain they'd never get exit visas. Finally they brought the child here to his brother, went home, and killed themselves. By gas." He broodingly watched his cigarette smoke spiral upwards.

"Oh, my God. I don't know what to say."

"You don't have to say anything."

61

After a while, I picked up a small olive-drab booklet, which was lying on the bed-table with his watch and the contents of his pockets. "What's this?"

"My internal passport. See how they control us?"

I opened it and a mug shot of Dima stared at me. "Read it to me."

"*Name: Kuznetsov, Dmitri Pyotrovich. Place of birth: Novosibirsk. Date of birth: 17 November, 1964. Nationality: Russian.* That's where it says 'Jew' if you are one. *Party affiliation: Not a member. Social status: Student. Military status: Not obligated to serve.* And that page is my *propiska*, my permit to live in Moscow."

I dropped the book and clutched him passionately. "Oh, my love, how can I leave you tomorrow?"

"Well, I have to leave too, for high-altitude training at Alma Ata. Anyway, it's only for three weeks, till Europeans. We'll be together in Paris then, that's something to look forward to, *milochka.* And in the same hotel!"

"What about bed check?"

"We'll get people to knock on the walls to warn us. No problem. And after Europeans, our Olympic team flies straight to Denver for two more weeks of high-altitude training. Where will you be?"

"I'll be back in Colorado Springs—just an hour's drive!" I exclaimed. "That's fantastic!"

"Then to Squaw Valley for two more weeks before the Olympics start. The team's traveling there by train—I think they're afraid of hijacking or a bomb on an American plane. Why don't you take the same train?"

"What a good idea. Then the Olympics, then Worlds a month later, then the tour for six more weeks. Oh, love, that's three or four months together!"

"Maybe more than that, maybe many more. Lesley, I am thinking of defecting. Will you help me?"

The Olympic Movement is a 20th century religion.
Here there is no injustice of caste, of race, of family,
of wealth. . . .
—Avery Brundage, IOC President, 1952–1972

People said it was degrading for an Olympic champion
to run against a horse, but what was I supposed to do?
. . . You can't eat four gold medals.
—Jesse Owens, track & field, four gold medals at
  Berlin, 1936

The tram jerked to a stop, and I was startled out of my memories. We had arrived at the terminus. My anger at Paula had evaporated, leaving only a residue of determination that my future belonged with Dima. I strolled slowly back to the Olympic Village, pausing to watch a mime troupe and an artist who was selling amateurish charcoal sketches for $3: "Your Portrait or an Olympic Champion's." The East German luge team in their conehead helmets and futuristic shiny suits were leaving the Village as I showed my ID to the guard.

Inside the Athletes' Center the game room was overflowing, as usual, for what some people rationalized as "concentration training."

An Arcade Triathlon was laid on for next week, an electronic game competition in Space Invaders, Pac-Man, and Dragon's Lair. The Russian and East German cross-country skiers clustered around their favorite video game, Submarine, picking off American battleships. East and West competed in Ping-Pong and pool.

In the TV room the Finnish hockey team were glumly viewing a videotape of their previous night's loss. On another set, the Russian team intently watched Sylvester chasing Tweety Bird.

Before the Olympics, I'd envisioned a multicolored panorama of national costume, but the athletes were generally dressed, disappointingly, in track suits or jeans. The most exotic things about them were their great variation in size and body type, from tiny skaters to burly bobsledders, and the unfamiliar inscriptions on their jackets like SUOMI or OSTERREICH. At the beginning of February, a tribe of Paiute Indians had come to do a "snow dance"; Japanese photographers pushed aside the international athletes to snap pictures of the Indians' colorful dress.

I went to the cafeteria for a quick lunch, during which Vinnie Luciano's accident was the main topic of conversation, then on to the hospital to visit Dima, after dropping off my skates to be sharpened at the waxing hut next door. Fyodor, a sulky watchdog, was at the door again. It seemed for a moment that he wasn't going to let me in, but he finally opened the door, scowling ferociously. "You don't stay long," he warned.

"Hullo, darling, how are you? Why is Fyodor so cross?"

"I suppose the team leaders, what do you say, called him on the rug," said Dima. "After all, he is here to prevent this sort of thing," gesturing toward his bandages.

"Prevent? You mean you don't think it was an accident?" At least that lets out the KGB, I thought. Or does it? Maybe Fyodor's angry he wasn't killed.

"Who knows?" he shrugged listlessly. "I am on the rug too. I can get up later today and go back to the dormitory, but they won't let me leave the Village at all anymore, with or without Fyodor."

"But why? Oh, Dima, do you suppose they know?"

He put his finger to his lips and glanced significantly toward the door. "I'm just being disciplined again. It's happened before. Like last spring, I was suspended for a year for too much partying during the tour, but they cancelled it after six months—just in time for this competition season. There are always letters in *Komsomolskaya Pravda* saying I have a swelled head and need putting in my place, so they crack down now and then."

"Why did they not let you be flagbearer, and keep you away from the Opening Ceremony? I meant to ask you last night."

"I think they favor Pavel now. I'm the white crow, the odd man out," he said gloomily. "They're going to make an example of me."

"Surely not! You are the world champion, after all. You'll feel more cheerful when you can get out of bed," I soothed him. "Can I bring you anything? Something to read?"

"No, I have the new sports magazines." He grimaced at a cover picture of Kimberly Cranford and Matt Galbraith with the headline GOLD DIGGERS OF THE XVITH WINTER GAMES.

"I wonder what Galbraith's coach had to do to get that cover," he said sourly. "I know that Zack Higgins promises them an exclusive interview if Kim wins."

I told him about Zack's misfired dirty trick and the other strange occurrences of last night. He didn't respond, and went on brooding at the ceiling. "I don't know what's bugging Nokitov and our other officials, but I can tell you this much: the pressure is on for a Soviet sweep of all four golds in figure skating."

"Bloody hell!" I whistled in surprise. "That *would* be a coup."

"Yes, it's never happened before, but they say we have the best chance ever this year. It would prove 'the triumph of the personality liberated by socialism,' you see," he said sarcastically.

"And impress the Third World," I put in.

"Pairs and dance are a sure thing, as usual, even though our dancers were out with injuries last year. But we've never had an Olympic gold-medal-winner in men's or women's singles. So they're really sticking it to me and Aleksandrova, since we're defending world champions. There's never been a Russian woman singles skater as good as Nina before, so they're on her case even more than mine. She'd like to retire from competition and become a coach, but there's no way they'll let her till a successor comes along. Just the opposite of my situation! Be very careful, Lesley. I don't think they stop at any dirty trick to give her an edge and screw you up."

"What can they do?" I shrugged. "If we both skate well, it'll depend on judging politics, as usual. I leave that to Paula. Anyway, Kim and Putzi could throw a spanner in the works."

"You might warn them too, if you feel generous. You know, Russians are famous for cheating in the Olympics—we don't think it's

65

cheating. Even our skating judges were suspended a year for bias. Think of all those male athletes masquerading as women. Remember the Press sisters?"

"Right," I grinned. "The Press brothers, everyone called them."

"In the pentathlon, the Russians dope the horses. And remember the fencer at Montreal with the electronically-wired épeé? Anything can happen in this sort of situation."

"Such as?"

"Oh, say, a skater or coach could meet with a nasty accident. I've heard of the things ballet rivals in the nineteenth century used to do to each other: putting ground glass in the toe shoes or sneezing powder in the talcum, cutting shoulder-straps almost through. They might try rotten stuff like that. Bootlaces could be cut or cassettes erased. I repeat, be ready for anything. And tell your coach, too."

"Good God," I exclaimed, "I can't go about expecting booby traps everywhere, poison in my food, or whatnot. PLAYFAIR's anonymous notes and the shambles in my room and Zack's sneaky tricks are enough to worry about. It would spoil the Olympics for me and my skating would fall apart. Just as always, I'm the only person I have to beat. All I can do is skate as well as I'm able, the rest is fate."

"Just take care, that's all."

Fyodor threw the door open. "You go now!" His beetle-browed glare discouraged argument, but I defiantly lingered a minute to kiss Dima good-bye.

It was time for my interview with Josh McDonnell. I met him at the coffee bar at Olympic House, and we took his espresso and my hot fudge sundae to a window table.

"That's very American of you, eating ice cream," he remarked, his smile illuminating his tanned, square-jawed good looks.

"Well, I suppose I'm mid-Atlantic now."

"Tell me, are you staying on in this country after the Olympics and Worlds are over?"

"I'll return to Britain eventually. Autumn after next, I hope to be up at Oxford reading PPE."

Josh took a notebook from his pocket. "For my readers' benefit, that's Philosophy, Politics, and Economics?"

"Yes. That's assuming I'm admitted, of course."

"And in the meantime? I imagine you'll retire from competition after Worlds."

I hesitated. "One hates to come right out and say these things. . . ."

"Especially if one is English," he put in dryly.

"Quite! But, of course, I hope for an offer from one of the ice shows. Assuming I have a medal of some color to show them."

"Gold, naturally, being the most impressive color. Tell me what you think your chances are."

I was flattered by the famous sportswriter's interest, which seemed genuine as well as journalistic. "I believe I do have a good chance at the gold this year, actually. My figures have improved a lot—they always kept me near the bottom of the list till last year, along with the injuries that seemed to haunt me: stress fractures, shin splints, tendonitis, and so on. Back when I placed 25th in the compulsory figures, no one paid any attention to my freeskating. One American reporter called me, 'Lesley Grey, whose skating is as gray as her eyes.'" I smiled, but it still hurt, even two years later.

"He'll go down in history with Dick Button's first coach, who said, 'That boy will never learn to skate!' What's your current ranking? I know a lot of this stuff is in your official bio, but I seem to have misplaced it."

I swallowed a big bite of ice cream, then replied, "In last year's Worlds I came 3rd, behind Nina Aleksandrova and Kim Cranford. This year Putzi Meier beat me in Europeans—I got the silver—which was a bit of a blow, since one likes to come to the Olympics as European champion. But I beat her in three pre-season competitions: Canada Skate, the St. Ivel in London, and Moscow Skate. And Aleksandrova hasn't placed higher than 3rd this year, except at Moscow, which is unusual for the world champion. I think each of the four of us has an even chance. It generally comes down to who makes the fewest mistakes under pressure. The other three are more weighted down with expectations. They're the World, the European, and the American champions, and I'm only the British champion. The underdog has it easier, nothing to lose and everything to gain." I sat back and looked through the window at a queue of black-clad New Zealand skiers waiting for the gondola.

I pictured my three rivals. Putzi: chunky, methodical, good-humored. Nina: icy, scornful, and precise. Kim: athletic, determined, rather scatty off the ice. I quite liked the German and didn't feel I knew the other two at all. I thought I should be able to outskate them, but this was the Olympics, where anything could happen.

67

"It's a similar situation to the men's competition, isn't it?" asked Josh.

"Not quite—they haven't seesawed back and forth so much. Dima's consistently beat all three of his main rivals over the last few years, though Matt Galbraith came jolly close to winning Worlds last time."

"To get back to what happens when you turn professional, have you thought of following John Curry's lead instead of Ice Capades and the like? Perhaps joining his company, or trying something similar of your own?"

"He already offered me a contract when I did that exhibition at Sky Rink last autumn, and there's nothing I'd rather do. But to be absolutely frank, he just can't pay enough. I'm hoping for one of those million-dollar-offers that gold medalists get from a big company so I can pay off my training debts. Some of them go back years."

"Even though you've had sponsors?"

"Oh, yes," I said, unable to prevent a smile breaking through, although my debts made me shudder. "Full-time figure skating training costs the earth. It takes at least ten thousand pounds a year. That includes coaching, ice time, conditioning, dance lessons, costumes, transportation for the coach to the competitions, and so on. Custom-made skates cost two hundred pounds a pair, and I wear out three pairs a year. Plus board and lodging. My family simply hasn't that kind of money."

"You were brought up by your aunt and uncle, I understand."

"My parents were killed in a car crash when I was very small—I don't even remember them. Auntie Mavis and Uncle Harry *are* my parents now, and they've been as supportive of me as they are of their own three daughters. But they've never been pushy or manipulative, as some skating parents are."

"Are they here with you?"

"No. Because of the money, it just wasn't on, though I hope to bring them to Worlds at Geneva next month. But they'll be watching the Olympic final on telly at four in the morning."

"I'm sure people all over England will be. But I thought your aunt and uncle manage an ice rink. Didn't that help with expenses?" Josh asked.

"Yes, the first few years were practically free."

"How old were you when you first put on skates?"

"As soon as I could walk, they tell me! Apparently, I just took to it straightaway. Figures were a bit stickier, though. I started learning them when I was only four, and the teacher had to tie a red ribbon around my right ankle so I could tell right from left. And I didn't understand the idea of tracing a circle back to its starting point, so she put an orange in the center of the figure eight. School figures were hard work, but I've always loved jumping and spinning, though I had many falls, of course." I thought back nostalgically to the relatively simple days of jump harnesses and foam rubber "Krash Pads."

"And after that?"

"Aunt Mavis and Uncle Harry's rink isn't Olympic-sized, and I needed higher-caliber coaching when I began winning primary and junior titles and working my way up the ranks. So for four years, from fourteen on, I lived in digs in London—a grotty bedsitter—and skated at Richmond before and after school." I licked the last of the hot fudge from the spoon.

"That must have been lonely. When did you move to Colorado?"

"Two years ago, after I won the British Senior Ladies title and finished grammar school. Oh, that has a different meaning here, doesn't it? A grammar school is a college preparatory high school, as opposed to a comprehensive school."

"I thought they'd been abolished by the Labour government," he said, signalling the waiter for a refill.

"When the Liberals got in, they were reinstated."

"So you didn't drop out of school, as so many American skaters do, and have private tutors?"

"Again, it was a question of money. But luckily one can still get an excellent free education in England."

"Could you manage a full academic schedule and not skimp your training? I always heard the grammar schools were very tough."

"It was a bit of a bind sometimes," I said, hoping I didn't sound too sickeningly modest. "They were quite helpful about letting me out of games and accommodating my competition schedule. I did manage to get my A-levels."

"That's typical British reticence," he said emphatically. "I don't know of an American skater, at least not recently, who's done the equivalent. Dick Button and Tenley Albright won their golds while they were at Harvard and Radcliffe, but that was long ago, when training didn't take so much time. I think Matt Galbraith had to drop out of school for several years. In the Eastern bloc the schooling is rigorous, of course, but it's tailored to the training schedule. Here, excellence in sports seems to pay the price of a good education."

"For me, it's a matter of priorities. As much as I love skating, it's not everything. My education's more essential in the long run—does that sound too sanctimonious? But there it is. I'm just lucky to have had both. I've had to forget about free time or a social life, but that's the same on both sides of the Atlantic for competitive athletes," I added with a laugh.

"Are you ever sorry you devoted your youth exclusively to skating?"

"No, not at all. Besides the world travel, skating's given me so much else: self-awareness, self-discipline, confidence, concentration."

"Was your early excellence a social handicap, as it is for so many women athletes?" he asked, scribbling in his notebook.

"A bit, I suppose," I said thoughtfully. "The only men I knew were skaters, and I was at a higher competitive level than most of them— which they resented."

I thought momentarily of my few fumbling affairs before Dima. I'd only slept with the first man to rid myself of my cumbersome virginity. Although the athletes I know don't have time for normal social lives, they're probably more interested in sex than the average person. Is it because of the central role that our bodies and physical sensations play in our lives? Or maybe it's because most of our youths were grimly spent in practice and competition, without any time for normal adolescent outlets. I thought that was probably the reason for Dima's past obsessive womanizing.

I glanced out the window again at the crowd on the infra-red heated deck. "Oh, look at that chap! He must be wearing two hundred pins."

A ruddy-cheeked man was showing off a collection of Olympic patches, badges, and pins that covered his parka and hat. Money changed hands as the pin-broker sold one of the crowd an enamelled badge inscribed SARAJEVO '84.

"I had a pin collection for a while," Josh said, "but people like that make it seem rather futile."

"Yet, you must have been at enough Olympics over the years to have accumulated quite a few."

"I've been covering the Olympics for *The New York Times* ever since the Aga Khan skied for Iran, of all places—to quote a well-worn line you've probably heard me use before!"

"When was that, exactly?"

"The first Innsbruck Games, 1964. He was probably the last true amateur, he and King Constantine of Greece who won a gold medal in yachting in 1960."

"How about Princess Anne at Montreal?"

"Right," he said. "Anyway, since '64 I've covered every Olympics and more world cups and world championships than I sometimes like to remember. But I was going to ask you about your stay in this country. You trained at the Broadmoor World Arena in Colorado Springs, didn't you?"

"Quite right. I simply couldn't get enough ice time in England. There are only about sixteen arenas in the whole country. They're set up for public rather than competitive skating, and I was able to get private ice only in the middle of the night. Patch takes six hours a day, and it's impossible during public sessions. So I followed John Curry's and Robin Cousins's examples—and most other English skaters', they're just the most famous—and came to Colorado for the facilities and coaching, plus the high-altitude training. Unfortunately, there's no way I could've afforded their coaches, the Fassis."

"Don't they charge fifty dollars an hour for private lessons?"

"More than that now, thanks to inflation. But I knew the Broadmoor had several good trainers, and I was lucky enough to be taken on by Paula Emery. She finished in the top ten at the Sarajevo Games. She hadn't had any worldclass pupils yet, so her rates were much lower. The British Skating Association weren't too pleased, understandably, so their grant stopped. But I was able to find a partial sponsor, and I got a couple of loans to support me. If you knew how much money I owe Paula alone, you'd be shocked."

"I doubt it. But I certainly understand why a lucrative contract means a lot to you," he said sympathetically. "Did you ever hear the story about Ina Bauer?"

"Is she the one the Bauer spread eagle is named for?"

"Right. She was the West German champion in 1960, and I understand she was a beautiful skater. At Europeans, she was in 4th place after the figures, which of course counted sixty percent in those days. She received a telegram from her father which said, 'I've put too much money into making you a champion, and you've wasted my efforts. Return immediately; this is your last competition.' So she never made it to the Squaw Valley Games."

"Maybe I'm not so badly off, after all! You're not going to print that about my wanting to make a packet, are you?" I asked.

"Don't worry, I won't make you look mercenary. But when you talk to other reporters, my dear, you ought to say that first instead of afterward. And remember that with most journalists, nothing is truly off the record."

"Oh, blast! I am a silly ass." I resolved not to relax so much during my next interview.

"Not at all, just a word to the wise. So—on deep background— you'll make a big killing with a one-year contract, then quit and go to Oxford?"

"That's my plan. I love Americans, especially their optimism, but I am English at bottom."

"I think that gentleman at the next table is eavesdropping. Shall we walk back to the Village?" We squeezed past a florid German in knickers and Tyrolean hat whose white mustache was smeared with mustard from the Polish sausage he was gobbling. "Let's hope he only sprechens Deutsch," Josh whispered.

We exited by the shoe manufacturers' showroom, full of athletes getting their freebies. Passing the tram station, Josh was almost struck by a pair of skis carried on the shoulder of a bronzed, blond tourist wearing a Sony Walkman. "Man, what a primo day," he was saying to his girlfriend. "I think I broke my ankle, but *it was worth it.*" I snorted and Josh laughed.

"You don't suffer fools gladly, do you?" he said.

"No, I'm afraid that's not one of my virtues."

As we walked on, Josh said, "I heard about Dima's accident. I do hope there'll be no medical repercussions—I must talk to the doctor. His competition with Matt Galbraith ought to be one of the most exciting of the Games."

"And don't forget Hans-Peter Koenig."

"No, never count out the East Germans. Or Pavel Marchevsky, Dima's heir-apparent. Let's hope history won't repeat Randy Gardner's misfortune at Lake Placid."

"Tai and Randy were the last pair to beat the Eastern bloc, weren't they?" I said as we strolled along companionably. "Fewer pairs are competing every year, except for the Russians."

"Yes, do they have a factory somewhere in Siberia turning them out?"

"If they do, it must be the only factory in the USSR that meets its quota!" I said with a chuckle.

"Was Moscow Skate your first time in Russia?"

"Yes, it was fascinating—and sad. What wonderful people I met. They deserve better than the government they have." We walked in silence toward the Village gate. The glass guardhouse was full of burly security men. One of Fyodor's colleagues was there, along with representatives of East Germany, Poland, China, Bulgaria, Romania, Hungary, and Czechoslovakia. Their watchful presence ensured that no athlete from a Communist country would leave the Village alone.

"Well, the Russian pairs certainly have discouraged their competition," Josh remarked. "Ever since the Protopopovs won their first Worlds back in '65, the only Western winners have been Tai and Randy, once. Rodnina and her two partners sewed it up for how long? Ten years, then a round-robin of various forgettable East bloc pairs, now Kulakova and Skachko for the last five years. But the French twins may give Katya and Kolya a run for their money this time."

"They are lovely skaters, aren't they? So lyrical."

"Yes, they take me right back to the Protopopovs, before all this athleticism took over. That reminds me—my daughter Zoe has a house here at Squaw, where I'm staying, and she's giving a party tonight. She asked me to invite you and Dima, if possible. I think she's already gotten in touch with the Carons and the Skachkos and some others. She's a great fan of you all, and is eager to meet you."

"I'd be delighted. How convenient of her to live here."

"She lives mainly in San Francisco, actually; her house here is just a ski condo. She's sort of a skating and skiing groupie—not in any negative sense. She's sponsored a few, and she enjoys meeting famous athletes she admires. She said eightish—will that interfere with your practice schedule or anything planned in the Village?"

"No, tonight my practice group's scheduled for midnight. And the entertainment is Part Six of *Star Wars* and a punk rock band. Oh, and a Jerry Lewis movie with French subtitles! So I'd love to come. What a shame Dima can't make it. He does love a party."

"Yes, so I've heard." He seemed about to add something, but only took my hand in a firm grasp. "Zoe will phone to confirm and give you directions. It's just a short walk. Till tonight, then."

I watched him go, wondering what had been in his mind. Surely, he was too sophisticated to rake up those salacious rumors that germinated like weeds around Dima.

The rest of my afternoon was free. I debated whether to take a nap or get in some extra practice. There were no events to see—the Alpine skiing, bob, and luge were finished for the day, the Nordic skiing wasn't within walking distance, and the 10,000 meter speed skating was about as exciting to watch as a phonograph record going round.

The weather was still enticingly warm under a brilliant blue sky, so I decided on skating practice at one of the outdoor rinks. It was difficult to stay in peak condition without my customary eight hours a day on the ice, but the demand for ice time on only five rinks from more than 100 figure skaters and 12 hockey teams made that impossible.

A hockey match was in progress at the east rink, but the west rink was unoccupied so I deposited my skatebag on the bench and sat down to lace my figure skates. I put in half an hour on my paragraph loops and counters, then changed skates to practice some of the short program's required elements, especially the spins. I concentrated mainly on the combination with its transitions from camel spin to broken-leg sitspin to scratch spin, oblivious to the crowd of onlookers and the constant stream of humanity around the rink. I thought I saw a black-coated figure watching me during one long series of spins, but when I came out of it I didn't see anyone I recognized.

The shadows were lengthening, and the increasing chilliness of the air began to penetrate my glow of warmth after an hour and a half. I sat on the bench and got my Nikes out of the skatebag, took off my right skate, and put my foot into the shoe. There was something inside it.

Puzzled, I turned the shoe upside down and shook it. A long black snake dropped into my lap!

I shrieked and leapt up and away in one convulsive motion. The snake fell to the ground. The nearby spectators jumped back, and several stifled screams.

While I tried to control my racing heartbeat, a little girl of about 10 came over and kicked the snake with disdain. It was now lying in S-shaped inertia. "I can't believe it scared you," she announced. "My brother has one just like it, and he puts it in my bed all the time."

"Did it ever drop into your lap? That might have startled you, at least," I said, a little ashamed. Now I could see the snake's rubber phoniness, but it had seemed realistic enough to stir an atavistic panic. The little girl handed it to me; a white label tied around its neck had been camouflaged by the snow.

In ominously familiar block capitals it read: NEXT TIME IT WILL BE A REAL ONE! A WORD TO THE WISE: DITCH THE COMMIE. BETTER DEAD THAN RED.

*The Olympics are a dinosaur, running out of cities.
. . . If you use the politics of a nation to judge whether
or not you compete with that nation, you might as
well say international sport is finished.*

—Sebastian Coe, track, gold and silver medals at
  Moscow, 1980

*. . . the world wants, needs, must have Olympics.
Munich was only the last Olympiad until the next
one. . . .*

—Erich Segal

I walked along Squaw Valley Road under a black planetarium sky, brightly pricked with innumerable stars. Overhead sparkled the Big Dipper, as Americans call the Plough. Blyth's glittering glass facade was lit up for a hockey match. In the meadow, I could see the faint glow from the luge run and hear the chorus of cheers at every descent.

After the snake had dropped out of my shoe that afternoon, I had stalked directly over to Security Headquarters. Fright had been succeeded by irritation bordering on fury. The sergeant at the desk gave me a form, THREAT TO ATHLETE, to fill out, but none of the boxes to tick off seemed to fit the case. ("What weapon was used? Was the threat telephoned? Was the caller's voice harsh? Inebriated? Disguised? Insane? Did the threat refer to nationality? Religion? Sex?")

A sympathetic but unimaginative Highway Patrolman interviewed me; I showed him the snake and described the note hidden in my pocket yesterday. The dormitory guard had already reported the vandalism in my room.

"You're British?" he asked. "It was probably IRA sympathizers. That's a 27 on our Threat Analysis Profile. There's really nothing to worry about—you're much safer here than in England. We've got five hundred Highway Patrolmen, five hundred Pinkerton guards, military personnel, forest rangers, local police and sheriff's deputies, customs and postal inspectors, and a K-9 corps of sniffer dogs. Then we've got metal detectors, spotlights and electric sensors in the Village fence, surveillance cameras, voice-stress analyzers, the works. No expense has been spared. See this?"

He showed me a picture of the FBI SWAT team in winter camouflage: white hooded snowsuits, backpacks with rifles, snowshoes and skis. They looked ridiculous, like the Snow Stormtroopers from *Star Wars'* Ice Planet. "They've trained for two years in the Rockies," he went on, "and they're ready for any kind of terrorist scenario or hostage situation. They're even equipped with infra-red night viewers and a nuclear detection device. So you can rest easy."

"No, I can't," I snapped. "If it is the IRA who're threatening me, they could plant a bomb in my bag as easily as a snake. In fact, they'd be much more likely to. But *they* wouldn't care if my boyfriend is a Russian. It must be one of these PLAYFAIR nuts who are all over the place, and you've done nothing to stop them. You have a one to one ratio of security people to athletes; can't you give me some protection?"

"No, ma'am, it doesn't work that way," he said wearily. "Believe me, we're doing our best to control PLAYFAIR. Now I suggest you keep an eye on your skatebag in the future, and be sure to let us know if there are any more reoccurrences."

With this cold comfort, I had to be content. Following Zoe McDonnell's directions, I passed the church called Queen of the Snows, straight on past 10 houses, then left at a totem pole and down the cleared path to an A-frame house with a snow-covered shake roof.

The door was opened by a petite woman of around 30 with cascading red hair, who grabbed my hands and pulled me in. "Lesley

Grey! I'm so thrilled and honored to meet you at last," she gushed. "And how is Dmitri? I'm so pleased that you could make time in your busy schedule to come to my little gathering. Dad, here's Lesley. Doesn't she look marvelous?"

In truth, I felt gawky and underdressed in my Fair Isle pullover and corduroy jeans, my hair casually pulled back in a barrette. I hadn't expected anything quite so posh. Zoe was dressed to kill in a low-cut and clinging white jersey frock, with what looked like real rubies and emeralds sparkling from her throat and hands.

Josh drew me toward a group of skiers and racer-chasers (ski manufacturers' representatives) near the crackling fire. I was relieved to see that most of them wore bib overalls and Nordic sweaters. Everyone was talking about the men's downhill, which had been won by a skier from "tiny Liechtenstein," as the reporters invariably called it. The talk was of waxing and tucking, prejumping and getting air.

"What a fantastic run!" exclaimed the Kneissl rep. "Just barely in control—the most exciting race since Klammer in '76. He really attacked that hill!"

"How much will his gold medal be worth in endorsements this year?" Josh asked.

"Half a million, easy."

"These *are* amateurs you're talking about?" I asked the rep incredulously.

"You don't expect them to dice with death for free, do you?" he said with indignation.

"Do the US skiers earn that much?" I asked Josh.

"No, and their expenses are much higher. They have to get to the World Cup competitions in Europe, and follow the snow and the glaciers year round for training."

"Also, they don't win so much!" hooted the racer-chaser.

"Yes, why is that, anyway?"

"Thousands of words have been written on the subject," said Josh, "many of them by me. I think the Europeans' motivation is upward mobility; it's about the only way for poor farm kids to make good. They have the incentive to risk their lives. The US skiers are usually pretty well-off already, or they couldn't be skiers. But it is puzzling, because our women do much better than our men."

"How'd the US men do today?" I asked.

"The highest was 9th."

"Well, I don't feel so mercenary anymore. At least I'm turning pro before I make my packet. And I don't sell advert space everywhere on my body except my teeth, like the skiers do."

Josh laughed. "At the finish today, Greiner had those skis up in the air with the brand name showing before he caught his breath or wiped the sweat away. Fastest skis on the mountain or off!"

"Very funny, but that sort of thing almost killed the Winter Olympics once, didn't it?"

"We're all more realistic now, even the IOC. Did you hear about the death today?"

"No, what happened?"

"A spectator had a coronary, a fifty-year-old man who'd climbed halfway up the course to get a better view. Poor guy, what a pointless way to die."

Josh excused himself to greet more guests, and I joined a bunch of skaters in the corner: Matt, Dany and Jean-Marc, Kolya and Katya, who were talking to the IOC member from Kenya.

"I am here as an observer for my country," he explained when Zoe introduced us.

"Oh, of course, the Summer Games are in Nairobi this year."

"Yes, the first time in Africa. We are very honored to host the Olympics."

"Will the altitude be a problem?"

"No, it's 1700 meters, 300 meters lower than here, and 500 meters lower than Mexico City, site of the so-called 'unfair Olympics.'"

"Can you tell us," Zoe asked, "why it's incorrect to say 'Winter Olympics' or 'Olympiad?' The IOC always seems to insist on Olympic Winter Games.'"

"Certainly, madame," he said in an impeccable Oxford accent. "The phrase 'Olympic Games' or '*Jeux Olympiques*' refers only to the primary event held in the summer. The term 'Olympiad' cannot be used in conjunction with the Winter Games at all. It is a measurement of time elapsed since 1896; this is the XXVth Olympiad, and they are numbered regardless of whether the Games take place. They have been cancelled three times, of course, because of world wars. The Winter Games, or *Jeux Olympiques d'Hiver*, on the other hand, are numbered only since the first in 1924, and only when they are actually held; thus, this is the sixteenth celebration of the Olympic Winter Games."

"Thank you," said Zoe, looking slightly confused.

Josh brought me a glass of wine and a heaping plate of smoked salmon on rye, pâté on toast, and brie on water biscuits. "Tuck in," he invited.

"Pig out is more like it," I said, sitting down with my plate. As I sipped the buttery Californian chardonnay I glanced around the luxurious room, appointed with bright Scandinavian rugs and overstuffed sofas covered with Haitian cotton. The laden buffet table was dominated by an ice sculpture of a skater in a layback spin.

Through the two-story window, I could see the twin Olympic flames and the floodlit Tower of Nations, the scene of the previous night's gruesome accident. The brooding, icy mountains accentuated the warmth and coziness within Zoe's house. It occurred to me that in two weeks this would all have disappeared, as if it had never happened. The house and all the other buildings would still be here, but this whole little world of the Olympics would have come together, existed briefly, and then vanished.

"What does Zoe do?" I asked Josh, who perched on the arm of the sofa with his martini.

"She sort of free-lances. Some designing, photography, writing, a bit of this and a bit of that. Whatever strikes her fancy."

"She must do it very well," I said dryly, looking at the spotlit Oriental *objets d'art* in glass-fronted cabinets.

"That's quite a collection, by the way; you must examine it closely. She's always loved jade and netsuke. Some of the pieces were given her by Avery Brundage when she was just a little girl. But to answer your implication, her financial position was considerably helped by her divorce settlement. It was extremely generous."

"Whom was she married to?"

"Old money. His name is Buckingham—she still uses it sometimes."

"Does she have some connection with the Olympics?"

"She's helping with protocol and entertaining the distinguished guests. For instance, she was involved in arranging the IOC meeting at Symphony Hall in San Francisco—an orchestra always plays at their meetings, you know—and she chaired the committee that put on the IOC ball last Saturday night at the St. Francis." He lowered his voice confidentially. "She told me afterward that she hadn't seen so much bottom-pinching since she was last in Rome."

"Did they really? The old goats."

Matt and Zoe sat down on the sofa next to me; he was asking why the IOC had chosen Squaw Valley as the Olympic site six years ago.

"The tourist and real estate interests here pushed it, of course," she replied. "I'd say most of the locals were opposed. They're not too pleased at having to wear ID tags to get home, and that sort of thing. A lot of them went away for the month and rented their houses for as much as $50,000. The accommodations committee didn't put any ceiling on rentals, as they thought that the people who wanted to stay nearby should pay premium prices. The others would have to spend more time and money to get here."

"I hear some people are even commuting from Sacramento and San Francisco on Amtrak," I mentioned.

"Yes, accommodations are very tight," said Zoe, "even though housing around here has increased a hundred times since 1960. Have you heard the definition of a '10' in Squaw Valley? A '4' with a room!

"But speaking for myself, I'm thrilled that the Olympics are here," she went on. "Squaw Valley needed a shot in the arm. For years, the owner'd put money only into new lifts, and the whole place had gotten run-down and tacky. It was losing business to all the newer resorts. A big development in the Village area fell through, just one of the many plans that failed. After all, this place has a seasonal economy with high unemployment in the off-season. Squaw Valley couldn't ignore all those construction jobs and millions of dollars in federal aid and TV money. Unfortunately, without the profit motive, no Olympics would even take place any more."

"But will they make any money?" Matt asked, quickly raising his eyes from her spectacular cleavage. "I read that they're costing $300 million. That's $25 million per day and $300,000 per athlete."

"That's not much," Josh joshed, "to prove that the American team is second only to the Soviet bloc!"

"The real surprise," said Zoe, "wasn't that Squaw Valley wanted the Olympics, but that the IOC would give the Olympics to the US again. Some of the members are *still* angry, after all these years, about the Denver thing and the Moscow boycott and all the problems at Lake Placid."

"The L.A. Olympics were a big success, though," said Josh. "And the USOC argued that there was less likelihood of terrorism here than in Europe, and an already established site. But there must have been heavy wheeling and dealing behind the scenes."

"Oh, tell them about Sapporo, Dad," Zoe said gleefully.

"In 1966 when Sapporo was bidding for the '72 Games, its Organizing Committee gave each IOC member a pearl—a real one—*before* the vote. That's nothing to some of the things that have gone on. The State Department and CIA usually get involved. Even the national Olympic committee meetings, where they pick the host city, can get pretty dirty. I sneaked into the USOC meeting in '77 when New York City and L.A. were competing for the '84 Games. The state governors were slinging mud—Hugh Carey brought up Charles Manson, and Jerry Brown countered with Son of Sam!"

"Oh, Dad, there's the Skating Union president—come and say hello."

I got up too, and wandered over to the art collection for a while, then to the buffet table for a glass of the renowned Robert Mondavi cabernet sauvignon. I eavesdropped on a ski magazine photographer griping to a Canadian skier about the hazards of his trade.

". . . the lenses fog, and the film freezes, which makes it brittle, then the camera chews it up. I've got to keep the battery in my pocket with a wire leading out to the camera, or it gets too cold to work."

"What kind of camera do you use?" the skier asked.

"Mainly a winterized Nikon F2A. But I'm carrying around tons of equipment. Today I fell on the mountain and sprained my knee—I had to wrap it with gaffer's tape. I was talking to a Russian photographer who covers their reindeer races somewhere up around the North Pole. He says vodka in the camera case beats a hand-warmer. . . ."

I circulated for a while, talking to athletes, skating officials, and a neighbor of Zoe's who told me how the peak called KT-22 got its name: when one of the original landowners first skied it in the thirties, it took her 22 kick turns to get down the mountain.

A TV commentator nearby was telling some Swiss bobsledders about his experiences as a cameraman at the Mexico City Olympics. "We had underwater windows in the diving pool to videotape the platform divers after they hit the water—very ingenious, we thought. But we found that the women went instantly topless when they hit the surface! Needless to say, the tapes were never shown. At least, not on the air," he said to a chorus of masculine guffaws.

I could barely hear the Modern Jazz Quartet on the stereo over the roar of the chatter as alcoholic relaxation set in. Sinking back into the fat sofa, I sipped my third glass of wine, reminding myself to take it easy at this high altitude. The wine was leagues above the plonk I was used to; I already felt a bit potted.

"The Greek Olympics were no Woodstock, man!" The loud, arrogant voice came from a booklined corner where Matt Galbraith was talking to a pony-tailed American ski jumper. "Haven't you read any history? I guess you believe everything you hear on TV."

"All I said, Matt, was that *if* the Greek Olympics were Woodstock, *then* Munich was Altamont."

"Bullshit, man, Munich wasn't the only bad trip—or the first, either. How 'bout Berlin in '36? Even an ignoramus like you must've heard about Hitler refusing to shake Jesse Owens's hand, and about the American Jewish sprinters being dropped from the team. Dachau was already open for business and Hitler had invaded the Rhineland. Sonja Henie was Hitler's favorite Aryan at Garmisch that winter. Or how about Melbourne in '56? Boycotts over Suez and Hungary, and blood in the pool at the water polo match.

"Remember Mexico City?" he went on, after a big gulp of wine. "Everybody thinks politics entered the Olympics when Smith and Carlos gave their one-fist salutes, but thirty years earlier, Hitler'd paved the way for Black Power and the PLO. And talk about bad trips: at Mexico, a couple hundred demonstrators were gunned down by police choppers just before the Games began! Have you forgotten? And the best distance runners, like Ron Clarke, dropped like flies because they hadn't lived at high altitudes, and couldn't get acclimated in the few weeks the rules allowed. The IOC ignored the doctors' warnings that people might die just 'cause of economic considerations. How about the running shoe scandals, $100,000 in cash payoffs to athletes from Puma and Adidas? And the suicide attempts? Remember Moscow—how'd you like that charade? IOC business as usual."

Josh joined them. "Do you think the US should've boycotted the Olympics in 1980?"

"No way," Matt said fuzzily. "Unfair to the athletes."

"I can't figure out whether you think political pressure ought to affect the Olympics or not," Josh said quizzically.

"It has to, and the IOC lives in a dream world to ignore it. They could have relocated the Moscow Games. Why can't they just make a rule that the host country can't be at war? Simple enough." He glared belligerently at the guests gathering around him.

I put in my tuppence worth. "Don't people who think that politics shouldn't affect sport play right into the hands of those who use sport for political gain, like Russia and East Germany?"

"Definitely." He hiccupped. "But to get back to the ancient Greeks— like someone said: beware of Greeks bearing gifts. Like the Olympics. There's nothing new under the sun; even back then, the businessmen and politicians were muscling in on the act."

"How?" I asked.

"The olive oil contracts."

"I don't understand—it sounds like *The Godfather.*"

"Oil to rub down the athletes. And there were under-the-table pay-ments—the shoe and ski manufacturers weren't the first ones to try that. The Greeks were no amateurs; winners were openly rewarded. The athletes said that winning a laurel wreath was okay for a goat, but they wanted better things, like houses, tax exemptions, free meals for life. After all, the ancient Olympics were run by city-states, political entities. Human nature hasn't changed much; each city-state claimed that their winners showed their political power and superior way of life. Sound familiar?"

Matt was in full cry now. "And they kicked people out, just like the IOC expelled Taiwan and South Africa. The Spartans, for instance— they never surrendered, so the other Greeks wouldn't let 'em play. Their specialty was the *pankration.* Ever hear of it? It was a combina-tion of free-for-all wrestling, boxing, and plain old dirty fighting. No holds barred except eye-gouging, and it wasn't over till one of them was dead. Athletic training in those days just meant learning wartime skills."

"What about the sacred Olympic truce?" asked the TV sportscaster. "You always hear that the Greeks stopped their wars for the Games, implying that we should do the same. Of course, we do the opposite."

"No such thing. That truce just meant a safe-conduct through the battle lines for the people going to Olympia. And most of 'em had something to sell. So there's your pure, holy Greek Games, the Wood-stock ideal we're all supposed to strive for! Maybe things started out well, but they went from bad to worse. Finally, after the Romans took over, Emperor Nero put the fix in—he insisted on winning all the gold medals—and that was too much for anyone to stomach. So they called the whole thing off for fifteen hundred years."

"Are you studying history, by any chance?" asked the TV reporter.

"Yeah, as a matter of fact, I'm working on my master's degree."

"Where?"

"Columbia."

"What's your thesis on?"

"Well . . . , 'Politics in the Olympics.'" Everyone laughed.

"You're the expert," Josh said. "Tell us more."

He needed no encouragement. "I bet none of you know when the torch relay started. The ancient Greeks didn't do it. It was first carried to Berlin in 1936, to show the world that Hitler's superman was directly descended from the Greek athlete. And Krupp made the torch."

"And Baron Coubertin?" Josh asked. "'The-important-thing-is-taking-part,' and all that? No doubt you've got a few choice words for him."

"You bet your ass. By the way, he didn't say that first—some bishop did, and Coubertin stole it. He didn't think up *Swifter, Higher, Stronger* either, he copied it off a building. He started the modern Olympics just 'cause he was mad that France lost the Franco-Prussian War, and he thought the French were too soft and had better get in shape for the re-match. Then they tried to keep Germany out of the Games."

"Come to think of it, that's not a bad idea," put in the ski jumper, who was ranked far below all the German competitors. "If you put East and West Germany together, they've won more medals than anyone else. Maybe that's why they divided the team."

"You don't know much about the Olympic movement you're supposed to be participating in, do you?" Matt snapped derisively. "They *didn't* want to divide 'em, in fact the IOC went on pretending that all of Germany was one big, happy family till 1968."

"Why don't you give us your opinion of the IOC?" said Zoe with a provocative smile. "But please remember that several members are here, and try not to be slanderous."

"Okey-doke. Anyone know where that distinguished geriatric group decided to hold the 1916 and 1940 Games before they were cancelled on account of war?"

"We give up," said Josh, who probably knew very well.

"1916: Berlin! Strike one. 1940: Tokyo! Strike two. 1940 Winter Olympics: Sapporo! No, it's not strike three yet, wait for it. When Japan backed out because it was already at war with China, the IOC picked—are you ready for this? Garmisch-Partenkirchen! Jesus, they're consistent, you gotta give 'em that. That was in June 1939, when everybody else in the world already knew what was going on in Germany. But the IOC president—the head ostrich—said piously that they were only interested in sport, not politics. In *November* of 1939 the Garmisch committee finally notified the IOC that the war was on and the Games were off. I think those are strikes three and four." He waved his glass, spilling some wine.

The International Skating Union president tried to get a word in, but Matt went right on: "Not to mention Avery Brundage's open fascist sympathies in the thirties when he was USOC president. He said the US should copy Nazi Germany and stop the decline of patriotism. And even in the seventies just before he died, he *still* said the Berlin Games were the finest ever."

"Your hindsight, as they say, is twenty-twenty, Mr. Galbraith," said the Kenyan delegate, joining the group which by now included most of the party.

"I'm not talking about you. You weren't in the IOC then—you're under ninety years old, unlike some of them in that wax museum. What's the median age now, seventy? How many titles are there? Thirty or forty?"

"Titles?"

"You know: count, baron, marquis, maharajah, duke, sheik, prince, like that." Matt grabbed the wine bottle by the neck and sloshed more into his empty glass.

"Not as many, proportionally, as thirty years ago. And the median age is now much lower. But those titled members have given generously of their time, and in some cases their fortunes, and served without financial reward to build the Olympic movement. I think many of your criticisms are more apropos of the period before the sixties. The IOC is capable of change, you know."

"I guess you're proof of that," Matt said grudgingly. "You were one of the first black members, weren't you?"

"Yes, but the first was long before my time. Of course we are not a democracy, no one claims that. And we are not responsible to governments, political regimes, and pressure groups, only to the Olympic movement and ideals."

"It's a movement of ideals, not ideas—that's the trouble," he retorted. "Let me ask you this: you aren't the delegate to the IOC from Kenya, but the representative in Kenya *from* the IOC, right?"

"Quite right."

"In other words, your first allegiance is to the IOC, not to your country, and the same goes for all the members."

"That is correct. That way we are not liable to governmental coercion," he said, a bit pompously.

"Like the IOC representatives in the US were not coerced by American policy in the Moscow boycott?" Matt pounced with an "Ah ha!" expression on his face. "Of course, the IOC promptly expelled the US from its membership and took the 1984 Games away from Los Angeles—or did it? Just as the IOC took the Montreal Games away when Canada refused to let Taiwanese athletes enter the country—or did it? Why don't you admit the truth: expediency and compromise is the name of the IOC's game." He shook his finger rudely in the delegate's face.

"Of course, we strongly deplore these political intrusions," the Kenyan said, "but we have to deal with the real world." Matt rolled his eyes at the ceiling. "Many of us in the IOC favor eliminating aspects such as national anthems and flags. We *have* shortened the anthems, which is a first step."

"Is that why the IOC wouldn't let that poor guy from Guyana compete on his own, under the Olympic flag, when his country joined the 1976 boycott?" Matt said triumphantly.

"I shan't try to debate you any longer, Mr. Galbraith. You seem to have an answer for everything. I'll just leave you with one thought: *Si la jeunesse savait, si la viellese pouvait!*" He smiled pleasantly and walked away toward the buffet, accompanied by the Skating Union president, who was also an IOC member. It occurred to me that Matt had just kissed his gold medal chances good-bye.

"What'd he say?" Matt asked, his eyes blinking blearily.

"'If the young knew, if the old could,'" I translated.

"Was that a put-down?"

"Yes, and you deserve it," said Josh severely. "Age has to acknowledge it can't cut the mustard any more, but youth *always* thinks it knows everything."

"Yeah, but age gets its revenge," said Matt, downing another glass of wine. "The old farts of the IOC put the Olympics in Mexico City at seven thousand feet, or in Rome in August, where the heat actually killed a competitor. And how about all the athletes the IOC has screwed? Like Karl Schranz? Jim Thorpe? Rick deMont? Eleanor Holm? Smith and Carlos? Matthews and Collett? As far as sports administrators are concerned, we're all scatterbrained teeny-boppers with no right to any say in things. Someone's making big bucks out of this commercial carnival, but you can bet your ass it's not an athlete. We're just the pawns, the unpaid entertainers who put on the biggest show on earth. Do you know most world record-holders in the US are on food stamps?"

"I could sympathize more easily with your poverty if you were a shot-putter or a steeplechaser," said Josh sharply. "The fact is, you *will* be rich, as soon as you sign your ice show contract."

"Not me. It's back to Columbia and my thesis, and my part-time job selling insurance."

"Then how about Karl Schranz, to use your own illustration? He may have been screwed by the IOC, but he did get rich from skiing; in fact, he already was. That was the whole problem."

"He was the scapegoat for all the other skiers," argued Matt.

"I agree, and I'm mentioning that in tomorrow's column."

"I didn't go along with the conclusion today in your column—"

"I'm crushed. Excuse me, I think Zoe wants me." He walked away.

"I think I've been put down again," Matt said to me. I was the only one still there, the others having moved away when the shouting stopped. Vintage Beatles had replaced the jazz on the stereo.

"You must be used to it."

"Somewhat. Anyway, I'm right about the IOC's situation ethics, and they know it."

"Tell me, if it's such a wretched mess, why are you here then?" I asked.

"I was wondering that during the Opening Ceremony yesterday, when Mutzenbecher and all the other old men were haranguing us like generals sending the troops out to die. Come back with your medal or on it! And then I found myself with tears in my eyes during the 'Ode to Joy.'"

"That happened to me too, but you still haven't answered the question. If something about the Olympics hadn't attracted or moved you long before that, you wouldn't be here."

"I guess it's that, underneath the horseshit mixture of religious ceremony and military pomp, this is the ultimate test. The crucible, if you will. After all, sports is the only field where the best from all over the world meet to test themselves. And I want to find out if I *am* the best, Numero Uno, in the eyes of my peers and nine implacable judges. How about you?"

"The Olympics are a human institution," I said after a pause for thought. "They mirror our society, the greatest and the worst aspects. You can't expect them to be any better than the fallible humans who put them on."

"Well said."

"But you seem to be concentrating on all the bad bits."

"Maybe I'm angry that we're *still* so far away from an ideal that *is* worth striving for," he said, his voice quivering with husky sincerity. "Or maybe we should forget it—desanctify the Olympics, and just treat them as a big sports festival."

"Would they get worldwide television coverage then?" I argued. "Would anyone care who won? And would all those governments bother to ante up the money? You disparage nationalism and commercialism, and the IOC pretend to, but aren't they what make the modern Olympics possible?"

"Hmm. You do have a point. Certainly, the world figure skating championships next month won't get the attention the Olympics do. If I were competing just for myself, not for the US, I doubt that I'd even be on TV. And I remember the Moscow Olympics—that is, I don't remember them. Since there was no US team, it was like they didn't even happen. There was a little media coverage, but no one really paid any attention. Well . . . are you ready to split? We can discuss whether the Olympics can be saved while we walk back to the Village."

"I've got practice in Blyth at midnight. What's the time? Ten to twelve? I must go."

"I'll walk along with you. Where's our hostess? I suppose we'd better thank her."

Zoe was talking to the Caron twins. "These two have been telling me that American food is inedible—"

"Oh, no, not again," Matt groaned.

"With the exception of your delicious buffet supper tonight," Jean-Marc interjected suavely.

"Oh, I think one could make a case for that point of view," Zoe said. "But there's quite a good little restaurant in Truckee that is not to be sneered at. French, of course. Will the four of you be my guests for dinner there on Saturday night? Perhaps Dmitri will be well enough to join us—I do so want to meet him."

"That's a bit dicey," I said. "He's out of hospital, but the team officials are cracking down and say he can't leave the Village."

"Oh, I'll have a word with someone," Zoe cooed. "You tell him to count on it."

As we thanked her and left together, I wasn't surprised to see that Matt didn't open the door for me or help with my coat. The courteous gestures to which Dima had accustomed me seemed unknown to him. But in spite of his boorish behavior earlier, I found myself drawn by his passionate sincerity and obvious intelligence. Like me, he couldn't suffer fools gladly. I decided we might not agree on much, but at least he was stimulating company. We walked through the starry night, snow squeaking under our moonboots.

"God, it's cold," said Matt in a cloud of frosted breath. "Cold as a skating judge's heart."

I smiled. "Who's Eleanor Holm? I'd heard of Jim Thorpe and the others you said were screwed by the IOC, but I don't recognize her name."

"Swimmer. Old Discus-Heart, Brundage that is, kicked her off the team in 1936 for drinking champagne on the boat to Germany."

"How absurd. By the way, why do you wear a beard?"

"Why not?"

"Well, I can't remember another skater with one, ever. Doesn't it put the judges off?"

"Tough shitsky for them, as your friend the Master of Sport would say. Well, what'd you think of Ms Zoe McDonnell-Buckingham?"

"The rich are different from you and me," I said, laughing.

"Yes, they have fewer morals. I'd be willing to bet that she manages to get Kuznetsov out of his Gulag, and probably maneuvers him right into her king-size waterbed. She's obviously hot for him, and he's interested in anything warm and moving."

I stopped and faced him angrily. "God, not again! Everybody seems to think he hasn't changed a bit in the last ten years. Can't anyone ever live down a bad reputation? You ought to look beneath the surface a little more, and not be so easily fooled by appearances and out-of-date gossip. I didn't think you were so idiotic. Ill-mannered and crass, yes. Now I see you're stupid as well."

"Oh, am I?" he snapped. "*I'm* not stupid enough to think the leopard can change his spots! My opinion wouldn't be any different even if—oh, forget it."

"Well, what were you going to say?"

"I guess you really don't know. Oh hell, I suppose I'd better tell you.

Someone's bound to, the way everyone's been talking about it."

"What?" I became faintly aware of a feeling of dread.

"Remember the bomb scare in the Village the day before yesterday?"

"I heard about it later," I said, puzzled. "I was out practicing."

"Yeah, most people were off practicing. There was hardly anyone there in the middle of the afternoon. I guess they didn't take the bomb threat—telephoned by the usual anonymous creep—seriously enough to order an evacuation. They just had a couple of guys with dogs go through the dormitories. I'm in Placid, and so is Kuznetsov, as you know. I was putting in some sack time because I'd been up till four A.M. in Blyth.

"Well, there's a knock on the door, and in comes a soldier with a German shepherd who's trained to smell explosives. He explains, and the dog sniffs around. The guy's wearing a big grin, and I ask him what's so funny. He tells me that a few minutes ago he'd knocked on a door down the hall, and gotten no answer, as usual, so he let himself in with the passkey. And there they were in bed, really going at it."

"Who?"

"Kuznetsov and Kim Cranford."

Look not beyond the sun for any brighter star
Nor beyond Olympia for greater games to sing.
—Pindar

Don't look back—something might be gaining on you.
—Satchel Paige

"I don't believe it!" I cried. "How did he know?"

"He said he'd seen them both on TV recently—'Up Close and Personal.' He recognized them right away, even though he closed the door fast."

"Oh, my God," I said in a faraway voice. "Paula tried to warn me. . . ."

"I asked the bomb squad guy to point out which door, and it was Kuznetsov's all right. I haven't told a soul, but he must have, because it's all over the place."

"That's why she wasn't at practice on Tuesday, no one knew why.

Zack was furious." Now why did I think of that? It really wasn't very important. I kept trying not to picture Dima doing all those lovely things to Kim that I had thought were ours alone. I felt dizzy, stunned.

"Are you all right? You're staggering a bit—not that I blame you. I'm sorry as hell to be the one to tell you, but better me than someone who'd do it with malice. It's a rotten Valentine's Day present, isn't it?" he said with concern in his voice.

"Don't worry. I appreciate your doing it, and I apologize for the nasty things I said just now. In fact, I owe apologies to a number of people. I honestly thought he'd sworn off since he met me—it seems everyone else was right about him. God, what a fool I feel," I said bitterly.

"Please don't. No one thinks that, least of all me. He's a louse and you're a nice person, and I don't want you to get hurt. Well, hurt any more, I mean." He put his arms around me and held me in a friendly embrace. "Cry on my shoulder if you want."

"I can't. I don't feel anything but sort of numb and giddy."

"Where do you want to go? I'll take you there."

"Practice, I must practice for the short program."

"Surely you don't feel like it now?"

"I must. What else can I do?"

He kept his arm around my shoulders as we walked inside the arena. The loudspeaker echoed, "Group four may take the ice for the ladies' short program six minute warm-up."

Matt glanced through the door and said, "There's your coach, I'll leave you with her."

"Would you tell her I'm just changing and I'll be there right away?"

"Sure. By the way, I hope you'll consider me a friend if there's anything I can do. An ear, a shoulder, whatever. I do care."

"Thank you, I will."

He gently touched my cheek. "Remember, time wounds all heels."

I didn't seem to feel anything as I plodded automatically down to the dressing room. I bundled up as much as possible, my wool skating dress supplemented with leg warmers, a heavy sweater, a knitted cap, and gloves. But I was still cold, and felt as if I were looking down at myself and the whole scene from a great height.

When I climbed the stairs from the basement 10 minutes later, the announcer was saying: "Your time is two minutes, five seconds. Next, Miss Hansen of Denmark. Miss Grey, please stand by." Music from

Carmen filled the arena as the Dane began her short program by falling out of a triple salchow. Six other women were practicing bits of their programs, moving hastily out of the way of the one whose music was playing with the skater's almost infallible radar.

I wondered if I'd be able to skate at all, but 10 years of training came to my aid as I stroked around the ice in a few quick warm-up laps. Before I'd had time for more than a couple of single jumps, the music ended and the loudspeaker announced, "Your time, one minute, fifty-eight seconds. Miss Grey of Great Britain. Miss Aleksandrova, please stand by."

Waiting in the center of the ice for my music, Elgar's *Enigma Variations*, I saw Paula sitting in the officials' box to get a judges'-eye view. From her sympathetic grimace, it looked like Matt must have told her the news. I hoped we needn't go into it again. Thank God, Kim wasn't in this practice group. I decided to ignore her in the next few days, to forget everything but what I came here for. Skating well is the best revenge.

Mechanically I proceeded through my program, managing even the tricky counter-rotational combination of triple lutz and double toe loop without trouble. The prescribed six-revolution flying change sit-spin finished the routine. When I skated over to Paula, I thought wryly that for two minutes and three seconds I hadn't thought about Dima and Kim at all.

"Good, Lesley. Now, at the end of the serpentine sequence, you weren't quite far around enough for the axel. . . ." As the coach wound up a few minutes later with ". . . stretch and extend more, and remember if you elect to do the double lutz instead of the triple, make up your mind well in advance," I realized that not a word of advice had registered. Aleksandrova's gypsy air had just ended, with Nina whirling in a full Biellman spin with one foot high over her head, and I hadn't been aware of that either.

I went on practicing, grooving the difficult moves more deeply into muscles and nerves. As my turn came round again, I repeated the complete program twice, finishing with cooling-down laps of the arena. I stopped only during resurfacing and once to blow my nose. It was only while I was skating that my mind could erase the taunting pictures that kept creeping back in.

At 2 A.M. we left the ice, our place taken by the Zamboni. Half a dozen pairs were getting ready to skate. Dany Caron greeted me:

"Quite a party, *n'est-ce pas?* It's still going strong."

"Yes, it was a good party," I replied. "Goodness, no gloves. Won't your hands freeze?"

"No, we cannot wear them," Jean-Marc explained. "We must be able to feel each other's hands in the lifts with nothing in the way."

"Oh, I see. Well, have a good practice." I wonder if they know, I kept thinking during the brief exchange. Maybe they're sorry for me, that's why they're being friendlier than usual. Matt said everyone knows, they're all talking about it, everyone knows, everyone knows. . . .

After a few hours of troubled sleep in the early morning, I had a late breakfast with Angela. I couldn't bring myself to pour out my troubles to my roommate. I'd been brought up by Aunt Mavis not to moan over things that were my own fault, and to overcome lifelong conditioning was impossible, as much as I longed for a sympathetic ear. Sometimes I wished I were an American, able to wail and howl and messily spill the beans to all and sundry.

Nigel stopped by our table as I finished pushing my bacon and egg around the plate. "What about a game of chess?" he suggested.

"I'll take you on in a bit," I said, determined to seem cheerful, keep busy, and ignore thoughts of Dima. "Just give me a few minutes for a look at the papers."

I settled down in the lounge with that day's *New York Times* (MR. GREINER OF LIECHTENSTEIN TAKES DOWNHILL; MRS. KLUGL, 2 OTHERS IN GDR SPEED SKATING SWEEP) and turned, as usual, to Josh's column.

. . . Plus c'Est la Meme Chose
By Josh McDonnell

Squaw Valley, CA, Feb. 13——"The more things change, the more they remain the same." In this space yesterday, I harked back to 1960's disputes and dissensions and found them pretty small beer.

Think of all the things that hadn't happened yet. Ski companies didn't emblazon brand names all over the (wooden) skis. Karl Schranz, the great Austrian skier in his first Olympics (he ultimately competed in three) hadn't yet been sacrificed as the manufacturers' scapegoat in his fourth by a vengeful old man.

Doping control wasn't even a gleam in the IOC's eye, although later in 1960, a Danish cyclist died of a stimulant overdose at the Rome Olympics. Shoe manufacturers were not yet buying runners and keeping them in their pockets like so many nickels and dimes.

According to what were not yet called the media, the athletes in

1960 were good clean kids, right out of *Ozzie and Harriet*. *The San Francisco Chronicle* carried a breathless description of Saturday night in the Squaw Valley Olympic Village: "Ice cream sodas, table tennis, and a nickel juke box blaring everything from rock 'n' roll to polkas! Some people took in a movie, some turned in early! Hot chocolate, cha cha, and jitterbug! 'Mack the Knife' and 'Moonlight Serenade.'"

Eat your heart out, Jerry Falwell. On subsequent evenings, the athletes were entertained by musical groups like The Vagabonds and Sons of the Pioneers, fashion shows by Esther Williams and Edith Head, Hawaiian Night, Disneyland Night with Roy Rogers and Dale Evans, and an Italian pop singer who had everyone singing *"Volare."* That is, when they weren't humming "A Summer Place." Art Linkletter was the entertainment director of this orgy of wholesomeness.

Were we really that naïve then? A look at the front pages of February 1960 was more disillusioning: the Finch murder-adultery trial spewed bad taste across the headlines for days. Governor Pat Brown of California (Jerry's father) couldn't make it to the Olympics because of his eleventh-hour consideration of a stay of execution in the Chessman rape-murder case. Jack Paar walked off his late-night TV show because the network censors wouldn't let him say "W.C." (Some people wanted naïveté protected.) Queen Elizabeth gave birth to the prince who would be known 20 years later in a cruder time as Randy Andy.

What some would think a major news story was, surprisingly, not on the front page: the US hockey team defeated the USSR, in a half-empty Blyth Arena at 8 A.M. Even when we later won the gold medal, one of only three for the US that year, it didn't make headlines—although the same cry was heard in the land as in 1980: "We beat the Russians!"

Maybe it'll happen again, the home-field advantage being pretty strong in this sport. There was no bobsled or luge competition then; the US is not among the top-seeded in either this time.

In 1960, the Austrian ski team was embroiled in the usual fracas over which skiers would make the cut. The American women's Alpine team was the strongest in years, and emerged with three silvers, though Penny Pitou and Betsy Snite were as downcast as those who've missed gold by hundredths of seconds always are. A tenth of a second can mean a skiing career. We're unlikely to do that well this time, though Stephanie McGregor could surprise.

Atypically, our speed skaters will probably be dominated by the USSR and GDR this time. Just as in 1960, none of our Nordic skiers has a hope. A host country that wins few medals is like a polite dinner party host: "family hold back."

Our champions dare not forget how slippery snow and ice can be to high ambitions. One fall in skiing costs an Olympic title. FIS

95

World Cup scoring depends on many races, but Olympic gold on only one. In figure skating, a fall doesn't mean elimination, but one performance determines a championship (though some observers think overall reputation equally important).

Kim Cranford and Matt Galbraith have a good chance of repeating Carol Heiss's and David Jenkins's 1960 winning feats in figure skating, but they won't find it quite as easy to cop the crowns. European champ Putzi Meier, world titleholder Nina Aleksandrova, and Britain's fast-rising Lesley Grey all are strong contenders in women's singles.

As usual, Galbraith will have his work cut out for him against world and European champion Dmitri Kuznetsov. Hans-Peter Koenig and Dima's teammate Pavel Marchevsky are threats as well. Our ice dancers Elinor Rhodes and Brent Reece could be dark horses, but the Russians, led by Kulakova and Skachko, will probably triumph in pairs.

It's hoped that Dima Kuznetsov's accident on Wednesday won't be a case of history repeating itself. In 1960, Austrian skater Norbert Felsinger had to withdraw from competition because of a head injury suffered in practice. The doctor assures us, however, that Felsinger's—and Randy Gardner's—fate will not be Kuznetsov's. We'll all be the losers if this classic US-USSR confrontation is scratched.

Monday: Olympic women

It wasn't going to be easy not to think about Dima. I got my coat and joined Nigel and some kibitzers, mostly ice dancers, at the big outdoor chessboard by the pool. The pawns were as tall as my waist, and my white queen looked me in the eye. A pile of checkers lay nearby, sawn-off sections of redwood tree trunks. I moved pawn to king's four with a large croupier's pusher.

Half an hour later, my forces were in retreat. I'd just lost my queen when Angela called me to the telephone from our balcony. I let Elinor Rhodes take over my pieces and ran upstairs, resolving that if it were Dima, I would just ring off.

It was the Tahoe City lawyer I'd tried to reach a few days earlier on Dima's behalf. His cousin, an acquaintance in Colorado Springs, had given me his name. Now, I didn't know what to tell him. I decided to pass it on to Dima, so he could do whatever he liked. Not daring to mention his defection plans on the phone, I rang him and said tersely that I had to talk to him privately, but didn't wish to come to his room.

"Then I take you to lunch. How about Pfeifer House in Tahoe City? Let's get out of this joint."

"I thought you couldn't."

"We have to take Fyodor. But I think they'll let me go. Nokitov was much nicer today, I don't know why." We arranged to meet at the bus stop near the Catholic church on the far side of Blyth.

There was a knock on the door, and Kim Cranford, of all people, entered—in the nude as usual. She seemed a bit disconcerted at seeing me, and said hastily, "Angela, could you call Elinor to the phone? She's right outside, and I can't find my bathrobe to go out on the balcony."

Angie was changing her clothes, so I seemed to be elected. I opened the sliding glass door to the balcony we shared with Kim and Elinor's room. The American ice dancer was still at the chessboard, with a few white pawns left. "Hallo, Elinor—phone for you," I called, leaning over the rail.

Suddenly I heard a thump overhead. A blast of cold air whistled past my head, and something fell with an ear-ringing crash. One of the enormous icicles dangling from the roof had fallen and shattered inches from my feet. Icy fragments littered the balcony floor, and the razor-sharp tip of the icicle glistened in the sun. It could have split me like kindling.

My legs were quivering and my heart pounding with fright at the close call. Angela ran out onto the balcony and Kim peeked around the drapes. "What the bloody hell—? Are you all right?"

"An icicle—it just missed me," I quavered.

"God! It looks like those BEWARE OF FALLING ICICLES signs are here for a purpose. I've never seen that happen before."

The thudding sound continued, and it wasn't my heartbeat—someone was running across the roof. I leaned back against the rail and craned my neck. A dark figure was just disappearing over the opposite end of the roof, probably into the stairwell. I raced along the corridor and down the stairs in pursuit, but when I opened the fire-door at the bottom, all I saw was the usual horde of athletes milling about. Many of them wore dark colors, and it was impossible to pick one out as the figure on the roof.

Back upstairs, I examined the icicle's shards. The thick end, though splintered into several pieces, was smooth, wet, and seemed almost warm to the touch. Had someone partially melted it with a lighter or something, then stamped on the roof to dislodge it? It looked like I'd never know for certain, and the evidence was melting fast. I set off to meet Dima.

My heart melted too, along with my good intentions, when I saw him standing there with his hands in his pockets, blond hair gleaming in the sun. He was so dear—how could I give him up? Stop it, I scolded myself, he's given *me* up. He only wants one thing from me—my lawyer. I smiled sadly at the feeble joke.

I greeted him coolly and said hello to Fyodor, bearlike in a *shapka* and huge blue serge suit. We boarded the Tahoe Area Rapid Transit bus, nicknamed TART, and I told him about my narrow escape. We chatted about the mild climate: "This Californian weather doesn't seem like winter, does it, at least during the day when it's in the fifties." How pathetic, I thought, disembarking; we have to talk about the weather. We walked along the lake shore in silence, its cold sapphire beauty unmentioned.

Tahoe City was gaily adorned with flags, bunting, and children's murals of the Olympic events. When we arrived at the chalet-style restaurant, Dima banished Fyodor to a table across the room, and we sat in a booth with mugs of St. Pauli, Dima's favorite German beer.

"All I had to tell you was that the solicitor rang up. I didn't know what to say, so I thought I'd pass him on to you."

"You know I can't talk to him directly!" he said angrily. "I thought you were going to meet with him and carry messages. Aren't you on my side anymore? Why are you letting me down?"

"Perhaps you'd better ask Kim Cranford to handle it for you," I said in a distant voice.

"So! Some big mouth has told you."

"No, a friend told me."

"It didn't mean anything, you know."

"What *does* mean anything to you?"

"You do. You know that. Look, it just, well, happened. I thought our team officials might be suspicious of you and me spending so much time together, so it wouldn't hurt for them to think I'm still playing the field."

"Sorry, that won't wash anymore," I snapped.

"And then I thought maybe she or her coach might be able to help me. Zack Higgins is a pretty important person. And you know I've changed my mind about living in Britain, since you told me what it's like there for skaters."

"Super. You can marry Kim, become an American citizen in three years, win the next four Olympics for the US, and live happily ever after," I said in a voice with ice cubes in it.

"No, no! I'm having no intention to do that. She got scared as soon as I even hinted at defecting. Besides, she has a boyfriend—he'll be here next week."

"So? That just makes her another coldhearted, two-timing sod like you!"

"No, it means she looks on these things as I do, that they have no importance. You must overcome your old-fashioned Puritan ideas."

"But how could you bring yourself to go to bed with her?" I hissed angrily. "She's so stupid! And so scrawny," I added spitefully.

"Lesley, we are not each other's property. Shh, *deushka*. Eat up your nice bratwurst and potato salad and that enormous pickle."

"Don't want any," I said sullenly.

"Give me your hand. Come, don't pull away." He put something in my palm and closed my fingers around it. "There. Happy Valentine's Day."

I opened my hand and saw a fat golden heart on a delicate chain. In spite of my rage, my eyes filled with tears.

"I give you my heart—see? Please forgive me. I promise it won't ever happen again if it bothers you so much."

"Oh, Dima, I don't know. All morning, I've felt like I was hit by a lorry. Weak and bruised and stunned. I don't want to feel that way anymore."

"Then don't," he coaxed. "Feel good. I need you, *milochka*—don't let me down."

"I'll have to wait and see. Let's put it on hold for a bit. I ought to concentrate on nothing but the competition right now. After the Olympics, we'll see."

"That's all I ask." He fastened the chain around my neck, brushing my breast casually with the back of his hand. "*Ya tebya lyublyu.* I love you," he whispered. It was the first time he'd ever said it to me.

We sat in silence holding hands for a few minutes, then I roused myself from my dreams and said, "I'll make an appointment with the lawyer for a week from today. My competition will be finished then, and maybe you'll have a more definite plan."

"Maybe the Mustang Ranch plan?"

An unwilling grin flickered across my face, remembering a hilarious afternoon in bed at the Broadmoor dormitory in my room. We'd been in ridiculous moods. Dima had suggested telling Fyodor that he was going to the Mustang Ranch, the most notorious of Nevada's legalized brothels, and then sneaking away to the Immigration and Naturalization Service office in Reno to claim political asylum.

I had begun to giggle. "No, *deushinka*," he explained, "don't laugh—that's the way a Russian writer did it in London. His name was Kuznetsov, too. He was researching Lenin's early life in London—stop laughing—and he told his *mamka* he was going to Soho to find a prostitute. Really! The idiot wished him a good time and went back to the hotel. So Kuznetsov ran to the nearest police station. It's true, I read it in *Newsweek*." I had actually rolled off the bed at that point, laughing helplessly.

"The problem is," I said now, "Fyodor would want to go along as well. I've a new idea: why not hole up in the Olympic Village church and claim sanctuary? The press would love it. What's the time? Oh blast, I've got patch. Paula'll have my guts for garters if I miss it. Let's push off."

"I've got practice for the short program. Are you going to watch the pairs' short tonight?"

"Yes, will I see you there?"

"Sure. Is there an athletes' section where we can sit?"

"No, I think we're meant to watch from the skaters' entrance. But Dima, let's not go together. Everyone seems to have heard about you and Kim, and I don't want to look a proper fool."

"As you like."

I tried not to feel too happy while I glided through my figures at the outdoor training rink, surrounded by the usual throng. Nevertheless, it was as though a great stone had fallen from my heart. I even found myself whistling the dated compulsory dance tunes like "Beer Barrel Polka" and "April Love" drifting out of the Blyth dance practice session. After I talked with Paula, who was much more encouraged by my figures than at yesterday's patch, I jogged along the snowy road for a while, then watched the women's speed skating sprints, enjoying the warm sun on my back and the festive scene.

The figure skaters' draw ceremony took place at 5:00 in the Athletes' Center lounge to determine the skating order positions for the first rounds of competition. One by one, or two by two, over a hundred skaters drew numbered cards from a velvet bag held by an ISU vice president. My number for the compulsory figures was 27, one of the last to skate the first figure. In the freestyle rounds, the skating order would be decided by how well we did in the compulsories, which gave the early events even more importance. Skating in the last group in the final was vital for a medal chance.

After a sashimi and rice dinner ("Japanese Night"), I walked to Blyth with a dozen other skaters, doing my best to ignore Dima. To my relief, Kim wasn't among us. This first figure skating event was sold out, and scalpers were hawking tickets for $70 each. The flag-bedecked arena was packed and humming with noisy anticipation.

We trooped down to the basement, then up again to the tunnel leading to the skaters' entrance to the ice. Autograph hounds hung over the rail from the audience, searching for their favorites. The Zamboni had just finished surfacing the ice, and coaches lined the barrier at the skaters' area, watching their pairs warm up like anxious mother hens.

In spite of years of exposure, I felt anew the thrill of fine pair skating: two skating as one. Here at rinkside, I could accurately gauge the speed of the man skating toward me, his partner held high by up-stretched arms, her head nine feet above the ice.

"God, I'd be scared way up there," I said to Gilly Herring, who was standing next to me. "The woman must have to have absolute trust."

"Yes, one must love to fly. If you're scared and tighten up, injuries are more likely. I skated pairs till I was fourteen. See?" She lifted her chin and showed me a faint crescent-shaped scar. "Most women pair skaters I know have that from being dropped on their faces."

"No wonder there are so few, only twelve pairs in this Olympics."

"Do you remember, Tai Babilonia wore braces till she was sixteen or so?" said Matt, who had overheard us. "They were to keep her teeth in! Randy dropped her once when they were kids, and about four teeth were knocked out, scattered all over the ice. They had to collect them and take them to the dentist."

"Did they grow back?"

"Yeah, he just stuck 'em back in."

I winced. "Look out, I think it's going to happen again!" As the Chinese pair attempted an overhead lasso lift, the man's arms collapsed.

"No, it's okay. She fell on top of him," said Matt. "Always a wise move."

"A spot of weight lifting's in order for them, don't you think?" I asked. "The poor Chinese skaters—it's rather embarrassing to be at such a low level in international competition."

101

"But it's so nice for everyone else. You know you'll never be at the absolute bottom. Anyway the Chinese aren't bad, considering that they only re-entered world competition in the middle seventies, and our musical rhythms and dances are completely foreign to them."

"Novice level now, would you say?"

"More like Junior. They're an interesting contrast to the Russians when *they* first entered, back in the fifties. They didn't try an event till they had a good chance of winning."

In the television area, across the short end of the rink, spotlights were being tested for the large camera in the flower-adorned interview corner. Several people in headphones watched monitors and fiddled with dials. The network was supplying a world television feed by satellite, so each competitor would be briefly photographed, regardless of standing, for the fans at home. Nine other cameras were spotted around the arena.

"One minute remaining," the announcer warned.

"Where are Dick Button and Peggy Fleming?" I asked Matt. I was trying to hide the embarrassment I felt over last night's encounter behind a casual manner. I hoped he wouldn't think I'd betrayed his kindness and concern. I resolved not to speak to Dima when he was around, but there wasn't much hope of fooling him for long—he was too sharp.

"They'll be here soon. It's a nice change," he remarked, "to see blank barriers with no advertisements on them, isn't it? Of course, they couldn't finance Europeans and Worlds without the ads—I hear those companies pay $250,000 each to get their names on the boards."

"Please clear the ice," boomed from the public address system, and all but the first pair returned to the dressing rooms with their coaches. The usual announcements were made in English, French, and German: "Please refrain from the use of flash attachments on your cameras, ladies and gentlemen. They're unnecessary under television lighting, and a dangerous distraction to the skaters. And I'd like to remind you that in the arena there is no skating, please. Uh, that's no *smoking*, please."

A delighted roar of laughter and applause filled the huge enclosure. "Your announcer gets a 2.9 for presentation," the red-faced official said ruefully.

After more laughter from the audience, he introduced Olympic and ISU officials and the nine judges, then listed the seven required moves of the short program and the skating order. Buffs hurriedly scribbled names in their souvenir scorecards.

The announcer consulted his phonetic pronunciation sheet again, and carefully enunciated, "Liang Mee-ling and Hsi Tse-tung, from the People's Republic of China." The two stroked out in tandem and stood poised at center ice.

At the resurfacing interval, I found myself near Dima in the milling crowd. "Do you think Katya and Kolya are worried?" I joked. None of the first half-dozen couples had received marks of much over 5.0 out of a possible 6.0, and several had botched at least one of the vital required elements. One pair had fallen disastrously, ripping their costumes, and missed two moves before they recovered.

"Well, I tell you, they *are* a little worried by the French and East Germans. They're both damn good, and maybe the judges think too many Russian pairs have won over the years."

"No, pair skating's considered a Soviet sphere of influence. Sort of like Eastern Europe."

"Now we see some real skating," Dima said with relish as the last six pairs—two Russian, and one each from France, Japan, East Germany, and the US took to the ice for warm-up. They immediately showed a precision and assurance that set them apart from the earlier, more tentative skaters.

Dany and Jean-Marc were first to skate in the last group, a dangerous position for top competitors. Even if they were flawless, no judge would risk giving them a 6.0 in case those following them were better. Room had to be left above them in the marks.

Regardless, they looked superbly confident as they skated out together to enthusiastic applause and fluttering French flags. They wore stylish black costumes decorated with vertical stripes of silver bugle beads changing to black ones along a diagonal line. Their short dark urchin haircuts enhanced their striking resemblance. CARON AND CARON, FRA lit up the electronic scoreboard as their haunting music began, the Second Suite from Ravel's *Daphnis et Chloe*. They were skaters of extraordinary purity and delicacy. As they leapt in absolute unison into double salchow jumps, they seemed, as the best pairs so often do, two halves of one person. Even the angle of their arms and hands and the tilt of their heads were identical.

Of course, I thought as I watched their tango camel spin, they once were one person. No, that's just identical twins, both of the same sex. But these two sometimes do seem the same sex, some new androgynous form with eerie ESP. Chills ran down my spine as they shadow-skated seamlessly into a prolonged lift.

Jean-Marc threw Dany up into a split double lutz twist, then they flowed into their incomparable death spiral. Holding Dany's right hand in his, Jean-Marc glided backward on a right outside edge, and then pivoted around the toe of his left foot. As he pulled her around in a backward circle, she arched her back and lowered her head till it brushed the ice. Her right skate mirrored his deep outside edge, her free leg high, and their outstretched left arms completed the diagonal line of their joined right hands. Only speed, centrifugal force, and the tension of their connected arms kept their cantilevered sculpture balanced on the fulcrum of Jean-Marc's toepick. On the ice they traced a wide spiralling circle like the center of a seashell.

"The best death spiral since the Protopopovs'," murmured Dima, his breath tickling my ear. "Smooth as whipped cream. . . ." He was standing behind me, and rubbed sensuously against me as I leaned back.

"Is that loyal to Kolya and Katya?" I asked, under cover of the tumultuous ovation. A memory nagged at the back of my mind, a sense of déjà vu, but his powerful ability to arouse me blotted it out. My breathing quickened. Now all I wanted was for us to be alone and become one.

"No, but true."

Roses rained down as Jean-Marc bowed and Dany kicked into the exaggerated skater's curtsy, a catlike smile on her face. Ice flakes still sparkled in her hair from the death spiral. The announcer warned the audience not to throw flowers onto the ice because of the danger to succeeding competitors, and was, as usual, ignored.

The pair finally stepped off the ice into the TV area, their arms full of flowers, to embrace their coach and talk to Peggy Fleming. Their interview with FR3 French TV was interrupted twice by enthusiastic applause and whistles when the marks came up: 5.8s and 5.9s both for required elements and presentation from all but the East German judge. A volley of boos and catcalls greeted his 5.4s.

"The Franco-Prussian war goes on," said Matt who was standing nearby eating one of the competitors' oranges.

I edged away from Dima and remarked self-consciously, "You

know, it took me a while when I first skated here to realize that whistling from the crowd is good. In Europe it means they hate you."

"In Japan, they don't whistle at all, only clap," said Matt. "And in Scandanavia, there's a long silence before the applause that makes you wonder what you did wrong."

"But what a responsive audience tonight! They cheer for the US, of course, but they recognize good skating, regardless of nationality. Thank goodness those PLAYFAIR people don't seem to be skating fans."

The audience was now applauding the young American pair who had just skated out. Their club, the Philadelphia Skating Club and Humane Society, waved placards, cheered and whistled. More booing ensued, however, as most of the judges sternly penalized them when the man tripped in the spiral step sequence and his partner fell over him. The Japanese pair never recovered from two false starts with the wrong music; their change-foot sitspins were wildly unsynchronized, and almost collided. The East Germans, whose program began with their customary electronic tone which made me think of behavioral conditioning and Pavlov's dog, were uninspired but made no mistakes and got marks similar to the Carons'. Only the French judge gave them a 5.6 and 5.5.

"Revenge!" said Matt to Jean-Marc. The twins had returned to the skaters' entrance to watch the rest of the competition.

"*Mais oui*, did you see how low that swine of a German marked us?"

"You two really do skate as one. How do you get such amazing unison?" Matt asked in a surprisingly respectful tone.

"We practice with mirrors and use our peripheral vision," Dany replied. "And we have skated together all our lives, after all."

The third-ranked Russian pair was now performing a one-armed overhead lift, the man holding up his tiny 80-pound partner as easily as a waiter carrying a tray.

"There seems something illicit about that pair," said Matt.

"One man and his doll, as they used to say about Sherkasova and Shahkrai," I said, laughing.

"*Zut alors!* But they are so good," enthused Jean-Marc. "She's a marvelous skater for only fourteen years old. Would you have stopped Mozart from composing?"

"Well, I don't think it's cricket," I said, "and I think it ought to be outlawed by the ISU. You and all the other men have to lift great girls your own age like Dany, who have to worry about slimming all the time."

"I'm hardly a great girl, at one-and-a-half meters and forty-six kilos," she said indignantly.

"That's what? Five foot one and a hundred pounds? And what are you, Jean-Marc, about five-eight and one-fifty?"

"I suppose," he said without interest. "I don't feel like working it out."

"*Eh bien*, time will take care of the Russian pair's problem," said Dany.

"Yeah," Matt said. "Remember the '81 Worlds in Hartford when Shahkrai could hardly lift his partner, even though they were the defending world champions? She'd finally outgrown him. They split up, but more one-and-a-half pairs keep coming along. Uh oh, look out: new Olympic event. Hammer throw with tiny Russian girl." I grinned; their death spiral did look like the girl was about to whiz out into the audience.

Matt went on speculatively, "I've heard that some of the Eastern bloc sports doctors give their girl gymnasts and pair skaters shots of testosterone, to retard puberty and keep their bodies light and child-like. You can tell by their big heads."

"God, the perversions that take place in the name of winning!" This was a subject on which I had strong views. "They say the East Germans start their athletes on sugar pills at ten years of age to get them used to taking drugs. Then they switch to anabolic steroids."

Matt interjected: "Do you remember that swim coach who was asked about his women swimmers' deep voices? He said, 'We have come here to swim, not to sing.'"

I laughed. "I can top that. Not only the East bloc uses, shall we say, questionable medical practices; I read that the *West* Germans at the Montreal Olympics injected compressed air into swimmers' backsides to make them more buoyant."

"No shit!" Matt whistled.

"Well, I don't know." I giggled.

Evidently the judges agreed that cracking down on disparately-sized pairs was in order. The Russians' marks for presentation were low 5s. "*Scandaleux!*" hissed Dany, shaking her head in disgust.

"By the way, you were *magnifique! Formidable!*" said Matt, receiving a bored "*Merci bien*" from Jean-Marc and a sniff from Dany. They moved away, arm in arm. Matt grinned at me.

"The last skaters, from the Union of Soviet Socialist Republics, Yekaterina Kulakova and Nikolai Skachko." Katya and Kolya skated with the authority and precision of the five-time world champions they were. Their speed and power transmuted the same elements we had seen so many times before with a kind of alchemy.

"Well, who do you pick?" Matt muttered to me.

"They're great, of course, and there's no doubt that they're technically superior. But I prefer the Carons' skating—if not their personalities. It reminds me of the old days before pair skating turned into a weight-throwing contest, when you could feel a relationship between the two of them. But a brother and sister team can't really convey a romantic or erotic relationship, can it?"

"With those two, I wouldn't be too sure."

The audience paid tribute to the Russian champions, but the applause was nothing like the ovation the Carons had received. As the Skachkos left the ice, Matt said, "I'd give the czar and czarina 5.7, tops."

Dany had returned and was standing at the barrier applauding. "*Oh la la*, Matt, you are joking. They must get a 6.0," she insisted.

"Don't you want to win?" he asked.

"We know there are heights to which we cannot aspire," Jean-Marc said pompously. "They are the masters."

The judges agreed, with one 6.0 and the rest 5.9s. Several people in the audience yelled, "Too high!" Within a few minutes, the computation-minded spectators had done their calculations, converting the marks into ordinal rankings by judges' majorities from 1st to 12th. Even before the computer printouts were handed to the press, the interim standings were buzzing through the arena: USSR, GDR, France.

As the crowd filed out, Dima caught my arm, "Come to my room now," he whispered. "Kolya won't be back for hours—it takes him forever to get through doping control, and then they're going to a party." He backed me against a wall, pressing his body urgently against mine.

"No. No, really."

"*Deushka, lyubov,* I want you so much. Only you, no one else. Please." He kissed the palm of my hand and stared ardently into my eyes, as he had at the picnic in Gorky Park when I fell in love with him.

Paula's right, I'm obsessed, I thought. I want to, but of course I shouldn't. If I give in to him now, there'll be no turning back. I opened my mouth to say no, and said weakly, "Yes, all right."

*[Olympic competitors] are mystery people. We have
our place in the sun once every four years and then we
disappear. We're forgotten. Nobody wants to hear
from us or about us. People understand Joe Namath,
but they don't understand us. . . .*
—Micki King, diving, gold medal at Munich, 1972

*I had never heard of Shirley Babashoff until last week
and already she's let me down.*
—Josh Greenfeld, writer

Saturday, February 15, 1:30 P.M.

The next day was again sunny and warm under a cerulean sky, and
50,000 day-trippers jammed into Squaw Valley. I stopped to buy a
falafel sandwich from a vendor's wagon, and watched a victorious
East German speed skater being tossed high in a blanket by her teammates. My free program practice had just finished, and I was on my
way to watch the ski-joring demonstration in the meadow.

I'd slept half the morning, after sneaking back to my room at 3 A.M.
after several hours of lovemaking more intense and abandoned than I
had ever known. Dima had sworn that he wouldn't even look at
another woman from now on. No doubt, I was a fool to weaken so

easily, but I was committed now—no backing out. Anyway, I felt so good, and Paula did say I'd never skated better. In for a penny, in for a pound, I rationalized.

Munching my sandwich, I walked along Squaw Valley Road, which paralleled the meadow. A knot of people by the split-rail fence were standing around a TV cameraman. The commentator who'd been at Zoe's house was interviewing a potbellied, elderly man in a broad-brimmed ten-gallon hat, whom I recognized from the Opening Ceremony as Ulysees S. Whitman. The Nevada millionaire had financed the building of the Olympic bobsled run and luge *bahn*, which he apparently thought gave him a proprietary interest in the running of the Games. Behind him circled a group of picketers with the familiar red, white, and blue PLAYFAIR signs. I drew near enough to hear.

"Would you tell us, sir, what the name of your organization stands for?" the newsman asked.

"Glad to, son. It's an acronym, don't you know. Our full title is Political League for Action against Your Foreign Athletes Ignoring Regulations. Spells out PLAYFAIR, see? The wife dreamed it up, and I thought it was right cute. Says what it means, too."

"And what are your goals?"

"I reckon you might say we're carrying on the torch for the late Avery Brundage, trying to keep amateurism in the Olympics. We're against government support of athletes from their cradles to their graves."

"Which governments?"

"Why, the Eastern bloc, of course," Whitman replied emphatically. "The Soviet Union and the People's un-Democratic Republic of East Germany are the worst offenders. Or maybe I should say the most successful, since all your Iron Curtain countries are tarred with the same brush. And their IOC members are the biggest supporters of the regulations on amateurism, don't you know. Those rules only handicap our Free World athletes, since the Soviet bloc pretends to have no professionals. The IOC's always ready and willing to kick out some poor American boy who might have gotten a free pair of shoes or skis. Meanwhile, the Reds provide special sports schools, living expenses, free equipment, and salaries."

"But these accusations of professionalism in the Eastern bloc came up when Brundage was IOC president, and he decided nothing could be done because there was no documentation."

"That's what we're aimin' to provide. Did you know the Russian soccer team in the professional World Cup is the same one they use for amateur competitions? Do you know what a Russian national team hockey player's monthly salary from the government is? Three hundred rubles! Your average doctor or lawyer in the USSR earns only two hundred rubles a month. When the Russian team beats our NHL All-Stars, each player gets a bonus equal to his annual salary!"

"What is your source?" asked the newsman.

"*The New York Times*," Whitman said smugly, "an article by a defected reporter from *Sovietski Sport*. Want the date?"

"I'm not sure that will satisfy the IOC—"

"What do they want, son, cancelled checks? All those Russki athletes sign an oath not to divulge their salaries or any information about their training. They protect their sports program like military secrets!"

"But the IOC doesn't even use the word 'amateur' anymore," the newsman protested. "In any case, what about American corporations paying the federation of an athlete who makes commercials for them? Or broken-time payments from the USOC? Rule Twenty-six now allows these, and each sports federation makes its own rules on amateurism. And how about athletic scholarships? Or under-the-table payments from equipment manufacturers directly to athletes?"

"That's private enterprise, sonny. That's not government subsidy. Our government doesn't give our athletes a dime. Which side are you on, anyway?" He shook a scrawny finger warningly.

"European ski teams are government-supported to aid tourism—"

Whitman went right on: "Our aim is to throw the Russians and East Germans, and all the others of that ilk, out of the IOC and all the international sports federations."

"Do you seriously think you have a chance of achieving that aim?" asked the commentator skeptically.

"Yes sir, every chance—in spite of the liberal-dominated news media. Our goal at this Olympics is mainly publicity. We're getting together enough documents to go before the IOC at their next meeting, and hopefully throw those Russian professionals right out of the Summer Olympics, and all the Games from then on."

"Aren't you injecting politics into sport? The IOC likes to keep them separate."

"That's mighty unrealistic. You can't keep politics out of something that three-quarters of the world is interested in."

"Well, that should be an interesting confrontation. Thank you, Mr. Whitman—"

"Just hold your horses, son. I want to say a few words about our hockey player, Vinnie Luciano. He's hovering between life and death at the hospital in Reno, and I want all good Americans to send up a prayer for him right now. Surely, God will not take from us such a fine, clean, young athlete." The old man added ominously, "And if He does, PLAYFAIR will know who's responsible."

"What do you mean, sir?"

"It was some of them Russian professional hockey players, the Red Army Club team, who dared Vinnie to climb the flagpole. And I think the police ought to check the top of that pole and see if it wasn't greased."

"Back to you, Jim," the commentator said hastily. When the red light on the camera had gone off, he shook his head.

"You'd better watch it, Mr. Whitman, if you don't want to be sued for slander."

"I don't think Russians sue American citizens, sonny. And if they have any other ideas, I have plenty of bodyguards. But U. S. Whitman is always happy to meet anyone in open court. In fact, I find myself in court pretty often." He winked at the spectators and adjusted the turquoise and silver eagle holding his leather thong tie.

Shaking my head in disbelief like the newsman, I walked on, trying to remember what I knew about the daft old man. I'd read that he wrote his name ULY$$E$ $. WHITMAN. Front page newspaper stories had described his bankrolling of Moral Majority groups, and his dispatching of his private army to various parts of the globe where he felt American interests were not being protected. I didn't care for the idea of being on PLAYFAIR's hit list, and glanced behind me once again to see if any black-coated men were following me.

I paused at a gap in the fence and showed my dog-tag ID to the park ranger who was checking tickets. A big crowd of Europeans had turned out to see this authentically Wild West sport. For a while, I watched skiers being pulled by lariats tied to the saddlehorns of galloping horses. They were racing, jumping from ramps, and spearing rings. After an hour, I glanced at the time, as I'd promised Angela I would watch the first two compulsory ice dances.

On my way back to the arena, I joined the long queue at the Spectator Center for what Americans called "the restroom." There weren't nearly enough women's toilet facilities, and to speed things up, the women in line had set up a competition for each to improve on the time of the one before her. All zipping and buttoning had to be done outside the stalls, and the queue counted loudly, cheered and booed. Only in America, I thought with a grin.

Blyth Arena was less than half full. Either the sunshine and outdoor events had enticed the spectators away, or they'd decided that compulsory skating events weren't very interesting.

The little boy sitting next to me in the stands kept whining, "Dad, I want to see the Zamboni man." His father took him away after 10 minutes. "This is a sport?" he complained peevishly.

At least compulsory school figures aren't set to saccharine music, I reflected, and the men don't have to wear monkey suits during them. I hoped the audience wouldn't be put off on ice dancing as a whole, since the final free dance was just as exciting as the other freestyle events. In fact, it had to be even more dramatic and theatrical, because of the restrictions against lifts and jumps. But I loyally stuck it out through 24 repetitions of the Viennese Waltz and 10 Yankee Polkas—played at earsplitting volume to enable the dancers to hear the beat—so I could applaud twice for Angela and Nigel.

After the first dance they were ranked 15th, without prospects of moving up very far. It didn't look as if Hartley and Dodson were going to follow in Torvill and Dean's footsteps to a gold medal for Britain. Once the compulsories had established skaters in the lower-ranking groups, it was almost impossible to break out of them—as I'd found, to my sorrow, in my first four years of international competition. Hartley and Dodson's usual "place" in the judges' minds seemed to be around 13th. The Russian dancers seemed to have a stranglehold on the first two places, with the Americans Rhodes and Reece 3rd.

After a word with Angela, I walked back to the Village for a long hot bath before Zoe's dinner party. I was looking forward to it—I hadn't had a good French meal since Europeans in Paris.

Paris—my happiest time with Dima. Soaking in the herb-scented Vitabath, I remembered us walking through the Tuileries and along the Seine with our arms around each other's waists. Unlike Moscow, Paris smiled on lovers in a passionate embrace on the quay. We sampled *la nouvelle cuisine,* liver with raspberries. Lounging at innumerable sidewalk cafes, we watched the Parisian world go by. We made love under a high gilded ceiling with staring cherubim, and I discovered Dima was a restless sleeper, thrashing and skating in his dreams. Sometimes he awoke from nightmares shouting, *"Nyet, nyet!"*

We talked for hours *dusha-v-dushu*, soul to soul, about everything under the sun. He had described his amazement during his first few competitions in the West—the miles of highways, more in one city like Paris than in all of Russia, the unguarded, glittering piles of consumer goods. How he'd naïvely thought at first that most of the Europeans must be poor, because they wore running shoes instead of leather ones.

"It was on my first trip to America ten years ago," he said once, while we were lying in my bed in the aftermath of love, "that I found out for certain that everything they ever told me about the West was a lie. Our officials say the black people are beaten and lynched; instead, I saw them mingling freely in society and driving big cars. In fact, the Soviet Union is much worse—visiting African students are always getting beat up. They told us we'd need bodyguards to protect us from the American gangsters with tommy guns.

"They said the shops crammed with food, clothing, televisions, were all for show—they couldn't be real because there were no queues! After a while, I realized they must be genuine. I could take photos anywhere, no one stopped me. They said the US has no culture; obviously, not true. The biggest lie of all is that the American Communist Party is going to start a revolution any day. I found out it's a tiny group, and if they did, no one would follow. Why should they? They had their Revolution two hundred years ago, and now they have freedom."

"I don't understand," I said. "Is it political or artistic freedom you want?"

"Aren't they the same thing? In Russia, all issues are political, whether or not the individual is. For instance, they're not going to let me compete anymore after this year, I'm sure of it. In the West, I could go on as long as I want, if I'm good enough."

"Aren't you afraid when you think of defecting, darling? It's so dangerous. It frightens me, I don't mind saying."

"Is a bird afraid when it flies out of a cage? That is what it must do."

"But your family—will you ever see them again?"

"*Nyet*. They will be interrogated and punished for harboring a traitor. And never to see my homeland again, the land of my birth and ancestors. . . ." Tears filled his eyes, and he once again began to make frantic love to me, to blot out the dark visions oppressing him.

Zoe and Josh arrived punctually at 8:00 that night in the promised limousine to pick up Dima and me, along with Matt and the Carons. Fyodor and another Russian security man followed in a black sedan; Zoe had obviously exerted her pull on the higher-ups.

"This is the life," said Dima, settling back luxuriously. "Driver, take us to Acapulco. Step on it, there's a good fellow."

"Capitalist beast," said Zoe, smiling at him. She was all tarted up again, in a strapless black velvet sheath under a silver fox coat and a cloud of Joy. I was wearing my favorite jade silk frock, and hoped I was keeping my end up. Dany's mauve dress set off her dark sultriness; the men wore blazers over turtlenecks.

"Now then," said Zoe, "I hope you're all fond of garlic. There's enough in the food at La Vielle Maison to keep you safe from vampires for the rest of your lives!"

"Yes, you'll still be tasting it next week," Josh said. "All you have to do is breathe on your opponents, and they'll wilt."

We all laughed and chattered happily, pleased to be out of the spartan Village atmosphere. As usual, we talked shop.

"Did you hear what happened to the American pair today in practice?" Dany asked. "They were doing the pair sitspin, the one where the woman's bent skating leg is between the man's thighs, and their free legs stretched out. Well, her skating foot slipped, and her knee hit him, quite hard, in the um, er. . . ."

"No kidding, right in the old um-er? Ouch, that smarts," said Matt. "*Tant pis*, as you were probably about to say."

"Will he be all right to skate in the final tomorrow night?" Josh asked.

"Oh, yes. Not that it will make much difference to anyone, I think."

"Incidentally," Josh said, "I just heard an hour ago that that kid Vinnie Luciano died. The hockey player who fell from the flagpole."

"Poor chap," I murmured, remembering him gleefully lobbing mashed potatoes in the cafeteria.

"Will they stop the Games, or what?" Matt asked.

"There's to be a memorial service tonight before the award ceremonies," said Zoe. "But the PLO didn't stop the Olympics—for more than a day—and neither will the accidental death of a steelworker from Pittsburgh."

"Is that what he was?" asked Dima.

"Yes," said Josh, "he was a true amateur, but he certainly would've been drafted by the pros after the Games. Scouts from several NHL

115

teams were watching him with interest. That political group PLAYFAIR is really up in arms, by the way, swearing vengeance. They're certain he was murdered to ruin the Americans' hockey chances." I told them about the TV interview with Whitman I'd seen this afternoon.

"A number of the hockey players are involved in PLAYFAIR," said Matt. "They have to keep it quiet, of course, because it's too openly political for the IOC. But I know that the captain, Bruno Novak, is a rabid anti-Communist." I recalled the anonymous notes, the snake, and the nearly-lethal icicle, and tried to ignore prickles of unease.

"That must be why he called me a Commie fag the other day," Dima said. "He and Vinnie were practicing goal-shooting in the arena when we were scheduled to practice, and he wouldn't leave the ice when I asked him. In fact, he threatened to make me the puck. I don't think he was joking."

The limousine passed under a railroad trestle, and Truckee came into view: a ramshackle small town sprawling over a little valley. Its boxy wooden and brick buildings along narrow streets gave it an agreeably dated look.

"*Elle est charmante, la village!*" exclaimed Dany. "*Regardes*, Jean-Marc. Just like the Old West."

"That's right," said Zoe, "you Europeans love cowboy and western things, don't you?"

"That's for sure!" Matt said. "Did you see the pairs' short program last night? The Hungarians' music was 'Don't Fence Me In.'"

"For them, that song might have quite a different meaning than for you," Dima said, a bit stiffly.

"What do you mean?" asked Jean-Marc.

"That they long for freedom, of course."

"Did anyone ever see Anett Poetzch's cowboy exhibition number?" I asked with a laugh. "The East German who won the gold at Lake Placid? She wore a ten-gallon hat and denim pedal pushers, and kept drawing imaginary six-shooters."

"Or Igor Bobrin's 'A Cowboy's Work is Never Done,'" said Matt. "That was a real showstopper."

The car pulled up in front of a red-trimmed shingle and stone building. At the back of the house was a round stone tower topped by a weathervane. "Nice old place, isn't it?" commented Josh. "It used to be a bawdyhouse."

The owners, friends of Zoe's, welcomed us effusively and ushered us to a round table in front of the rock fireplace. Zoe put Dima on her left and Jean-Marc on her right, then me, Josh, Matt, and Dany to complete the circle.

"An aperitif, madame? Cinzano? Dubonnet?" The waiter placed a wooden bowl of garlic mayonnaise on the table.

"*Aioli!*" exclaimed Dany. She and Jean-Marc began to eat it with French bread, explaining that it was known in the south of France as Provençal butter.

"Don't worry about ordering," said Zoe. "It's prix fixe, and we get whatever they're cooking tonight. I've chosen the wine—ah, here it comes—so *bon appetit*, and enjoy." She tasted and approved the 1978 Puligny-Montrachet.

Jean-Marc toasted her: "*A votre santé!* Ah, this is excellent. I was afraid we might be served Cold Duck or root beer."

"Please, we're not total barbarians."

As I savored the first course of salmon in avocado, I looked with pleasure around the crowded, candle-lit room. Reflected firelight sparkled in the tulip wine glasses. Josh called my attention to the wall posters: "Fight mouthwash, eat garlic," "Chez Panisse Garlic Festival," "Visit Gilroy, Garlic Capital of the World." I squinted at the Art Nouveau lettering.

"I have actually heard of Gilroy, but what's Chez Panisse?"

"It's a restaurant in Berkeley that pioneered California Cuisine, one of the finest in the country," replied Zoe. "If you're ever in the Bay Area, I'd love to take you there. In fact, please do let me show you the City some time. What are your plans after the Olympics? If you join an ice show, they always come to the Bay Area sooner or later."

We were served a salad of butter lettuce and walnuts in a Dijon mustard dressing. After I, then Matt, had briefly described our immediate futures, Zoe asked the others.

"We'll also retire from competition," Dany said, "but we won't join a show. We don't like them—they are too much like vaudeville or the circus. Mmm, this is *delicieux!* I will return to my studies, and Jean-Marc also, to the Sorbonne where he's doing an economics degree."

"It's true," I said, "the ice shows are sometimes cheap and flashy, but not always. And one doesn't have to wear a Las Vegas-style costume, and do only waltz jumps. For instance, Peggy Fleming kept her integrity. And she designed her costumes, did her own choreography, and so on. *I* think the main drawbacks are living out of a suitcase for months, and always having to be careful of one's image. But, at any rate, I really have no choice, for financial reasons."

"And you, Dima?" asked Zoe.

"I, too, have no choice in my future," he said. "But my pressure is not economic like Lesley's, but physical. I will be told what to do—maybe coaching in Siberia! Or training the bears on skates for the Moscow Circus."

"Do you want to go back?" she asked.

"I don't think we should talk about it here," he said to her in a low voice. "As we say in Russia, rumors stick like birch leaves in a *banya*." They began to whisper.

"Have you been watching the ski jumping practice?" Josh said to Jean-Marc. "There's a good French prospect in the 90-meter, isn't there?"

"*Pardonnez-moi*, what did you say? I did not hear. Ah, this looks good." A trout, cooked with garlic and a pine bough en casserole, was set before him. He efficiently filleted it and, with much lip-smacking, pronounced it "*superbe*."

I decided that he took no interest in anything but his stomach and his sister, and gave up conversation with him as a bad job. I caught sight of Fyodor and his companion at a table near the kitchen, demanding blini and vodka from the waiter. Hiding a smile, I turned to Josh. "I'm looking forward to your next column, on Olympic women. Can you give us a preview?"

"If I tell you now, you won't read it on Monday," he said, smiling at me affectionately.

"Oh, don't worry, I never miss it."

"Well, without giving too much away, I can say that this column also springs from the research I did on the 1960 Squaw Valley Olympics. It was surprisingly fascinating, in terms of the attitude changes this society has gone through since then, especially toward minorities and women. For example, *Look*, one of the big picture magazines of the day, did a whole issue on California as publicity for the Winter Olympics. Included in it, which was normal for that era, was a picture story on the girls—in quotes—of two private California universities, USC and Stanford. Even back then, Stanford was an excellent college; in fact, it admitted three times as many men as women, so the women had to be top-drawer intellectually. Well, these 10 "typical coeds" were photographed in bathing suits or sweaters, and every single one of them said her life's ambition was to be a good wife and mother. Those who wanted to work only planned to do so to put a husband through graduate school, or to fill time before assuming her real career, motherhood."

"Incredible!" I exclaimed.

"I can believe it," said Matt. "Nineteen sixty was really still the fifties. My mother was at Vassar around that time. She once said that not having an engagement ring by the time you were a senior was cause for serious loss of face."

"Did she?" I asked.

"No, she was always a non-conformist. She got a Ph.D. in mathematics and didn't marry till the late sixties."

"Times had certainly changed by then," put in Jean-Marc. "Our parents met on the barricades during the French general strike in 1968. Our mother did time in jail for hitting a pig of a *gendarme* with a cobblestone. What a decade!"

"Are your parents here at the Olympics, Matt?" asked Josh.

"No, my father died when I was a kid. My mother was planning to come, but she had a bad automobile accident earlier this winter, and is still laid up with several broken bones."

"My parents both died in a car crash when I was very small," I said to him. "We have something in common."

"My father was killed in an avalanche; that's why I'm not a skier instead of a skater. My mother never skied after that, and she wouldn't allow me to as a kid."

"How did you start skating, then?"

"Went to a birthday party at an ice rink when I was seven. I liked it, and my mom bought me a pair of skates at a sport swap for five dollars. Little did she know. . . ."

"But what has all that about the magazine to do with women in the Olympics?" Dima asked Josh impatiently.

"Women athletes were still considered freaks in 1960. I won't give you the best examples, because I'd rather you read the column. I write better than I talk."

"You're certainly right about women athletes, Dad," said Zoe. "I've got a book about the '60 Olympics—I was glancing at it the other day, and the comments were absolutely patriarchal."

"I'd like to read that," I said with interest. "Recent social history is fascinating to me. It's not covered in school, because it's not in the textbooks yet."

"I'll loan it to you—I have all the official Olympic books, if you'd like to see them. We'll stop off and pick it up."

"But to get back to the subject of women in sports," Matt said, "I think it's a mistake to believe that attitude is completely in the past. I don't know if Lesley and Dany will agree with this, because they're in a sport that's socially approved for women. They look graceful and feminine while they're skating, and the spectators don't know how hard they have to work. The smile makes it all look easy, like in ballet. So they don't get the hassles a woman weight-thrower or hurdler *still* gets."

"*C'est vrai*," Dany said. "When I'm training—running or weight-lifting—I often get whistles and suggestive remarks."

"Me too," I added, "or condescending ones, at best."

"And how many husbands and lovers," said Matt, "are psychologically strong enough not to be threatened by their women's Olympic medals?"

Dima yawned and looked at his watch.

"Now then, who's for dessert?" asked Zoe. "There's brie or boursin, a nice garlic cheese—for a change of pace." There was a chorus of good-humored groans; every course had been redolent of the "stinking rose."

"Or perhaps a Grand Marnier soufflé?" suggested the waiter. "And cafe filtre?"

After a final cognac we piled into the limo, breathing genially at each other. When we reached Zoe's house around midnight, everyone regretfully declined her invitation for a nightcap, so she went inside and returned with several volumes on the Olympics for me. We bade her good-night, the Carons especially thanking her for showing them "an oasis in the great American wasteland of food."

The driver dropped us at the Village gate. Dima and the other KGB man had to support the stumbling and singing Fyodor, much the worse for vodka, as we walked to the dormitories.

"He's in good spirits," Matt said.

"Or vice-versa," I answered with a grin.

"Dmitri Pyotrovich," groaned Fyodor. "Don't . . . don't run away tonight. You would not do that to me. Right now, I could not stop you." He belched and stumbled.

"Shut up, you fool, you're drunk. I'm not going anywhere."

"Dima, my friend, promise me. We're in too much trouble already." He flailed his arms, then lurched into a bush, muttered something in Russian, and passed out.

The Olympic Movement is perhaps the greatest social force in the world. It is a revolt against 20th century materialism, it is a devotion to the cause and not to the reward. . . .
—Avery Brundage

There are only two places in a race, first and last. I only want one of them.
—Buddy Werner, Alpine skiing (died in avalanche, 1964)

Monday, February 17, 8:55 A.M.

"The next skater, representing Great Britain, Lesley Grey." To a polite spattering of applause from the few hundred spectators, I skated forward to a patch of clean ice well away from any hockey markings, lined myself up, and indicated my long axis with my arms. The referee nodded. I took a deep breath and pushed off into a counter on my right forward outside edge. The women's compulsory figures had been underway almost two hours.

I had awakened at 5:45, an hour before the draw to determine the starting foot for the three figures. After meeting Paula in the arena for the draw ceremony, we went to the skaters' lounge to discuss strategy and wait for my turn.

"The right's your stronger starting foot for the counter and loop, so that worry's taken care of," Paula reassured me. "Fortunately, the judging panel for the compulsories is fairly neutral, neither heavily German nor Eastern bloc. Because if you get a strong start—4th or above—in the figures, nothing can keep you from the gold."

"Just keep telling me that!"

"It won't be easy. On the freeskating panel on Thursday, you've got to face the East German, the West German, the Austrian, and the Swiss judges—all German-speaking, and possibly leaning toward Putzi. Then you've got the Czech, the Russian, and the Hungarian, plus the East German again—probably favoring Nina. Don't kid yourself it isn't a cold war on ice! That just leaves the Finn and the American, who will naturally mark Kim high. There might be some wheeling and dealing with you and Kim getting squashed in the middle. But I know them all, and my spies and I will keep our ears to the ground. I haven't heard anything suspicious yet, except what I told you about Zack and the short program."

"Who's on the compulsories panel today?"

"The judges are the best we could've hoped for, with just the usual lower marks from the West German, Russian, and American to worry about. The others are Canada, Britain, Netherlands, Italy, Yugoslavia, and Japan. No axes to grind there. If the British judge doesn't try to prove he's above nationalism by giving you a deliberately low mark, we'll be all right. *Provided* you don't let your concentration slip for a single second, and skate your figures as well as you've shown you can over the last two years."

"How are the tracings showing up?"

"Very well. The paint under the ice is gray, and the lighting's good— not too glary. Only the tiniest skaters will have any trouble seeing their tracings. I'll go watch for a while, to get a feeling for how the judging's going."

I ate an orange and sipped tea while I read SportsMonday. (Russ Duo Takes Pairs; miss mcgregor dominates downhill)

Olympic Women
By Josh McDonnell

Squaw Valley, CA, Feb. 16——One of my predecessors on these pages, Arthur Daley, wrote not so long ago: "The Greeks had a word for dames in the Olympics. The word was no." He went on to say that they had the right idea. Avery Brundage publicly agreed.

As Leonard Koppett pointed out in *Sports Illusion, Sports Reality*, women will never participate fully in the mass-spectator sports that attract the greatest investment of time and money: football, basketball, and baseball in this country, and soccer everywhere else. Sexism and the macho mystique are integral components of the commercial sports establishment, with its ties to advertising, gambling, and the media. And these sports were designed for the male physique, and even the best women players cannot compete on an equal basis with the best men.

But amateur sport, especially the Olympic variety, is a different story. We've come a long way, even if full equality of hearts and minds has not yet arrived. Consider the Greeks: women—or slaves —who dared even to watch the ancient Olympics were thrown off a cliff.

Not because of the fact that the Games were conducted in the nude, as the popular wisdom has it. (The audience in Rome included Vestal Virgins.) The nudity was to ensure that the competitors would include no women ringers. The early Games were quasi-religious rites, mysteries too sacred for the eyes of a woman except those of an anointed priestess.

After the modern revival of the quadrennial festival in 1896, women competitors were not allowed in any numbers until the 1920's. A few years before the first Olympic figure skating competition (in the London Summer Games of 1908), Englishwoman Madge Syers-Cave nearly defeated the great Ulrich Salchow in the unisex World event. The ruling body hastily created a female division in 1906, and magnanimously allowed the women to skate in skirts short enough to show their feet!

In the 1920 Olympics, American Teresa Weld was penalized for an "unfeminine" single salchow jump. Up till 1948, figure skating was the *only* women's sport in the Winter Olympics. Women's speed skating was not contested till as late as 1960; its inclusion then was partially to fill the void left by bobsledding's absence.

One of the United States' alltime great athletes, Babe Didrikson, was allowed to enter only three events in the 1932 Games, though she held many world records, and there was no similar restriction for the men. Women's sports have always been fewer and initiated later into the Olympics; women were not included in the early Olympic Villages.

Nineteen sixty seems recent in chronology, but still medieval in attitude. Here in Squaw Valley in the eighth Winter Games, the downhill contenders in one of America's strongest women's ski teams (which ultimately won three silver medals) were labeled in a straight news announcement: "a three-gal team of two brunettes and a blonde."

Double gold medalist (in 1952) Andrea Mead Lawrence was their chaperone, not their coach. That honor was reserved for her husband, although he had never won an Olympic medal of any color. As well as technical mentor, the women's ski coach was supposed to serve as big brother, father confessor, and sex symbol. Canadian ski champion Nancy Greene said that a coach has got to make his "girls" fall in love with him. She married hers.

The few women journalists covering the Winter Olympics in 1960 were permitted to report only on fashion and social events. One had to file her story under the headline "A Girl Reporter's Snow Job." Male journalists graded women in print on their looks in stretch pants—each wrinkle counted minus one from a perfect 10. A *San Francisco Chronicle* sportswriter commented, inaccurately as well as rudely, "The ladies don't do so well on the icy runs. They fall flat on their fannies and are ornaments only at the hot-rum hour, they in their skin-stretch tights."

The European skiers and speed skaters were routinely described as "big strong gals," "strapping lasses," "husky tomboys," and other such condescending terms never applied to muscular male athletes. Despite a few well-publicized cases of Eastern European competitors who later announced they had been men all along, or discreetly dropped out when femininity testing began in 1966, treating female athletes as "bull dykes" is unfair and demeaning.

At best, women were damned with faint praise in 1960, as in this account: "These three Russians [Nordic skiers] pushed their narrow skis as fast and as fantastically as any career girl clicks her heels on Fifth Avenue." American "skating beauty" Carol Heiss received more approval when she said, "I want to think about the next dance as the most important thing in my future" than when she won her gold medal. *Time* said skier Betsy Snite "cut corners like a man."

Sportswriters and ski coaches would barter their last jockstrap for a reasonable explanation of American male skiers' poor showing in the Winter Olympics compared to the "US cuties." During the sixties a lot of poppycock was written about how American girls didn't have anything more serious than ski racing and husband-chasing to occupy their time, while the men had to get on with their careers.

Bob Beattie, former US ski coach and TV commentator, came up with this example of doublethink in 1980: "The competition among women skiers is not as severe, and it's harder for a man to get to the top because many more men enter the sport." The over-all record stands. US men: three medals, none of them gold; US women: 11 medals, including four gold ones.

More tomorrow.

When Paula came back, I asked her, "Did you read Josh's column today?"

"Yes, wasn't it terrific? At last, a man who takes women seriously!"

"And a man in an influential position, too. Reading that's given me a big boost."

At 8:30, we entered the hushed arena and I began my warm-up. I spotted Angela and Matt in the audience, but didn't see Dima. Six skaters shared the practice third of the ice, inscribing meticulous geometric patterns with the compasses of our skates and bodies.

In the center third of the ice, divided on either side by a line of orange traffic cones, a Japanese competitor in spectacles was surrounded by nine well-wrapped judges and four officials. They looked like ice fishermen waiting for a bite as they inspected her figure. On the far third, two men with shovels and scrapers were patching the ice. Then a mini-Zamboni, tiny and silent, restored it to a pristine sheet.

At 8:45, those of us warming up moved over to what had been the competition area, the judges and next competitor moved to clean ice, and the first third, now covered with a lacy pattern of tracings, was resurfaced.

I was a bit surprised at my calmness, especially after the row I'd had with Dima last night. The atmosphere here today was so exactly like every competition I'd skated over the last 10 years, that I kept forgetting, then remembering with a start, that this was it—the Olympics. The only chance to grab the brass ring.

The handful of spectators marked their programs and punched their pocket calculators to compute standings. The only noise in the cathedral hush was a crying baby, quickly taken out, and an occasional walkie-talkie squawk from the Zamboni storage area. Someone in the audience sneezed in the middle of a figure, and several spectators turned around and glared. Wimbledon must have been like this in the old days, I reflected. No, it's more like a cricket match—the same polite applause after the marks. Except to dedicated skating fans, the compulsories are as exciting as watching paint dry.

The referee blew her whistle, and the judges pulled their plastic number cards from the boxes they wore suspended from their necks like popcorn vendors. They each held up a card in either hand, except for the last judge who was holding only one number.

"The marks for Miss Fredericks of Australia: 2.9, 3.4, 3.1, 3.3, 8.2. . . ." The announcer paused and the fifth judge quickly changed hands, to a ripple of laughter. "Correction, that's *2.8*, 3.3, 3.1, 3.2,

3.0. Thank you. The next skater, representing Great Britain, Lesley Grey."

Concentrate, concentrate, I repeated silently like a mantra through the crucial first half-circle. I executed the initial difficult and complex counter turn, rocking my blade into the new lobe I was now tracing backwards. Don't anticipate, I told myself as I completed that circle and pushed off backward into a new one on my left foot, remembering to scissor the free foot on the turn. After gliding around the third lobe, I began the exacting task of superimposing my layout print twice more, ideally without a centimeter's deviation.

Returning to center for the third time, I skated straight away from the figure without disturbing it. As I joined Paula at the barrier, to my surprise the audience applauded.

"They could tell from your form that it was a good figure, even from the bleachers," she said, looking pleased. "Your carriage and speed were excellent, and your flow was nice and smooth."

The referee brushed away the snow with a child-sized broom, then placed two vertical markers at the counter turns. The Russian judge paced off the figure in her Eskimo mukluks, while the Japanese got down on hands and knees and inspected the tracing for any misplaced edge changes, looking as if he'd lost a contact lens. After several minutes of intent scrutiny and scribbling, the nine formed a ragged line. Tweet! squeaked the referee's whistle, and out came the cards with a clatter.

"The marks for Miss Grey: 4.0, 4.2, 3.8, 4.3. . . ." Paula hugged me as the applause swelled. All were over 4.0 except for the Russian and American marks, quite a high score in the compulsories, unlike the freeskating.

"Thanks to you," I said, beaming exuberantly as I put on my skate guards, "I think those are my highest school figure scores ever! I'd better cut out that chunk of ice and take it to Worlds."

In the dressing room, Paula kissed me on both cheeks and said, "It's a good omen—you can feel how the judging's going from the very first figure, and they seem to be well-disposed toward you. Just keep it up."

"Thank God, I don't have to keep it up for two days and six figures, like the last Squaw Valley Olympics."

"*Twelve* figures back in Sonja Henie's day."

I pulled on warm-up pants under my green striped woolen skating dress, and replaced my skates with ballet slippers. "Imagine sixty percent of the score for figures—I wouldn't be here at all."

"It was still fifty percent after the '72 Olympics at Sapporo, when Trixie Schuba got 5s for her figures and stole the gold from Janet Lynn —even after she placed 7th in the free with only single jumps. The man who won that time was an uninspired freeskater too, so the ISU was forced to start the short program the next year. Eventually the scores were weighted thirty-twenty-fifty percent, as they still are."

"Do you think they'll ever get rid of the compulsory figures? They seem to be moving in that direction."

"Not as long as the Eastern bloc does well in them and their ISU representatives vote accordingly. A lot of people think that anything that demonstrates control is a good thing, like scales on the piano or dressage on a horse. It's just too bad that the qualities needed to do good figures are the opposite of a great freeskater's. Well, see you later—your next warm-up will be about ten o'clock."

She returned to the arena and I lay down on the couch and closed my eyes, ignoring the comings and goings of the others. I tried to think about the next figure, but Paula's reference to Sapporo had awakened a nasty memory from the night before that had ruined my concentration.

Dima and I had been walking back to the Village after the pairs final. Katya and Kolya had taken the gold medal, as expected, the East Germans the silver, and Dany and Jean-Marc the bronze. Other pairs met with mishaps, several competitors collapsing at the end of the four-and-a-half-minute program from the altitude.

The Carons had skated last, and we were still tingling from their extraordinary program which had concluded with the *Liebestod*, the Love-Death from Wagner's *Tristan and Isolde*. I was bewitched by my memory of the luscious music and the skaters, in white and mother-of-pearl, in their final gorgeous death spiral. There had been a hush afterwards, the mesmerized audience reluctant to break the mood, then a standing ovation and shouts of "Six! Six! Six!" But the 6.0s—three of them—had fallen only to the Russian pair.

The erotic music and images had powerfully affected Dima as well. "Come to my room, *milochka*. Let's go to bed."

"Darling, no. I'm sorry. It's midnight—I should be asleep already. I have to get up at five-thirty."

"Please, you must. We have hours before Kolya gets back from the press conference." He whispered hoarsely, "I must have you tonight. Don't you want to?"

"Not tonight!" I said, irritated by his insistence and bad timing. "My first event starts early tomorrow morning, and I must get a good night's sleep."

"But I told you about all the pressure on me. I'm so nervous about the competition coming up. I must release the tension or I'll go crazy. Is okay to screw before the figures, just not before the short program. Ha ha, joke. Come on, don't you love me?"

"It's you who don't love *me* if you want me to jeopardize my chances tomorrow," I said coldly. "You know how important the compulsory figures are! If I don't do well in them, I can say good-bye to the medal."

"Well, *I* have to skate them the day after, and you know how much more depends on *my* gold medal." He kicked a pine tree sulkily. "Damn it, I wish the Olympics were in Sapporo or somewhere civilized instead of this hick town!"

"What on earth are you talking about?" I snapped.

"The Worlds were there three years ago. You could go to Turkish baths where there were human washrags—women who covered themselves with soapy foam and washed you. Or the bar hostesses— they'd go to a hotel with you for an hour. *Tsure-komi-yado*," he said reminiscently.

"What does that mean?"

"Take-girl-in-love-hotel. They had hourly rates. I once came three times in an hour. It was fantastic! I heard that during the '72 Olympics in Sapporo, you had to go all the way to Tokyo to buy a condom."

"Good God. Well, I'm sorry you're not there, too. Or anywhere but here, badgering me. Don't you see, I don't need this right now!"

"All right!" He scowled at me. "You're either with me or against me. Now I see what's important to you. Is your fucking medal, not me. Good night, I call you after you win—maybe."

He stomped off angrily. I fumed over his appalling egotism for a while, then shrugged and went up to bed. He'd get over it. But had it been a mistake to say no to him? Anyway, it was his own fault, and it couldn't be helped now.

"Come on, Lesley. Time to warm up for the bracket." Paula was gently shaking my shoulder. I dragged my mind back. The paragraph bracket—that was the important thing now.

I received slightly lower marks than on the previous figure; the "blind" part of the tracing, where I had to face outside the circle unable to see where I was going, as usual proved my downfall. But I held 3rd place, as we'd hoped, behind Nina and an East German who always fell many places later in the freeskating. Behind me were Putzi and then Kim.

The rest interval was longer this time, with my group being second to skate the final figure. As I sat in the sunshine outside the arena, my mind wandered back to the men's freeskating practice I'd watched yesterday afternoon. After the warm-up stroking, Dima had taken off his red team jacket and Matt his blue one at the same time. Underneath, they were wearing similar dark blue jerseys with a red stripe down the sleeves. They noticed the likeness and began to skate in tandem like a pair team. As the watching crowd cheered them on, they leaped into simultaneous double axels, then synchronized flying camel spins. Dima bowed and Matt curtsied, to laughter and applause.

The memory made me smile. Dima could be so funny and dear. Why did he have to be so bloody-minded on occasion? Especially now, of all times.

I recalled another scene, from last year's Worlds at the Scandinavium Hall in Gothenberg. A little blonde Swedish girl of about nine, one of the caddies, came out onto the ice to pick up Dima's flowers while he took his bows. As all skaters will do sooner or later, she had forgotten to take off her skate guards and fell sprawling on the ice. She tried to get up, and fell again. Dima saw her predicament and the tears spilling from her eyes. He skated quickly to her, picked her up and swung her over the barrier, then kissed her cheek. The crowd cheered even louder, and his teen-age coterie of followers screamed at the top of their voices: "Di-ma! Di-ma! Di-ma!" and waved their heart-covered signs.

I sighed. He was a crowd-charmer, right enough. Whenever he was on the ice, his charisma drew all eyes to him.

More spectators were present for the third figure, the loop, either because of the later hour or because it was lovely to watch. The abrupt change of speed and direction, and the leg swing as the skater gracefully twisted to inscribe a small oval within a larger circle, made it look something like modern dance.

Again, I came through with a majority of marks around 4.0, and the standings were more or less unchanged. Nina, the East German, and I, along with Putzi and Kim, would all be in the highest-seeded final group for the short program Tuesday afternoon. The skating order within each group was decided by a draw held after the compulsories; I drew number 25, first to skate in the last group. That meant

I wouldn't get the full warm-up, and the judges would mark more strictly.

I went back to my room for a nap, trying to stay loose and not think about the mounting pressure. As soon as I dozed off, the phone rang. Dima! I thought. But it was Josh McDonnell, inviting me to lunch the next day before the short.

I went back to brooding about Dima. Why hadn't he been there for me today? I always watched his compulsory figures. Hoping that reading would make me drowsy, I glanced through Zoe's Olympics books. But looking at pictures of Tenley Albright, Carol Heiss, Peggy Fleming, and Dorothy Hamill increased my depression. It seemed so unlikely that I would join that glittering gallery the Americans call Queens of the Ice. Wrong nationality for a woman and wrong sex for a Brit, I decided wryly. The only Englishwoman ever to win Olympic gold in figure skating was Jeanette Altwegg, a school figures specialist, way back in 1952.

The silver and bronze medalists of the sixties and seventies caught my eyes as I flipped through the pages. I wondered if anyone remembered Gaby Seyfert, Karen Magnussen, Dianne de Leeuw, or Christine Errath, even though they'd all been world champions. Who would now recognize the name of Megan Taylor, or of Cecilia Colledge who was the first woman to do double jumps? The two Englishwomen had been perennial also-rans to Sonja Henie in the thirties. Was I myself fated to be buried in the Soviet sweep of Aleksandrova and the rest, or to become a footnote in the record books next to Kim Cranford's name? Does nothing count but the gold, I wondered as my spirits sank lower. Coming 2nd seems like not being here at all. Or is it the taking part, the quest, that matters?

Unable to fall asleep again and tormented by more memories of Dima, I finally telephoned his room. There was no answer.

I got up restlessly and walked down the corridor to the bathroom. In the cubicle, I heard again the familiar sound of vomiting. Curious to find out who was possibly pregnant, I peeked through the crack in the door till the woman emerged. I saw curly black hair and a blue USA warm-up suit: it was Kim Cranford.

To hell with waiting around for Dima to ring, I decided that night. After dinner, Angela and I watched part of Leni Riefenstahl's epic *Olympische Spiele 1936* at the Village cinema, then looked in at the Red Dog Bar, upstairs from the dining hall. It had been transformed, more or less, into the Olympic Village disco by a mirrored ball and a strobe light that flashed occasionally. There wasn't much action yet, only a few serious Chinese and Romanian athletes learning dance steps from the hostesses to the music of Abba. Hans-Peter, Putzi, Pavel, and Nina were sitting together near the roaring log fire, and the friendly Germans beckoned us over.

"Join us for some good German beer," invited Hans-Peter. He brought us bottles of Dortmunder Union.

"From the wrong side of the border, *nicht wahr?*" teased Putzi. "Doesn't Karl Marx-Stadt export beer to the States?"

"Well, this capitalist brew is better than the watery American stuff, anyhow. We were just wondering why the Americans seem to tell one their most intimate problems on first acquaintance. How does one reply?"

"Yes, it's very strange," Angela agreed. "I'd say, 'No emotion please, I'm British!'"

"Have any of you been to the army surplus store in Truckee yet?" Hans-Peter rambled on. "I bought two dozen pairs of *klasse* Wrangler jeans to take home."

"A little black marketing on the side?" I said with a grin.

"Of course not. One needs a lifetime supply, isn't it? Well, what about a dance? Come, Pavel, snap out of that black Russian mood, my friend. We are here for a happy time. You dance with Lesley and I'll dance with Angela, and we'll step all over their feet and ruin their chances for tomorrow."

Pavel followed me gloomily onto the dance floor and we shuffled around together to an old Blondie song.

"Are you ready for the compulsory figures tomorrow?" I asked inanely. I could never think of a thing to say to this sour and taciturn boy who kept himself to himself, so completely Dima's opposite.

"*Da.* I'm going to whip Kuznetsov's arse. I'm tired of playing—second violin, is it?"

"Second fiddle. Well, you've got to beat Matt and Hans-Peter too, you know, and that Japanese chap Hiroshi looks good."

"No sweat," he boasted. "Is all arranged."

131

"What on earth do you mean?"

"Kuznetsov was told is time to step aside. He can't go on forever, and is my turn now."

"You mean he's throwing the competition?" I asked incredulously.

"*Da.* Though I could win anyway, of course."

"No bloody fear," I said firmly. "He'd never agree to that—you know what he is."

"Wait and see. Is our system, not the individual who counts. He did not understood that sometimes. He is no longer acceptable model for New Socialist Man. There he is now, drunk again."

I looked over my shoulder. Dima swayed in the doorway, glowering at me and Pavel. As I started toward him, he growled, "Well, I see you're not too tired tonight!" then turned and lurched away.

"Look out, he's pretty jealous," said Pavel smugly. "He can fool around, but not his women."

"Oh, belt up, can't you?" I snapped, and stalked back to the table. Matt and Kim had joined the other skaters, and they were all talking about the latest PLAYFAIR demonstration.

"Did you see their signs today?" asked Matt. "They said creepy things like 'Vinnie Luciano is a martyr to Red oppression' and 'Vinnie's death was no accident.'"

"The grossest ones went 'Vengeance for Vinnie' and 'An eye for an eye,'" said Kim with an excited shiver. "The IOC asked the police not to let them in any closer than the highway, but I saw them when we were driving over."

"So has everyone else, and they're all over the TV, of course," Matt said. The disco was getting noisy and he had to shout. The American ski team at the next table were singing and thumping their beer glasses in time: "Downhill racers sing this sing, doo-dah, doo-dah. Downhill course is goddamn long. . . ."

Matt went on: "Some of the PLAYFAIR members are privately making rather ugly threats toward all the Soviet bloc athletes. So be careful, you three," he warned Pavel, Nina, and Hans-Peter.

"*Quatsch!* Nonsense!" said the latter. "They have nothing against the German Democratic Republic."

"Don't be so sure. Haven't you heard that there was a sabotage attempt against an East German bobsled? Fortunately, the driver noticed the bolts had been loosened before the run. It could have been fatal—like loose screws on a skate. Ring a bell?"

"But the police announced Luciano's fall was an accident," protested Pavel, "and there was no—what? Foul playing."

"PLAYFAIR's screaming whitewash and cover-up."

"*I* am not worried," said Nina haughtily. "What could they do to *me?*"

"You know who Bruno Novak is?" asked Matt. "The captain of the US hockey team? Well, he's a member of PLAYFAIR—secretly, of course —and he's also a computer genius, a hacker from way back. I've heard he's been tampering with some of the competition scores." I remembered, ashamed, that I'd assumed that Matt was the one who had been playing tricks with the computer.

"You should inform the authorities," said Pavel pompously.

"The person who told me has already taken care of that, and the guards at the data processing building are on the lookout for Bruno."

"That's probably no use, he could be doing it by phone," I mentioned.

"That's true. Uh oh, speaking of the devil, here he comes now."

The hockey team swarmed into the disco. They had beat the Canadians tonight and were celebrating, ordering drinks for the house and slapping everyone's palms as if they were in a television beer commercial.

Bruno and some of the others strutted over to our table. "We wanna dance with these fine-lookin' ladies," he announced. I found myself dancing with the goalkeeper who'd replaced Luciano. He was actually quite nice, once he'd dropped the rowdy-boy act.

No one had invited Nina to dance, so Matt, with remarkable tact for him, led her onto the floor. "Hey, Galbraith, or Badbreath, or whatever your name is," Bruno shouted. "That's carrying Olympic brotherhood too far, even with a girl shortage. Ditch the Commie broad and dance with one of them foxy Swedes."

"Buzz off, Novak. This lady's our guest, and your manners stink."

"You know who I hate even more than Commies?" the hockey captain growled belligerently. "Fellow travelers—the scum of the earth."

"Get stuffed."

The atmosphere was growing ugly. Bruno squared off and started to throw a punch, but his teammates hustled him away.

"See what I mean?" Matt said. "I apologize on behalf of my country. We're not all like that turkey; in fact, hardly any of us are." Nina, unappeased, marched out the door with her nose in the air, followed by Pavel.

I went to the ladies' room. While I was combing my hair, Kim came in. My green eyes and her brown ones locked for a moment in the mirror.

I turned around. "Look here," I said abruptly. "I know you and Dima had it off. Are you pregnant?"

"No!" Kim squeaked. "It was just once, and I'm on the pill, okay?"

"You mean last week was the only time? But you're having morning sickness. I've heard you being sick, over and over."

"Oh, that. No, I always make myself barf to control my weight. I was just gonna stick my finger down my throat to get rid of all the beer I've drunk tonight, okay?"

"Well, that's a relief." I studied Kim's slender figure, which she'd displayed often enough nude in the dormitory. "I think you're getting carried away. You don't have a weight problem."

"That's what you think," Kim said bitterly. "Zack keeps a scale in his car and weighs me twice a day. Every glass of beer or doughnut or whatever shows up." She swallowed. "Listen, I'm sorry about Dima . . . and stuff. It didn't mean anything, it just sorta happened. I guess I thought I'd be one up on you, or something. I just get so tired of Zack and Mother always telling me 'do this, do that.' But I didn't mean to bum you out."

"Well, it's over and done with now, let's forget it. But I think you should talk to a doctor about this weight obsession. If you lose too much, you won't have enough strength for jumping. And it can be dangerous and self-destructive if it goes too far. Isn't it called bulimia or anorexia? You should have some counseling."

"Oh, get off my case. Butt out, or you'll be sorry!" She flounced into the cubicle and slammed the door.

Skating is a decade of hard work and sacrifice.
And even then all you might get is heartbreak.

—Maribel Vinson Owen, figure skating, bronze
   medal at Lake Placid, 1932 (Died in 1961 plane
   crash with her two daughters, both US champions,
   and the entire American skating team)

Olympic Women . . . and Men

By Josh McDonnell

Squaw Valley, CA, Feb. 17——Yesterday, I wrote about women
athletes' long struggle to compete in Olympic sports on a separate
but equal basis. They were usually treated as "bull dykes" and aggressive "emasculators," but there were other hazards too.

   During the 1960 Rome Olympics, Pope John XXIII worried that
the women competitors might tempt his priests to unclean thoughts.
He warned them not to attend events where they would be exposed
to scantily-clad female bodies.

Jacqueline du Bief, French figure skating champion of the fifties, revealed in *The Times* of London that she was sometimes offered generous marks by male judges "in return for amorous adventures." This sort of episode is the other side of the coin, just as nasty.

Society prefers to keep women in neatly defined categories or boxes: madonna, trollop, lady, or jock. In the 1968 Olympics, a Dutch runner was disqualified for being pregnant—apparently she had tried to put herself into the wrong box, or two at once.

The winner of the most gold medals in a single Winter Olympics was Lidia Skoblikova, USSR speed skater, until Eric Heiden broke her record in 1980. She won four golds in four days in 1964 (after her first two in 1960). But news reports on the "speed skating matron" featured her dimples, blonde curls, and understanding husband. The male reporters seemed more comfortable with this image.

Figure skating is a case in point. Before Elaine Zayak put seven triple jumps into her program in 1981, women's athleticism was journalistically downplayed in favor of grace and style, though these are important too (for men, as well). As in gymnastics, diving, and pole vaulting, great strength must be coupled with restraint and elegance.

A skater like Britain's Lesley Grey has it all: she performs fewer triples per program than some, but only the most difficult ones—axel, lutz, loop. And she has a lyrical expressiveness and a dancer's sense of her body that we haven't seen since Peggy Fleming. In Grey, figure skating has reached its ideal amalgam of sport and art.

Few people realize how demanding a sport it is. Skating a four-and-a-half-minute free program has been compared to running a four-minute mile. We're fooled by the smiles and the sequins, and don't see the sweat and pain and long years of single-minded training (which includes road work, stair-running, weight training, and eight hours a day—or night—on the ice).

A carping few even complain that ice dancing and pair skating are not true sports, and don't belong in the Olympics. Not so. In the final, ice dancers do four non-stop minutes of extremely precise and complicated footwork, at top speed in unison—without separating more than arms' length, and without tripping each other up.

The woman in a pair skates a longer program than in singles, and must have the nerve to be thrown 10 feet into the air at high speeds, and the agility to land like a cat. She has to learn these feats in childhood or the fear is too great; at that speed, it's like being thrown off a train. The man must smoothly lift and hold as much as 120 pounds over his head while turning on the ice, sometimes one-handed. And it's supposed to look like fun; if you can tell how much work they're doing, they've failed.

This society finds it difficult to reconcile masculinity with grace or emotionalism, femininity with ambition and self-actualization. In sports, especially, women are still on the defensive. And in figure skating, unfortunately, men are too. On the whole, Americans don't trust men who wear rhinestones to work.

To review yesterday's historical survey, patriarchal attitudes are less firmly institutionalized now than in the ancient Olympics in 776 B.C. or the "modern" Games of 1908, 1932, or 1960. But think of how many years it took to get a woman into space, the Supreme Court, or the IOC, and a women's marathon into the Olympics. Think of the flap over "effeminate" male skating in 1976, and two women tennis stars' private lives in 1981.

Of the nine Winter Olympic sports, women compete in only five. There are still no Olympic women bobsledders, ski jumpers, biathletes, or hockey players, though some women do compete in these sports. Is this IOC intransigence, or is it superior female common sense to eschew the most dangerous and aggressive activities in the Olympics?

No matter what people's private feelings are now, at least "sissy skater" and "husky gal skier" are no longer enshrined in print. Athletes in all sports get more respect, whether they happen to have one X-chromosome or two.

Tomorrow: Luge, winter sport's stepchild

"**Y**our column was superb, Josh! It made my day." I took a sip of Perrier and a bite of cold chicken leg. Josh had brought a picnic, and we were lunching at a redwood table at the beach in Tahoe City. The bright overhead sun and the blue water lapping at the sandy shore made the snow seem out of place, as if scenery for two plays set in different seasons had been mixed up.

"But I hope you don't change your opinion of me this afternoon," I added.

"You ought to have more faith in yourself—I do."

"But the short program's so unforgiving; it's make or break." I was nervy and keyed-up. I hoped I could use all the adrenaline flooding through my system to work for me, instead of against me. "Missing just one of the required moves can put you well and truly out of the running. No do-overs! If you make the same mistake in the long, the judges hardly notice because you can make up for it. And it does happen, especially in the combination jump if you gamble on a triple. People can even fall on something like a flying sitspin they haven't missed in years."

"I know—Janet Lynn, Dorothy Hamill, and Elaine Zayak all lost titles on that move. But would you really like to go back to the days of sixty percent of the score for figures and forty percent for just one free-skating program?"

"N-no, I suppose not," I said dubiously. "There must be some alternative, though. Every skater I know hates the short. The only ones who do well are as consistent as robots, and take absolutely no risks."

"But there should be a standard of comparison, some moves everyone has to do, shouldn't there?"

"You're right," I conceded. "I just wish it were over so I could concentrate on the long program for Thursday. That's my forte."

"How'd the men's figures go this morning?" Josh asked, tearing off a hunk of sourdough bread. "I was watching the slalom."

"Pavel was 1st, then Hans-Peter, Dima, Matt, and Hiroshi."

"Kuznetsov's 3rd? That'll be more of an uphill battle than usual."

"Yes, he's usually 1st in the compulsories. It's the first time Pavel has beat him. The judges seemed to think Dima lined up one of his figures with the hockey blue line, which is forbidden of course, and that really hurt him. Also—not for publication—he acted hung over."

"Is he worried?"

"A bit, I think. There's a lot of pressure on him. I only saw him for a moment, then his coach grabbed him."

"So you're both in 3rd place. Yet, you don't seem too anxious about the final result."

"Mathematically, it's quite possible to win from that position in the compulsories," I explained. "It depends on how consistent each skater is; if someone places high there but not in the freeskating, which counts more, then she can be overtaken. I'm not sure I'd want to be 1st after the figures, myself—too much pressure. Anyway, there's a saying that success is a tranquilizer and failure an amphetamine. We'll both be more motivated now."

"But Pavel is a good freeskater. With a 1st in the figures, he's a real threat."

"Yes, he's a black horse, as Dima would say. Could I have more of the quiche and ratatouille? It's all so delicious, by the way." I tried to change the subject, superstitiously afraid of jinxing Dima or myself.

"Won't you have some wine? It might help your jitters."

"Thanks, no. Even one glass on competition day would show up in the doping test—speaking of amphetamines and tranquilizers."

"Good God, I'd forgotten," Josh exclaimed. "But why do they bother to ban alcohol? Surely, no one would risk blowing an Olympic competition by being smashed."

"Apparently, in the Summer Games the archers and the pentathletes tend to think a wee dram will steady their hands for shooting. I don't know about the biathlon, maybe they'd do it here too if they could."

"I'm so glad you remembered—I'd never forgive myself if I were responsible for disqualifying you!" he said remorsefully.

"No fear. Anyone who's not familiar with the doping rules runs a big risk. You can't leave it to the team doctor. Remember Rick de-Mont's disqualification in '72 because of his asthma medicine?"

"That's right, he lost his gold medal. What if you get this Olympic flu that's going around the Village?" he asked.

"There isn't much you can do for it, because even a lot of over-the-counter drugs are banned. Just the other day, Jean-Marc offered Dima some miracle French cold medicine that turned out to contain ephedrine; luckily, I read the fine print on the label before he used it."

"What is that, adrenaline? It's a good thing you were there to save them both from the consequences. I'm surprised Dany didn't set him straight."

"And I always take codeine for a cough in England, you can get it without a prescription there, but it's a no-no because it's converted to morphine in the body. I brought some along in case I needed it before competition began, but it was taken when our room was vandalized. What's the time?" I asked restlessly. "I don't want to get held up in traffic. Didn't someone once miss his event because he was stuck in a traffic jam?"

"Yes, at Mexico City. It's 2:00—two hours to go. Shall we?"

As I helped him pack the picnic hamper, I asked, "Could we pop in to Zoe's house on the way back? I want to return those books on the Olympics she lent me. I might forget later in the week when things get frantic."

"Sure. I have to speak to her anyway about the IOC luncheon she's giving tomorrow, since I didn't see her this morning."

"She's jolly generous, isn't she? Offering to show me around San Francisco, loaning those books, taking us all out on Saturday. I must thank her again for dinner; I haven't had a chance to write a note. I'd be afraid to admire her dress for fear she'd insist on giving it to me."

"Yes, she is generous. Of course, like most of us she's a mixture of altruism and selfishness. I'm afraid she can be a bit of a schemer sometimes." I wondered what he meant.

Driving north on Highway 89 in the sluggish stream of traffic, we chatted about the British bobsledding team, now in 4th place, one of whom was related to the royal family.

"Did you know those bobsleighs go a hundred and ten miles an hour, and pull four Gs on the turns?" I commented. "Trevor says the adrenaline rush is fantastic."

"So I hear—what an incredible sport! The bobbing federation rules don't allow anyone under eighteen even to get into a bobsled." Josh turned left at the Squaw Valley Road.

"Thanks ever so much for taking me out for a while," I said. "I get cabin fever after being in the Village for three and a half weeks, especially on competition day."

"It's not a village, it's a collection of egos in egg boxes!"

When he pulled into Zoe's driveway behind a red Mercedes 450 SL, I gathered up the books and walked with him to the front door. "Her car's here, she must be in," he said, unlocking the door and calling, "Yoo hoo, Zoe. It's me."

There was silence, then a scuffle and a thump overhead. As we walked through the foyer into the living room, we heard footsteps running down the stairs. Zoe appeared with disheveled hair, clutching a white satin dressing gown around herself.

"I'm sorry, dear, did I wake you? Are you ill?"

"It's okay, Dad. I just have cramps. Thought I'd go to bed with a heating pad. Oh, Lesley, hi. Aren't you competing today?"

"In a bit," I said, wondering why anyone would put on eye make-up and lipstick to go to bed with cramps. They were smeared all over her flushed face. "Sorry to disturb you. I just wanted to thank you for the books—they were so interesting." I felt a little embarrassed to intrude without telephoning first.

"My pleasure. Well, good luck this afternoon." She was obviously eager not to prolong the visit.

Josh told his daughter he'd call her later about the IOC luncheon. I put the books on the coffee table and turned to go. Something red caught my eye. Draped across the back of the sofa was a red warm-up jacket. As I stared at it, frozen, the penny dropped. I knew everything. It was a Russian team jacket—I could see part of the white CCCP on the front. It was undoubtedly Dima's. In fact, I recognized the first three Cyrillic letters on the back: КУЗ. KUZNETSOV. He was undoubtedly upstairs without his jacket or indeed any of his clothes on. Zoe wasn't in bed with cramps, she was in bed with Dima.

. . . I imagined the spectators asking one another
how, for heaven's sake, could this Czech girl be en-
tered. They just did not know how easily one failed;
they could not understand.
—Olga Fikatova Connolly, discus, gold medal at
  Melbourne, 1956

Tuesday, February 18, 3 P.M.

I turned on my heel and walked back to the car, robotlike. I didn't
feel anything yet, but I knew that I would any moment. It was like the
instant after you smash your finger or burn yourself, before the message gets through to the brain. I wanted just to keep walking, but that
would involve some sort of explanation to Josh. Apparently, he
hadn't noticed the jacket, nor had Zoe confessed. A few minutes later I
got out at the Village gate, mechanically thanking him for the lunch
and for his assurances that I would do splendidly in the short.

In my room, I yanked at the chain around my neck and threw the
small golden locket in the wastebasket. Pain stabbed at my heart—I
had to keep moving, or I might collapse.

141

An official sort of envelope lay on my pillow, too important-looking to ignore, so I ripped it open. It was from the Highway Patrolman whom I had told about the anonymous note and the snake. He had sent them to the Sacramento crime lab for testing; the snake's rubber surface was too rough for fingerprints, but the accompanying note had borne several distinct prints among many smudged ones. They belonged to Kim Cranford.

God! I thought in despair, everyone's hand is against me. Moving on auto-pilot, I collected my skatebag, cosmetics case, and seafoam chiffon costume in its garment bag. I walked stiffly downstairs and over to the arena, picking my way automatically through the crowd I didn't see. A religious cultist handed me a flower and a leaflet, which I dropped in the snow. Ignoring the stares and cries of "Good luck!", I trudged down to the empty dressing room, sat down, and looked at the death mask in the mirror.

My mind was still blank, but occasional thoughts streaked across the blackness like evil comets: Sod the bastard. How could he? I hate him. How could I be taken in again so easily? I'd like to kill him.

Competitors began to flock in. Nervous laughter, chatter, and the noise of blow dryers filled the room. Kim listened to her positive-thinking tape through earphones while the make-up lady applied pancake to the bruises on her legs.

I pulled on my tights, zipped up my dress, and found a place at the mirror. Without looking myself in the eye, I yanked my hair into a knot and slapped cosmetics onto my ghostlike face, then I laced up my skates and went to the practice rink to warm up.

Unlike the night I'd heard about Kim and Dima, this time I couldn't forget anything while skating. It was a nightmare. After falling for the fifth time, I went back to the dressing room. I tried a mental visualization of my program, but kept picturing myself failing the vital required moves. For the very first time, the crowd and the cameras seemed malevolent presences. I felt they could all see into my mind. I was going to fall and they'd jeer, all 8,000 of them. My stomach clenched into a cold lump. Unlike so many skaters, I had no anxiety-reducing exercises or tapes to fall back on. I was totally unprepared for pre-performance fear.

Paula came in and took one look. "Lesley! My God, what's wrong?" She pulled me into the temporarily deserted lavatory and put an arm around my shaking shoulders.

"I might as well tell you." I did so in a dreary monotone, not leaving out the episode with Kim either.

"Well, now you know," Paula said distractedly, pulling on her hair. "God, what timing. It's probably one of the worst things that's ever happened to you. You're at the bottom now. What are you going to do? Reach down, or give up?"

"Yes, I'll have to pack it in. I tried to skate and I can't."

"Then you wouldn't deserve the gold, even if you'd been lucky enough to get it. Are you a competitor or a quitter?"

"I just don't think I can do it. I can't go out there in front of everyone." I clasped my hands together to keep them from shaking, wondering how they could be cold and sweaty at once.

"No, you'd better not," the coach snapped. "If you're so spineless that you're nothing without some man, you'd better quit right now! Don't waste my time any further—I have skaters who want to win, and who need me. Crawl into a hole and feel sorry for yourself like the self-centered wretch that you are!"

My face and temper blazed—this was too much. "How dare you speak to me that way? Fuck you!"

"That's the spirit! But don't get mad, get even. Come on, time to go."

I found I could walk again without stumbling. Clenching my jaw stopped my teeth chattering. I could even skate, heated by anger. I'll show them. I'll show them all, I thought, pasting a pretend smile on my face as my music began.

But it was a mechanical, leaden performance. The first layback spin was uncentered and left me dizzy and disoriented, facing the wrong way. Gritting my teeth, I soldiered on. I singled out the planned triple lutz in the combination, though I at least got through the required part, the double toe loop. Just in time, I did remember to leave out the illegal Bauer spread eagle. At last, the final flying sitspin. As I jumped into it, I caught a flash of red hair in the front row, and lost my edge on landing. Stricken, I sprawled on the ice and stared at the place where I'd seen Zoe. It was a stranger.

I sketched a perfunctory curtsy, then skated off quickly to lukewarm applause. Paula was shaking her head at Dick Button to indicate no interview, and I heard him saying, "Let's look at that fall on instant replay. . . ."

Zack Higgins gave me an obviously insincere sympathetic look as I brushed past him. He was barely hiding a smile. "Choked, huh? Sorry about that."

Paula and I left the arena floor before the marks came up, but we could hear the relentless loudspeaker from the basement corridor: "The scores for required elements for Lesley Grey are 5.0, 5.2, 5.1, 5.1, 4.9. . . ."

Paula's arm encircled my shoulders as we walked outdoors. "I'm sorry, dear. You know I didn't mean any of those things, I just had to snap you out of it. I thought that if some emotion started flowing, even anger, you could use the adrenaline in your skating. You were like a zombie. If you'd stayed in that depression—"

"Yes, I see. Don't apologize. Well, I'm afraid that does it. I've mucked it up."

"Not necessarily. You only completely muffed one move, well, one and a half. A lot will depend on how the others do. You'll have to play catch-up, and you'll have to win the long program decisively to show the judges you deserve the gold. But I believe you can do it. As Yogi Berra said, 'It ain't over till it's over.'"

"Hey, wait, you guys! Lesley, Paula!" Matt was dashing toward us.

"I thought you'd want to know—Aleksandrova just two-footed her triple sal and fell out of the combination. Her marks were as bad as yours. And the altitude's getting to everyone—a couple of the earlier ones collapsed at the end, and I just saw the Swede throwing up. They're all gulping oxygen like mad. Now, what the hell's going on with you? Obviously, something's wrong, and by your face, it's not the altitude."

Paula looked at me and I nodded listlessly. "Tell him." The coach drew Matt aside and talked to him in a low voice, while I stared blindly at the illuminated ski run on KT-22.

"The son of a bitch! I'd like to kill him!" Matt shouted, his face contorted. "Just before her short program—God, how rotten." Paula went on whispering.

I turned to them. "You were both right, you tried to warn me and I ignored you. He used me, and then he threw me away when he found someone more useful to him. But, at least, now I know who my friends are. Bless you both. Let's not talk about it anymore. I'm going to take a long hot bath and try to forget everything. No, don't worry, I'm not going to slash my wrists."

Paula looked dubious.

144

"No, really. I do have *some* pride, after all. I'm not going to let him treat me this way anymore—it's almost a relief." To my surprise I actually felt an extraordinary lightening of the spirit. I managed a tentative smile. "I'm finished with breaking my heart over him, this is really the end. So I'll see you later, Paula—practice tomorrow morning at nine? Right."

"Don't forget to stop off at doping control. Got your green card? Good-bye, dear. Hang in there."

Matt fell into step with me, and we walked through the Village toward the medical building. "I really don't like to leave you, unless that's what you want."

"Thanks, but you can't come through doping control with me—only the matron can do that. I'll see you later, if you like."

"Good. Want to catch a movie tonight? They're showing the *Tokyo Olympiad*—if it's the same one I saw a long time ago, it's a masterpiece."

"Just the thing to get my mind back on the job. Thanks, see you after dinner."

"Keep your chin up, or is this an appropriate time to say keep your pecker up?" He grinned impishly.

"Right. I intend to—the British are good at that."

After I left the urine specimen and came back to my room, Angela greeted me with the pink score sheet. The standings showed me in 5th place for the short and 4th overall; I had only slipped one place. Kim had won the short, then came Putzi, an Italian, and Nina. The over-all rankings going into the long program were now Nina, Putzi, Kim, and me. I was still in the race, with a longshot chance to win if I came 1st in the free. Grateful for the reprieve, I decided that fate had sent me this second chance as a sign that it would be kind if I didn't allow myself to be distracted by men and sex.

"Matt called," Angie said, "and told me what happened. He thought you might need someone to talk to. I'm frightfully sorry, love."

"Did he really? How thoughtful of him. I don't know how I ever could have thought him nasty and cynical."

"He said to warn you that tonight is 'Russian Night' in the cafeteria —he thought you might not have much appetite for borsch and stroganoff. He said he didn't even have the heart to scramble the letters on the menu. I must say, I like him a lot. He's really a hunk, too," Angie added slyly.

145

"I supose so. I was too busy disliking him to notice."

"How little one can tell about people from first impressions," she philosophized.

"That is so true!" I said in a vehement burst. "Dima has a wonderful facade—all charm, sweetness, and good manners. And underneath, just selfish appetites and ruthless opportunism, looking out for Number One. To hell with him—I'm going to cut him right out of my life, starting now."

"Good for you!"

"I don't love him anymore, I don't even like him. And he doesn't need me now. Zoe's connections will make his defecting a snap. He can be a star in America or rot in Siberia. I don't care, it's all one to me."

These are the Olympics. You die for them.

—Al Oerter, discus, four gold medals at Melbourne,
1956; Rome, 1960; Tokyo, 1964; Mexico City, 1968

"The marks for Hans-Peter Koenig for presentation: 5.5, 5.5, 5.3, 5.1, 5.4. . . ."

I squinted at the electronic scoreboard and tried to remember Pavel's short program marks. The two skaters' scores were very close. Each had failed to perform every compulsory move perfectly; the short program nerves had struck again. I felt a little better about my debacle 24 hours earlier.

The atmosphere was electric. The opportunity to forge ahead was there—room had been left at the top for higher marks. Of the leaders, only three were left: Matt, who was now skating around the near end

147

of the arena in tense circles, Dima, and Hiroshi. Dima hadn't appeared yet. He had skipped the group warm-up, as he often did; he was probably in the small adjacent rink.

"Representing the United States, Matthew Galbraith!" The partisan crowd went wild as Matt took his place at center ice. "Dueling Banjoes" filled the arena. The audience gasped as he exploded into the first required jump, a triple salchow, which he did on one foot. He had the rare quality of *ballon*, much prized by dancers and skaters, the ability to seem to hang in the air at the highest arc of the jump. This, together with his extraordinary elevation, made his triples look as effortless as singles. I hoped they didn't seem too easy to the judges; great skaters sometimes have to make it look like hard work to get the marks they deserve.

The staccato, fast-paced music ideally set off Matt's exuberant flair and dash. From his serpentine step sequence, he swaggered without a pause into a combination triple axel-double toe loop. The necessary check against the terrific torque of the three-and-a-half revolution axel showed impressive strength. The spectators jumped to their feet, roaring adulation in a single voice as he blurred into a cross-foot spin, stopped suddenly as if in freeze-frame, and flipped one arm aloft in a nonchalant shrug as if to say, "Nothing to it!"

Applause was still ringing out and Matt was collecting flowers when the first marks went up: one 6.0 from the US judge and eight 5.9s. The nearby fans gathered him into a tumultuous mass embrace. The second set of marks was identical, with a 6.0 from the British judge and all the rest 5.9s. Dima would have to pull out all the stops to beat this, and I vengefully hoped he couldn't.

Where was he, anyway? He should be on the ice by now. Not that I cared, of course. As the thunderous ovation finally died down, people began looking around for the next skater. The pause lengthened, and a curious hum rose from the crowd.

After a few minutes, the dour Russian team leader Sergei Nokitov pushed through our group of skaters milling around the entrance onto the ice. He walked carefully on crepe soles to the referee, sitting between the fifth and sixth judges, and whispered to him. The buzzing in the audience died away as the hushed crowd, sensing some sort of disaster, watched the two. The referee beckoned a caddy and handed her a note, which she took quickly across the ice to the announcer. You could hear her blades scrape in the silence.

"Dmitri Kuznetsov of the Soviet Union will not be competing at this time. He has withdrawn because of injury."

Murmurs of consternation swelled in the arena. "Flashback to Tai and Randy!" said Angie, her blue eyes round with surprise.

I tried to catch Nokitov's attention as he passed us, but he ignored everyone; walking quickly with a set face and gazing straight ahead, he vanished down the stairs into the basement. I looked across the ice at Matt, still talking to Dick Button. He met my gaze and raised his eyebrows, shrugging slightly.

"The last skater, from Japan. . . ." Hiroshi, looking bewildered, was hustled onto the ice as the samisen's twanging began.

"I'm going back to the Village, Angie. I must find out what's happened."

"I'll come too."

We walked in silence. As we approached the Athletes' Center, Angela said, "I wonder if anyone here knows why Dima withdrew."

"Bad news travels fast." I had a feeling of foreboding that chilled me.

Nigel called to us as we walked into the crowded lounge. He drew me aside and said, "You'll hear it in a minute anyway, love. Everyone's saying he's dead."

"Wh-what?" I stammered.

"Maybe it's just a rumor, I don't know where it came from, but about five people have already told me. It's spreading like wildfire."

"Let's switch on the telly," suggested Angie, looking at me in concern. "Are you all right? You're white as a sheet."

In the television room all three sets were on, and crowds of athletes bunched around them. Dick Button was winding up his interview with Hiroshi.

The anchorman interrupted: "We have just received confirmation of the death of world champion figure skater Dmitri Kuznetsov." A few watchers gasped, and some turned to look at me. "The Soviet team officials have refused to verify it, but we have a reliable report that he died earlier this afternoon in the Olympic Village hospital. There have been many rumors over the last half-hour, but we waited to make this announcement till we received independent confirmation. The cause of death is unknown at this time.

"Kuznetsov suffered a head injury as a result of an accident in practice a week ago today, but we do not know if his death has any con-

149

nection with that incident. Yesterday he placed 3rd in the compulsory figures, somewhat low for him, but appeared in good health. Stay tuned for more details as we have them. On our late-night wrap-up of today's Olympic coverage at 11:30, 10:30 Central and Mountain, we'll show you highlights of Dmitri Kuznetsov's career." A commercial for the official yogurt of the Winter Games filled the screen.

"Bloody hell!" Nigel said in disgust. "They must have obituaries ready for all of us."

I felt absolutely nothing, as if the series of shocks over the last week had finally short-circuited my emotions. "Christ, I just can't take it in. It makes no sense. I'm going to talk to that Russian doctor. She'll tell me what happened, she's a good sort."

"Do you want me to come with you?" asked Angela.

"Yes, please." People parted to let us pass. Some awkwardly patted my shoulder, murmuring words of sympathy.

We found the Quonset hut hospital beseiged by reporters. "There's a back door—come on!" Angie whispered.

We sneaked inside. I saw Dr. Sologubova's broad back outside the Russian team clinic down the hall. "Doctor, please, I must talk to you," I said urgently.

She hesitated, then motioned me past the OFF-LIMITS sign on the door. Inside the small room were an examining table, oxygen cylinders, a refrigerator, and locked glass-fronted cupboards of instruments and medicines. A tiny bathroom with two toilet cubicles, visible through an open door, adjoined the clinic; I had used it for my doping test yesterday because the main bathroom was too crowded.

"What on earth happened? He'd recovered from his fall, he was fine the last time I saw him!"

"When was that?" Her face was drawn and weary.

"Yesterday morning, just after the compulsories."

"He was fine this morning, too."

"Well, then?"

The doctor sat down and buried her face in her hands. She rubbed her reddened eyes, then looked up, her mouth trembling. "The head injury must have been more serious than I realized. Maybe there was a subdural hematoma after all, bleeding inside the skull."

"But you X-rayed him, didn't you?" I probed. "You kept him here for two days, and surely you did all the necessary tests."

"Of course, but no tests are completely accurate. There are still unknowns."

"You're not telling me everything." I decided to bluff. "I think some-one deliberately killed him. Maybe the KGB, maybe someone else. God knows, plenty of people had reasons. Maybe you were involved."

"No, it was an accident! It wasn't me!" she cried.

"What? What accident?" I pounced.

"I can say no more. I dare not! There will be a great trouble if any-thing gets out." Her eyes darted from side to side.

"You'd better tell me about it," I insisted. "I have a right to know—I loved him."

"*Da*. You and others. But I think he really did love you, as much as he could love anyone." She hesitated, then said in a rush, "I must talk to someone or I go crazy. All right, I tell you, but it must go no further. It was that damned blood doping that killed him!"

"I . . . I don't understand," I stammered.

"You've heard of it? An athlete has a unit of blood removed and stored for a few weeks before he competes. Then just before his event, he has a transfusion of his own blood. Meanwhile, his body has re-placed it. So, now he has extra red blood cells, the hemoglobin, to carry more oxygen to his muscles. He has added stamina, an edge over his opponents."

"Oh, I remember. Like people thought Lasse Viren did?" The Fin-nish long-distance runner, winner of the 5,000 and 10,000 meters at Munich and Montreal, had been widely suspected, along with others, of the practice. "Isn't it banned by the IOC?"

"*Da, da*, but impossible to detect. The athlete has only his own blood in his body, you understand, no foreign substances."

I floundered, trying to understand. "But Viren and the others were distance runners, they needed stamina and endurance that a figure skater doesn't. Maybe cross-country skiers or speed skaters might think they needed that, but Dima—why?"

"He worried about his age and this altitude. He say he didn't feel as young as he used to, that his rivals in their teens and early twenties would eat him up. I say nonsense, twenty-seven is not old, cut out the vodka and cigarettes and late nights, and you be fit as fiddle. But he wouldn't listen, he insisted on it."

That sounded like Dima, right enough. "When did you take the blood out?"

"The day he arrived, on the first day of this month. Then he decided later he'd need two transfusions, one before the short program and another before the long. So the day before the Opening Ceremony, he had another unit drawn."

That had been a busy day for Dima, I recalled, what with getting Kim into bed as well. But how could this blood business have led to his death? "Maybe the bleeding from his head injury, together with the two units that were removed, weakened him . . .?" I ventured.

"*Nyet,* the bleeding from the accident was minor, it looked like much more than it was."

"What time was the transfusion this morning?"

"About nine. It started to go wrong as soon as the blood was all in."

"*What* went wrong?"

"He must have had a transfusion reaction, I can't imagine why. I was so careful." Her face crumpled and she buried it in her hands again. "It was terrible! That poor boy—I really loved him like a son, you know. He died so quickly and I couldn't prevent it."

I ignored her sobs and pressed on. "How long did the transfusion take?"

"Ten or fifteen minutes. He began complaining of pain and nausea, and he vomited. Then he had a chill and his temperature shot up."

"What did you do then?"

"Nothing, because I thought it was a feverish reaction to bacteria on the needle or tubing. The symptoms are the same as the early symptoms of a transfusion reaction—but that is the last thing I suspected then. They usually go away quickly and need no treatment." The relief of confession made her words spill out like a dam bursting.

"What happened next?"

"I kept him here all morning to keep an eye on him, though he began to feel better, which made me think I was right. About eleven he called me from the lavatory next door. His urine was bright red."

"Oh, my God," I murmured in horror.

"It's called port-wine urine. Kidney failure can be the result."

"What did you do?"

"I had to call the team officials first. Then I started an IV and lab work on his urine and blood samples, but almost before I'd begun, he was comatose. I started medication to raise his blood pressure, it had fallen to almost nothing. . . ." She swallowed painfully.

"Was it irreversible?"

"Maybe not, if I'd given an injection of epinephrine hydrochloride at once."

"Why in God's name didn't you?" I gripped the edge of the desk and leaned over, staring fiercely into her eyes. She wouldn't meet my gaze.

"The officials, mainly that shit Nokitov, wouldn't let me! He said epinephrine might show up in the doping test."

"Is that like adrenaline?"

"*Da.* I said he would be dead long before that if they didn't let me treat him, or else transfer him immediately by helicopter to the nearest real hospital."

"And the bastards wouldn't allow it?" I asked incredulously.

"Perhaps they were afraid he'd defect, once out of their hands. They said they'd have to get permission to hospitalize him from the consulate in San Francisco, they didn't know who would pay for it, they'd need an interpreter at the hospital, and so on and so on. Maybe they didn't believe it was serious, or else they wanted to cover up the blood doping at all costs. Nokitov said the entire Russian team could be disqualified if it leaked out. *That* was the important thing to them; Dima was balanced on one side of the scale against the whole team on the other. *Vse boyatsa za svoyu shkuru,*" she said dolefully.

"What?"

"'Everyone is afraid for his own skin.' They were still arguing with me when he died."

I stood in silence. What a senseless waste, what a stupid way to die! A fatal combination of Dima's vaulting ambition, the doctor's passivity, and the bureaucrats' inept or malevolent fumbling.

"But I still don't understand what caused it in the first place." I tried to jog my mind into working again. "How could someone have a transfusion reaction to his own blood?"

"*Nye znaiyu,*" the doctor snapped. "I don't know. I can't think straight, I'm so tired. I was up all last night with Fyodor Viktorovich."

"Fyodor? Why?"

"He seemed to have alcohol poisoning or DTs, but it turned out to be an overdose of codeine."

"Codeine—!"

"Yes, the urinalysis confirmed it. He's not completely recovered yet."

"How could that have happened?"

"I've no idea. He denies taking anything. Dima said this morning that Fyodor was fine at dinner—he had four helpings of borscht."

My thoughts returned to Dima. "There will be an autopsy, I suppose."

"That's the last thing they want! They took the body away right afterwards to Reno, and they took me with them—I just got back. I was supposed to sign the death certificate for the undertaker, so he could be cremated immediately. But they decided that was too risky, so they took him to the Reno airport where an Aeroflot jet's always standing by. It's on its way home by now."

"He's gone? That's not possible! When did the plane leave?"

"Sometime around three, I suppose. You see, they wanted him just to seem to disappear, as if they'd withdrawn him and sent him home. They never intended to let it out that he was dead. There must have been a leak to the press, but they're still denying it."

"I wish I knew what to do, whom to go to," I said distractedly.

"If the truth about the blood doping gets out, the team will be ruined. I will be, in any case," she said heavily. "They will blame me for the disaster, though you can see it wasn't my fault. But you promised to say nothing."

"Yes, but that might make me an accessory to a crime."

"*Shto?* What crime?" Dr. Sologubova's mouth dropped open in fright.

"I'm sure that a sudden death like this has to be investigated. By whom, I don't know—the local police, or perhaps the FBI. I've no idea if Soviet officials are bound by American law. But I'm sure you're guilty of no wrongdoing; you acted responsibly, and did all they would let you."

"This is flea-chasing," the doctor said impatiently. I remembered with a pang that Dima had often used that expression, the Russian equivalent of "nit-picking." She went on, "You said earlier you thought he'd been killed deliberately. That means murd—" She clamped her hand over her mouth to cut the word off in mid-syllable.

"Dr. Sologubova, what would happen if he'd been transfused with the wrong blood group?"

"It would kill him," she said flatly. "It would be a foreign protein. He was type O, a universal donor; he could give blood to anyone, but he could not receive any other type. But that sort of mix-up is not possible. It's all carefully labeled, see for yourself." She opened the refrigerator door. About two dozen plastic bags, each tautly bulging with dark red blood, were piled on the shelves, along with racks of test tubes and bottles of medicine. She picked up the top bag and pointed to its white label, handwritten in Cyrillic letters.

"I have a system. See, this is Anatoli Mikhailovich Ivanov, the cross-country skier. Here's his name and number, his blood type, and

154

the date the blood was drawn. He is to have his transfusion early tomorrow morning, before his fifty kilometers of *langlauf*."

I remembered the gaunt flagbearer. "I see there's a lock on the refrigerator," I said. "Why didn't you use it?"

"Nokitov thought it would seem too suspicious. If anyone saw it, I was to say that it was our blood bank, for transfusion in case of injury. We must bring as much of our own equipment as possible, to prevent hospitalizing our athletes. Once they go to an American hospital, they are out of our control. This room was supposed to be locked up whenever I or the other doctors weren't here. But too many coaches and trainers needed access, so. . . ." She threw out her hands and shrugged.

Typical bureaucracy, I thought. East and West are just the same, the right hand not knowing what the left hand is doing. Which is probably why Dr. Sologubova and the blood are still here. "The IOC Medical Committee could have called in anytime and found this, you know. I was in that lavatory just yesterday for doping control when the main room was full. Any athlete or official could walk in and open that refrigerator."

I looked closely at the pressure-sensitive label on the bag of blood, then pulled up the corner. It peeled off easily. We looked at each other in horror.

"Can you test this blood to see if it's the group it's supposed to be?" I asked quickly. "Or better yet, do you still have any of the blood you gave Dima?"

"I'll test them both. It's very simple." The doctor took two glass microscope slides and labeled one I and one K with a grease pencil. Into a small glass tube she poured a fluid, and mixed it with a few drops of blood from the refrigerated bag. She did the same with the small amount of blood from the bag hanging on a stand by the examining table, presumably Dima's.

"Now I put typing serum on both ends of each slide. They will show clumping if A or B factors are present. I mix a drop of each blood cell suspension with each serum—so—then wait half a minute and look."

She put the K slide on the microscope platform and adjusted the eyepiece. "This is Dima's—type O, no A or B cells—so we'll see no clumping of cells on either side. . . . *Bog moi!*" she cried with a gasp.

"What is it?"

Dr. Sologubova replaced the slide with the one labeled I, looked again, and shook her head in disbelief. "But this is not possible.

155

Ivanov has type A, and should react with that fluid. But there is no clumping. Dima had type O and shouldn't react at all. The other slide shows what this one should!" She switched the slides again.

I peered through the viewer. The cells on the left side were bunching angrily.

"ABO incompatibility! I should have known," said the doctor in a hollow voice. "But how could it happen? I was always so careful."

"Someone changed the labels, it's the only explanation. Ivanov's blood, or someone else's went into Dima. And we saw how easy it would be to switch them. Didn't you ever realize that this blood doping business was just asking for foul play?"

The doctor shook her head wearily. "We have a proverb: 'When you live with wolves, you must howl like a wolf.' I had no choice."

A sudden loud pounding on the door made us both jump. Dr. Sologubova looked like a rabbit paralyzed by headlights. The door crashed open against the wall. Fyodor, Nokitov, Dima's coach Bogachev, and three other hard-faced Russian officials I knew only by sight filled the room. Nokitov glared suspiciously at me and the apparatus on the table. He barked rapidly in Russian in a harsh voice, then grabbed the doctor's arm to pull her from the room. She let out a squeak of fear.

Angela, looking frightened, was peering through the doorway. "All right, Angie, I'm just coming," I called, and walked casually toward the door. I was guiltily aware that I was abandoning Dr. Sologubova to her fate, but what could I do to save her? Fyodor, looking pale and unwell, barred the way.

I summoned all my presence of mind, smiled at him sympathetically, and said, "I'm so sorry, Fyodor Viktorovich. I know how terrible you must be feeling. You were fond of Dima too." I dropped my voice to a whisper: "I'm still *nasha*—on your side."

He lowered his eyes sheepishly, and I walked around him into the hall. I grabbed Angela's arm and muttered, "Straight out the back door, and don't say a word."

We strode quickly from the building, and I began to run toward our dormitory. "Christ, now I know what it was like under Stalin. Big boots and the knock on the door!"

"Tell me what happened!" Angie panted. "It seemed you were in there for hours, and then, all of a sudden, that bunch of secret police types marched down the hall and burst right in."

"Let's just get upstairs to our room, okay? They can't come after me there."

We dropped onto our beds. "Right. Tell! I'm dying of curiosity!" Angie begged.

"He was murdered. And since the doctor is probably on her way back to Russia right now, I'm the only one left who knows."

. . . the Village had been a refuge, admittedly im-
perfect, from a larger, seedier world in which individ-
uals and governments refused to adhere to any humane
code. For two weeks every four years we direct our
kind of fanaticism into the essentially absurd activities
of running and swimming and being beautiful on a
balance beam. Yet even in the rage of competition we
keep from hurting each other, and thereby demonstrate
the meaning of civilization.
—Kenny Moore, marathon, 4th place at
Munich, 1972

The day I had been awaiting for 10 years, the Olympic freeskating final, had at last arrived. And here I was, distracted and half-crazy. I'd spent a good part of the night tossing sleeplessly after my first long crying spell, alone in the darkness with pain and loss.

Now I had to take a decision. Should I call the police or the FBI? Tell my story to someone in the IOC, or perhaps the British Olympic Association would be more appropriate? Maybe I should confide in Josh. However, I had a feeling that any non-police person or group would pass this hot potato right back to me, not that I'd blame them.

But was there any real reason to tell the police? They'd probably

159

already tagged me as a complaining nutcase. And Dima was gone, nothing would bring him back. Dr. Sologubova was the only one to point the finger at, but she was a helpless cog in the KGB machinery. The only charge that could be made against her or Nokitov would be negligence. Finding the real murderer seemed an impossible task. What was the point in doing anything? My mind went round and round on its treadmill.

At breakfast the athletes, a superstitious lot, were speculating uneasily about the "jinxed Olympics"—first Vinnie Luciano, now Dima Kuznetsov had died. Who would be next? Several bobbers, lugers, and jumpers had been seriously injured, and a tourist had suffered a fatal coronary. A woman spectator had passed out last night at the outdoor award ceremony, arousing terror among the crowd, but it proved only a fainting spell. Matt suggested cynically that she probably couldn't stand listening to the GDR anthem one more time. He'd made great strides in sensitivity and consideration, but still lapsed into bad taste.

The Soviet delegation had made no comment whatsoever about Dima. They seemed to think they could deny it indefinitely—the Big Lie. For lack of any fresh news, conversation moved on to the living.

The American skaters were still high on the upset victory over the Russians in last night's ice dancing final by Elinor Rhodes and Brent Reece. It was the first gold medal ever for the US in dance. The Russians' brazen flouting of the rules in this event had finally caught up with them. The Americans had come into the free dance lying 2nd, won the free with the top Russian couple 2nd, and won under the tie-breaking rule. Angela and Nigel finished 13th. I felt the added pressure; if Great Britain were going to win a gold medal in skating, it would have to be mine. The weight of the entire country's hopes seemed to descend onto my shoulders.

Finally, I decided to do nothing about Dima's death for 24 hours, to try to put it out of my mind, and to concentrate only on tonight's final freeskating. I planned a light workout in the gym; perhaps exercising my body would whip my mind back into shape. The phone rang just as I was leaving.

"Miss Grey? My name is Duane Oglethorpe, FBI. I'm the special agent in charge of the investigation into the Dmitri Kuznetsov case. I'd like to ask you a few questions."

"Of course. When would you like to meet?"

160

"Right now, ma'am, if it's convenient for you. I'm in the lobby of your building."

"I'll be right down."

I looked around the lounge and spotted him immediately, a pudgy man in a brown suit. He wore a narrow tie and a tiny American flag pin in his lapel. A newspaper on a table next to him stared up at me: MYSTERY DEATH OF RUSS SKATER.

"How do you do, ma'am," he said, showing his FBI identification. "Is there any place private where we can talk?"

I led him to one of the alcoves off the lounge. He doffed his hat, but not his sunglasses, and took out a notebook. "Care for a stick of gum, ma'am? No?" He inserted a piece of Juicy Fruit into his mouth. "Now, I understand you knew Kuznetsov pretty well." His face wore a faint suggestion of a leer.

I decided to be frank. "Let's not beat about the bush. We've been— had been—lovers for the last two months, as I'm sure you know. I'm also sure you know that he had others."

"Yes, ma'am. When was the last time you saw him?"

"Tuesday morning about eleven, very briefly. I found out about his latest affair later that day, and decided to break off our relationship. I never saw him again. Would you mind telling me why the FBI is involved? Murder isn't a federal crime, is it?"

"The Placer County Sheriff's Office has called us in to work with them. It's funny you should use the word murder, seeing as there's not even a body. All we definitely have is a disappearance: a possible kidnapping of a guest of the US government across a state line, a possible felony committed on US government property, possibly involving foreign nationals who are all claiming diplomatic immunity and screaming their heads off about harassment. They're madder than ticks on a scrawny dog. The Rooshans change their story every five minutes, and they haven't really told us a thing. Without his body, we don't know how, when, where, why, or even *if* he died." For a moment, his impassive mask fell to reveal an irritated human being underneath. "Would you tell me your activities from Tuesday night through Wednesday night?"

"Yes, if you like. But wouldn't it save time for me simply to tell you what I know?"

"Just give me a chronological record of your whereabouts and what you did, please."

I did so, adding to the account Dima's defection plans and what Dr. Sologubova had revealed.

"Where can I reach this Dr. Sologuva?"

"Siberia, I should think." I repressed a wicked impulse to add, "Frozen Tundra 555—" I must have been spending too much time around Matt.

He did a double take. "How's that again?"

"You'd better tackle the Soviet brass again, but I don't think you'll learn much even if they will talk to you. I've an idea it was a KGB operation. They must have got wind of his plans to defect, or else they thought he was going to lose the competition. In either case, he'd be an embarrassment to them, and they had to get rid of him."

"So I have only your word for this whole blood mix-up."

"Why would I lie?" I asked uneasily.

"If you have any witnesses to corroborate this story, I'd like their names."

"Only the Russians were there; I told you the names I know. Wait—my roommate Angela Hartley saw them burst into the clinic and take the doctor away."

"Where can I reach her?"

"She's gone to the MGM Grand in Reno with a bunch of dancers, but she'll be back tonight. When was Dima last seen?"

"At breakfast Wednesday morning," he replied grudgingly.

"That fits," I said. "Dr. Sologubova said he had the transfusion at nine in the morning."

"Did Kuznetsov have any connections with terrorist organizations?"

"Certainly not."

"Was he a member of the Communist Party?"

"No."

"How do you know?"

"I saw his internal passport. It said 'not a Party member.'"

"Could you read it?"

"No, he translated it for me."

"Was he spying on team members or foreigners for the KGB?"

"I'm sure he wouldn't do that. Why do you ask?"

"That's usually a condition for travel abroad. Were you ever approached by any member of the Soviet delegation about doing intelligence work for them?"

"No."

"We've heard you were planning to marry Kuznetsov and defect to the Soviet Union."

"That was just the cover-up he used with his KGB guard. The truth was exactly the opposite. The story seems to have got around, though. I suppose you know about the anonymous notes?"

"Would you consider moving to the USSR?"

"Under no circumstances. Am I considered disloyal to the West for falling in love with a Russian?"

"But you have visited there," he pressed.

"Only for a skating competition. Believe me, if you've seen Moscow once, there's no way you'd ever want to go back, or become a Communist."

"Who else might confirm this defection story?"

"You'd better talk to Kim Cranford and Zoe McDonnell," I said wearily. "You might ask Kim why she's trying to scare me by sending me nasty notes. And why haven't the police done anything about it?"

"Miss Cranford is being interviewed this morning. What was the other name? Thanks." He asked skeptically, "If Kuznetsov *really* wanted to defect, why didn't he just come to Security Headquarters?"

"His bodyguard would have stopped him, by force if necessary. And he wanted to wait till after he'd won the gold medal, for the maximum publicity value."

"Did y'all know Vinnie Luciano personally?"

"Not really, we just knew who he was."

"Now, there was an athlete! Goldarn, what a hockey player." He showed a bit of warmth for the first time.

"Do you think there was some connection between their deaths?"

"I couldn't say, ma'am."

"Are you investigating Bruno Novak? Haven't you heard of the threats against the Russian athletes?"

"I can't say anything about the progress of the investigation. That's all for now, but I'm sure we'll want to talk to you later on. I advise you not to leave the area in the near future."

"You *do* know what I'm doing tonight, don't you?"

"We know all about you, don't worry, ma'am. Good-bye for now."

Seething with irritation, I ran upstairs for my leotard, banging all the doors as hard as I could, and jogged to the Village gym. After a warm-up at the ballet barre, I did some calisthenics and aerobics. A half-hour workout finally calmed me down. I lay on the mat in a light sweat and considered what to do next. I had to conserve most of my energy for tonight. A sauna, swim, and massage, then the final on-ice practice should fill the time nicely till late afternoon, when I'd have a meal, then a nap. The door opened and a lanky form flopped down next to me.

"Matt—am I ever glad to see you!"

"Me, the ugly American?"

"Don't be so silly. Now, you may get a call from a Mr. Oglethorpe of the FBI—"

"Yeah, he's just finished 'interrogating' me," he said sarcastically. "The Fuller Brush boys are in pretty bad shape if that clown's the best investigator they can come up with. He couldn't find Kuznetsov's murderer unless the guy confessed and spelled out his name very slowly."

"So, you think it's murder too." I told him about Dr. Sologubova's revelations and my interview with Oglethorpe. "The FBI seem to consider *me* a suspect," I finished.

"Of course. You've got the most powerful motive: sexual jealousy, a dangerous and destructive emotion. Hell hath no fury, etc. And they might see you as a Burgess-Maclean Commie-sympathizer type, recruited from your cell at Cambridge and all that. But take a number and get in line—I'm a suspect too."

I sat up and stared at him in astonishment. "No! That's absurd!"

"Sure—he wormed it out of me that Kuznetsov and I were competitors, and his tiny brain added up one plus one. Also, some helpful stool pigeon told him that I was heard on Tuesday afternoon shouting that I'd like to kill the son of a bitch."

"Oh, right, after the short." I felt warmed again by his championing of me. It was good to have someone on my side.

"I didn't do it, by the way," he said, his brown eyes gazing directly into mine.

"You don't have to tell me that. I know you'd never kill anyone."

"I thought the way he treated people was shitty, but that doesn't mean he deserved to die. Do you know, I've had a picture of him up on my wall for a couple of years?"

"Why?"

"To remind myself who I had to beat. It's as though I've been pushing against a strong wind all these years. Suddenly the wind stops blowing, and I fall flat on my face. I'll miss him," he said feelingly. "And I don't want whoever killed him to get away with it."

"At first I didn't see any purpose in getting involved, but now I feel the same way."

"Well, the FBI's suspect club is large," he said more lightly. "Oglethorpe let it out that the scorned women's division includes Nina, Kim, and Zoe. Then there's Pavel and Hans-Peter, doubly suspicious as dirty Commie rats, and all our coaches too."

"Coaches? Why?"

"Why not? Protecting their ducklings from the big bad wolf, I guess. Paula would cheerfully have killed Dima. No, I'm not serious. But I think you and I are tied for first place in the suspect sweepstakes."

I lay down on my stomach and propped my chin in my hands thoughtfully. "The obvious one seems to be Bruno Novak."

"Oh, yeah, I told Oglethorpe about Novak's connection with PLAYFAIR. I think he thought I was being pretty un-American."

"I tend to think it was the KGB, myself," I said.

"I think that's a Red herring, as it were."

"No, I've a gut feeling that the motive was political, not personal, but from which end of the political spectrum I'm not certain. Matt, we're going to have to work this out ourselves. We know everyone involved, and we're right on the spot. On the other hand, Oglethorpe's been brought in from Reno or San Francisco—"

"Mississippi originally, I suspect from his accent, by way of the Sacramento office. They brought him in by chopper in the middle of the night. Maybe he won't seem such a clod when he gets oriented, but he doesn't know anything about 'figger skatin'.' He confided tactlessly that he's pretty sure all male skaters are gay, by the way."

"Well, a few of them are." I pulled my single braid over my shoulder and began to replait it.

"Yeah, but if he thought Kuznetsov or I were, it would really throw him off. Maybe he's picturing a bisexual triangle or gay lovers' quarrel, or something along those lines. Furthermore, he gets the names of the 'ath-a-letes' all wrong. 'Da-me-try Kuznotsky,'" Matt said sarcastically. "He doesn't follow 'Rooshan' sports."

"If we don't at least clear ourselves, they won't let us leave after the Olympics. Also, mind you, I don't think the FBI has much incentive to find the murderer of a Russian. They probably think the fewer Reds, the better. I don't think he believed me for a moment about Dima's planning to defect. So—shall we have a go?"

165

"Get serious, we only have four days before the Olympics are over."

"We may not get anywhere, but it's better than doing nothing."

"Okay, Sherlock, I'm game. We'll play detective. But you take today off, you've got other fish to fry, and I'll start in. Tomorrow, you spell me till after I bag the gold."

"Right! This makes me feel more in control now, not so much at the mercy of events. I think I'll have a word with Josh McDonnell too."

"Good idea. He has connections we don't, and he's pretty sharp. I'll try to talk to some of those people I mentioned, and find out where they were at the crucial times. Maybe you could tackle some of the Russians tomorrow."

I stood up and stretched. "Carry on, Watson. I'm off to the sauna."

"Oh, Lesley, about tonight: don't worry, you'll knock their socks off. I'll be there rooting for you." He flashed a smile up at me, his teeth startlingly white in his auburn beard, and I returned it.

"Don't, you'll jinx me."

"Then how about *merde*, as they say in ballet? Or break a leg, if you prefer."

At 8:00 that night, I was sitting in my tights at the arena dressing room mirror, applying green eye shadow with a steady brush. I mentally contrasted the self-confident image in the mirror with the pathetic creature of Tuesday afternoon, and felt good about myself.

Paula came in. "Nervous?" I heard the applause for the first skater in the penultimate third flight and the announcer's voice before the door closed.

"Not much, just keyed up and ready to go."

"Good. You *are* ready, so just get out there and do your thing. You've skated the whole program twice through without a break, so you know you have the stamina. We've rehearsed everything that could go wrong. You know Kim's going to get a standing ovation just before you come out, and her marks may get booed, so that won't faze you. You're prepared for anything." She lowered her voice confidentially. "And you've got the look of a champion again; you'd lost it for a while. You're convinced you can win, so the judges will be convinced too. Everyone else knows you're the one to beat, and I think they're all pretty worried. Shall I zip you?"

I pulled on my shimmering teal-blue costume with its tight bodice and flowing sleeves, and Paula fastened it. She handed me hairpins as I brushed my hair and piled it up carefully in a ballerina's knot.

"Too much blusher?"

"No, just right for the TV lights. Wow, look at all your telegrams! Going to warm up now? I want to get back and watch that little Eskimo girl on the American team everyone's raving about. She should've beaten Kim in Nationals, but US champions don't get dethroned in an Olympic year—princesses have to fall in line behind queens. You've got half an hour yet."

By back stairs I made my way to the practice rink and warmed up gradually, first off-ice, then on, working my way up to the triple jumps. Then I flowed easily, not full-out, through my program minus the jumps, while the music sang through my head. Other skaters in the last group had come in: Putzi and Nina accompanied by their coaches, and Kim by her mother as well.

"*Viel Glück!*" said the chunky German with a smile.

"Good luck to you, too," I replied, silently adding "for the silver." I wished luck to Aleksandrova, whose delicate fairness was set off by a red Ukrainian embroidered dress; the Russian said nothing, but shot me a scathing glance and rudely turned her back.

Kim skated over. "Did the FBI ask you questions today?" she whispered.

"Yes, a Mr. Oglethorpe."

"Mr. Buggins or something talked to me. It was so gross, I couldn't even believe it. Like, totally weird. Then Matt Galbraith finds out where I'm staying, and comes and asks me more junk. He goes, 'Where were you Wednesday morning? Have you ever been in the Russian clinic?'" She glanced in her mother's direction and lowered her voice even more. "Oh, wow. I mean, forget it. I feel so hassled, I almost dropped out of the competition. Really."

Not bloody likely. "About the notes and the snake—"

"Those were sent to me first!" Kim squeaked.

"What?"

"Just like I told the FBI. The first note was in my message box the night before the Opening Ceremony, and the snake was on my pillow the next day—I almost died! That's one reason I moved out of the Village. And I definitely didn't see Dima again."

"What did you do with them?"

"Gave them to Zack."

"Your fingerprints were on the note, not his."

"Okay, he usually wears gloves, even indoors, haven't you noticed? He has a circulation problem in cold weather, or something."

"I wonder if he passed them on to me, thinking that if they were traced, it wouldn't be to him?" Of course—the mysterious black-coated figure I kept half-consciously noticing. He must have been planting the notes.

"I wouldn't put it past him—that's the kind of thing he'd do." Kim giggled. "He's into recycling."

What a fun-loving chap. So PLAYFAIR was after Kim, not me. Perhaps the falling icicle was meant for her too. The phone call had been for her roommate, after all, probably to entice Kim onto the balcony. Had my paranoia been misplaced?

"Well, I'm going now. Good luck." She didn't repeat the wish.

I went back to the dressing room so I wouldn't see the others' run-throughs and possibly get psyched out. Stuck into the mirror along with the telegrams, many from strangers, was a note from Josh expressing his sorrow over Dima's death. He offered his help to me and Matt, who'd evidently already talked to him. "I'm developing a source within PLAYFAIR," he wrote, "and I hope soon to pin down what their role is in all this." I reread the note, cheered by his adamant faith that I would triumph over the obstacles that fate kept throwing in my way.

Paula opened the door. "Last group's warm-up is starting. Let's go!"

I skated onto the arena floor a little after the other seven women, and was startled by the cheers. Kim looked around uneasily. As I glided backward in rapid crossovers toward the broadcasters' area, I heard Peggy Fleming say, "The charismatic English champion Lesley Grey lies 4th in this competition, but a strong performance tonight could give her the gold medal. Dick?"

"She has great athletic jumps, Peggy, plus her own lyrical, balletic style with line and extension, and it's this combination which makes her one who might leave the sport different and better, just because she was in it."

I 3-turned into a triple salchow and crashed to the ice—I'd leaned off-angle in the air. Serves me right, I thought ruefully; shouldn't bother about other people's opinions. I resisted the temptation to throw everything into the practice, thus possibly leaving my performance in the warm-up; instead, I coasted through the six minutes and returned downstairs. Since I was the very last to skate, I had more than half an hour's wait.

I filled the time by exercising to keep my muscles stretched out, then squirted honey into my mouth for energy. As I re-laced my boots to compensate for the harder ice, the right skate first as always, it occurred to me that when I next unlaced them I might be the Olympic champion.

I put on my mental videotapes; two perfect run-throughs of the program produced a semi-hypnotic state of concentration. Skating conservatively wouldn't be enough for top marks—I'd have to go all out and take all the risks. There could be no doubling out of the triple jumps, no holding back. Finally, I thought of all the years of competition stretching behind me, the lonely battle against myself in pursuit of excellence, my family's steadfast support, and the pile of gold that could release me from my debts. On top of it glistened the gold medal.

Paula called me while Kim's ovation echoed through the building. She was in the interview corner with Dick, the lights striking sparks from the rhinestone-trimmed yoke of her dress. Matt gave me the thumbs-up sign and whispered, "Go for it, champ!" Skating in tight circles near the barrier, I scanned Kim's second set of marks: 5.7s and 5.8s with two 5.9s.

"Putzi averaged 5.6," Paula hissed, "and Nina 5.7 with a few 5.8s. They've left room for you at the top. Go for broke, kid—you can do it!"

As my name was announced, I skated to the far end of the ice. I *can* do it, I thought, staring up at GREY, GBR in lights. Ten years of preparation, and it'll all be over in a few minutes. This is it, and no one can stop me—not the FBI or Kim or Zoe or Dima or anyone. There is no next time. I'm going to win.

When I heard the violins' opening theme of Saint-Saëns' Third Symphony, I closed my mind to everything but the music, my heartbeat and friend for the next four minutes. I was oblivious to the volleys of applause, but instinctively sensed the crowd's excitement as I leapt from a spread eagle high into a double axel, stretching immediately into another spread eagle. A mazurka jump, then a series of spins into a low Fratianne catchfoot sitspin with my free leg extended straight out to my pointed toe. I was the still center of the turning world. Then came a triple axel, a jump first performed in international competition only in 1978, that few women did yet. I felt the height, cold, and wind, then landed lightly, in perfect control.

The cheers drowned the beginning of the slow Andante section. I glided in a long spiral, a dancer's arabesque, around the perimeter, then down center ice as strings and woodwinds played exquisite arpeggios over the organ's meditation. It was considered unusual and a bit daring to hold one position so long, but both Paula and I believed that could be one of skating's most expressive aspects. The arena was hushed, and I reveled in the feeling that every pair of eyes was on me.

As the organ thundered the finale, I counterpointed it with a high open axel, then a crisp triple loop-triple flip combination, then a powerful triple lutz. Each jump, taken at full speed, was timed to emphasize a climax in the music, but the moves were not telegraphed; the preparation was always camouflaged in a graceful attitude. We had choreographed the program to show that I still had the stamina after almost four minutes for the very most difficult moves. I threw in a flying sitspin just to show any doubters from the short program that I could do it, then finished with falling leaf split jumps, Arabians, and an illusion spin in a brilliant whirl. Energy still surging through me, I felt that I could do the whole thing again.

I knelt panting on one knee, my arms upraised, and the air was filled with falling flowers. The audience leapt to its feet with cries of "Bravo!" then chants of "Six! Six!" Union Jacks waved frantically, dozens of them. The tumult cascaded down on me, louder than I'd ever imagined while practicing alone on chilly winter mornings in deserted rinks. Flashbulbs exploded like sheet lightning, and icy thunder resounded through the arena.

Minutes later, I stepped off the ice with a great armload of flowers. The scoreboard lit up: four 6.0s and five 5.9s for technical merit. I hugged Paula and the team leader, then Dick Button, Peggy Fleming, the BBC commentator, and everyone else within reach.

"Here are the marks for composition and style," cried Dick. "One, two, three, four, *five* 6.0s and all the rest 5.9s! And both of the Russian judge's marks were 6.0s! A total of nine perfect scores might be an Olympic record—I'll have to check. Terrific! You've won the gold medal! How do you feel right now?"

The dizzying whirlwind didn't subside till after the exhibition of last night's dance medalists, when I stood on the top step of the red-carpeted podium with the solid heaviness of the gold medal presented by IOC president Mutzenbecher around my neck. The arena fell silent for the measured strains of "God Save the Queen." The Union Jack slowly rose, with the Hammer and Sickle below it on one side and the Stars and Stripes on the other. Tears filled my eyes—for my country or myself?—till all I could see was a blur of red, blue, and white. When the three of us had waved our bouquets to the final ovation, I bent for the customary kiss to Kim on the left and a flinching Nina on the right.

After our skate-around, I was putting on my guards at the barrier when Nina darted up behind me and hissed, "You don't get away with this!"

"What did you say?"

"You kill Dima and you don't get away with it. I go to police and tell them everything!"

*I just can't wait to be normal again. But you know,
I suppose people will never really let me be normal
again, will they?*

—Anne Henning, speed skating, gold and bronze
medals at Sapporo, 1972

Questions, always bloody questions.

—Ingemar Stenmark, Alpine skiing, bronze medal at
Innsbruck, 1976; two gold medals at Lake Placid,
1980

Thursday, February 20, 10 P.M.

I sat down in the center—the gold medalist's place!—of the micro-
phone-laden dais in the arena's press room. Paula and an Olympic
official were next to me. Flanking us on one side were Kim and Zack
Higgins, and on the other, Nina, her coach, and a black-mustached interpreter. Reporters began taking seats, but a half-dozen still pointed
their tape recorders toward Elizabeth Cranford, who was giving them
an earful in the back of the room. As the crowd quieted, her shrill
voice could be heard: "The judges are the ones who should have doping tests!"

173

The officials recognized a Reuters correspondent, who asked, "Miss Grey, did you expect to win?"

Same old questions, I thought, as I tried to answer informatively but briefly. I remembered Josh's plea five minutes earlier: "Please tell me what to ask Aleksandrova. These Russians are always the same—when you ask them if they're happy with the results, they come out with some cliché like 'I have accomplished the task set by my coach.' And if you ask them anything more complicated, they talk for five minutes and then the interpreter translates: 'Yes.'"

Nina was now rattling volubly into the microphone. Finally the interpreter leaned forward and said, "She is pleased with the silver medal, and plans to go on competing till she wins another gold one."

A reporter from Japan's *Yomiuri Shimbun* said, "Miss Cranford, there has been some criticism of the judging of the compulsory figures. If you had been a place or two higher there, you might have won the gold tonight instead of the bronze. Any comment?"

Kim turned to her coach, who kept his poker face and remained silent. Everyone in the room knew that he and Mrs. Cranford had been the critics the reporter alluded to. She said hesitantly, "Okay, I'm not into judging, and I wouldn't want to accuse anyone at this point in time. But I can say that the harassment I got today from the FBI, and some others, might have affected the results."

"Was that in connection with the investigation into Dmitri Kuznetsov's sudden death?" asked *Newsday* avidly.

The Olympic official hastily cut in. "Any comment here on the progress of a police investigation is neither appropriate nor advisable. Will you please confine your questions to the women's figure skating competition?"

"Miss Grey, what were your feelings after you knew you'd won?" asked the London *Daily Telegraph*, an old friend.

"Relief!" I said bluntly.

"Not pride or patriotism?"

"Those came next."

"Miss Grey," the correspondent from the East German newspaper *Neues Deutschland* said, "you skated badly in the short program, and some observers think that you were overmarked there. What is your explanation, and do you feel that you really deserved to win the gold tonight, in view of your lack of technical content—only four triples, fewer than the other medalists?"

"On Tuesday, as tonight," I replied, trying to hide my annoyance behind an even tone, "I skated as well as it was possible for me to skate at the time. I believe I was marked fairly on both occasions, and I think I deserved to win."

"Oh, the judges are always right, then?" asked the correspondent sarcastically.

"I think they have a difficult job. As well as the jumps, they must look for interpretation, phrasing, changes of tempo, variety, use of time, use of space, and much more. They have to ignore the audience reaction and be dispassionate, unpatriotic, objective, the lot. No, I don't expect them to be infallible."

"Would you still say all that if you hadn't won the gold?" asked Josh with a twinkle in his eye.

"I hope so. That's not to say there's never been bad judgment or collusion."

"To go back to the original question," Paula added, "there is much more to Lesley's program than jumps, and her four different triples *are* the most difficult ones. There was no lack of content; rather the contrary. Neither of us sees any point in repeating triple toe loops ad infinitum." Elizabeth Cranford rose abruptly and stalked out the door, followed by several reporters in search of more colorful copy.

"What are your future plans, Miss Cranford?" asked *Die Welt*. "Will you compete in the Worlds next month?"

"We don't know yet," Zack said. "We're considering several different possibilities, including a movie offer."

"About your music: Miss Grey skated to Saint-Saëns, right?" asked the *Toronto Globe and Mail*. "And Miss Aleksandrova? Shostakovich, Prokofiev, and Mussorgsky. Thank you. Miss Cranford, you opened with Strauss's *Also Sprach Zarathustra*, then what?"

"No, it was *2001*, okay?" Kim replied. "Then *Flashdance* and. . . ." She looked blankly at Zack, who quickly filled in: "*Firebird*, by Stravinsky." Several journalists smothered snickers.

"Miss Cranford, will you miss competition?"

"No. Doing six figures for six hours a day, six days a week, for years and years is *boring*."

"Miss Grey," *Rude Pravo* asked, "since your victory was made possible partly by others' mistakes or inconsistencies, would you attribute it to luck?"

"No. Who was it who said, 'Luck is the residue of design'?"

"Your design or your coach's? In other words, is she responsible for your success?"

"Lesley always had three things no coach can give a skater," Paula said. "Superb balance, natural grace, and strong character. I helped her develop them to the fullest, but I just polished the diamond that was already there."

"Miss Grey," said *The Sunday Times*, "did you watch the others skate, and were you affected by their marks and the ovations they received?"

I went on answering questions to the constant obbligato of clicking shutters, trying not to squirm. The four glasses of water I'd drunk just after the award ceremony to expedite the doping test were taking their toll.

"Just one more question, please," the official said. "The competitors still have to go through doping control, which we postponed till after the press conference so you wouldn't have to wait so long."

A representative of the Polish news agency PAP stood up. "Miss Aleksandrova, give us your reaction to being the first woman singles skater from the Soviet Union to win an Olympic medal."

The interpreter translated the question, and Nina jabbered in staccato Russian. Her coach cut in with a long whispered comment. Then the interpreter said, "She feels that her victory brings honor to her government and its progressive athletic system. She is happy to have furthered the glory of socialist sport through cascades of complicated elements. Careful observers could see in her complex and meaningful program the basic elements of all Soviet art—"

Nina grabbed the microphone and shouted, "No! I say that *I* should win gold, but was cheated by English-speaking alliance of skaters and judges. And one of those somebodies also cheated Dmitri Pyotrovich —of his gold, and of his life!"

A gleeful buzz of exclamation and conjecture filled the room. "That's all, and thank you," said the official quickly, ignoring a forest of raised hands, and turned off the microphone. The two Russians hustled Nina from the dais and out the door.

Josh joined us as Paula was saying, "Well! Did she mean you?"

"Too right," I answered ruefully. "Can she make trouble?"

"No, they'll put her into seclusion," Josh said. "You saw how they shut her up immediately. They don't want an investigation."

"Well, she'll have to do the doping test or she'll be disqualified. Let's not hurry back to the Village—I don't want to bump into her or Kim in the loo."

After a final hug from Paula, who had to stay at the arena for the late-night practice of one of her male pupils, I strolled to the Village with Josh under a laser and fireworks display that lit up the night sky and reflected my mood. The American biathlon team increased the noise and confusion by firing their rifles into the air to celebrate the end of their competition. I tried to tell Josh about Matt's and my ideas on Dima's murder, but I was repeatedly interrupted by a stream of fans, autograph seekers, and newsmen with "just one question, Lesley." A small girl, open-mouthed, reached out shyly to touch me, as if to make sure I were real.

When the clamoring horde finally left us at the gate, Josh said, "Big news! Bruno Novak was caught red-handed earlier tonight, stringing wire at ankle level across one of the Nordic ski trails—the one the Russian relay team would use tomorrow."

"My God! Was he arrested?"

"He's being held for questioning at Security Headquarters. I'm going there to get more information as soon as I file my piece for the last edition. This is the break I need to get my PLAYFAIR source to talk, even if Bruno won't. Incidentally, I've learned that Pavel Marchevsky was the leak—the one who told a newsman that Dima was dead. I wonder why?"

"So do I. Work on that, will you?"

"Sure. It's good to do a bit of investigative journalism again, instead of pontificating all the time."

On arrival at the medical building, I was asked to wait in the crowded hall. In addition to the top six finishers, 10 others chosen at random were to give samples, and a technician had to observe each competitor in the act so she couldn't smuggle in a tiny vial or plastic bag of uncontaminated urine. Two hockey teams were also lined up outside the main bathroom, labeled "Doping Control Station." Outside the East German clinic, several lugers waited to have blood samples drawn from their earlobes for their own computerized lactic acid and glycogen comparisons.

After what seemed hours, a white-coated female technician checked my ID, entered the time on my green card, and ushered me into the small lavatory that adjoined the Russian clinic. Thankfully, I urinated into a cup, then poured the specimen into two bottles which the technician sealed and labeled with a code number. She rushed them out the hall door.

I tried the other doorknob. It was open! The small clinic was lit only by one gooseneck lamp. I tested the door to the hall, and it too was unlocked. Obviously, anyone in the building could enter from either door and find the room unsupervised. I opened the refrigerator; the bags of blood were gone.

The hall door banged open and the ceiling light snapped on.

"What are you doing here?" Nokitov, the Soviet team leader, glowered at me.

*The Olympic Movement appears as a ray of sunshine
through clouds of racial animosity, religious bigotry,
and political chicanery . . .*
—Avery Brundage

*The Olympics could be beautiful if they just let the
athletes get together and run it, instead of having us
all stand up on some podium so the world can count
how many medals each country won.*
—John Carlos, track, bronze medal at Mexico City,
  1968

"So what'd you tell Nokitov?" asked Matt through a mouthful of wholewheat pancakes. We were breakfasting at "Coffee And," a Truckee restaurant, for a change from the Village as well as to avoid possible eavesdroppers.

I bit into a hot biscuit and licked the honey dripping from it. "I just acted a bit thick, though it was hard to hide my fear. I told him that I was waiting for my doping test, and was looking in the fridge for something to drink."

"And he believed you?" asked Matt incredulously.

"I don't know. He did seem rather suspicious. I said I'd already drunk four bottles of mineral water and still couldn't—then I looked embarrassed and said, 'Um, er, you know.'"

"And then he let you leave?"

"I said, 'Do you know, I think I *can* do it now' and made a quick exit into the lavatory, taking a hockey player by surprise! I suppose I should've tried to get some information from Nokitov, but he scares me, the way he stares out from underneath his eyebrows like Brezhnev. Do you want some of these hash-browns? I'll never finish them."

"Sure, I'm carbo-loading. You've got to talk to the Russians some time, you know."

"I think the only one I might get anywhere with is Bogachev, Dima's coach. He seems more human than the others, and I think he was fond of Dima." I had somewhat mixed feelings, both disappointment and relief, that he didn't tell me it was too dangerous to interrogate the Russians. I still had chills, remembering the KGB's stormtrooper tactics with the doctor.

"Well, I haven't produced much in the way of hard information yet," Matt said. "Yesterday I talked to Bruno, Kim, Zack, Pavel, Hans-Peter, and Zoe. I tried to find out everyone's whereabouts on Opening Day, because I think we can safely conclude that Dima's accident that day was no accident, but the first murder attempt."

"Yes," I said thoughtfully. "I'm sure you're right. And it'll be so much easier to pin people down to that short a time span—say an hour before the parade. I don't know how we can find out who could or couldn't have sneaked into the Russian clinic over the last few weeks. And even if we rule out everyone on the list, we only know that it was probably the KGB, and we'll never pin anything on them."

"Or that our list wasn't long enough."

"Oh, blast."

"We can but try." He pulled an untidy sheaf of papers from his duffel coat's large patch pocket. "Here are my boy-detective-kit investigative records. I've even got a mini-tape recorder for taking down important clues and confessions." He grinned sheepishly as he pulled it out of his other pocket and showed it to me; it was smaller than a pack of cards, and the tape itself was no bigger than a matchbox.

I giggled. "You astonish me, Holmes."

"I generally only use it for dictating thesis notes and stuff, but it's really a marvelous device—Japanese technology is amazing. The internal microphone picks up the nearest voices in a crowded room, within eight feet or so, and filters out the background noise completely. Listen." He demonstrated it, playing back what we'd just said; no sounds from the busy restaurant were audible.

"Okay, back to work," he continued. "It seems to me that we have several possible motives, each pointing to a different group of people who might have wanted Dima dead. First, his nationality and the fact that he could win a gold medal for the Soviet team. PLAYFAIR might want to prevent that. Second, his possible defection. That points to the KGB. Third, his love life, which brings in the three other women. Once we decide who has a viable motive, then we have to consider opportunity and means."

"I'm the obvious suspect in the third category," I said, "which does seem to have occurred to the FBI. And there's a fourth category you mentioned yesterday: professional rivalry, which probably makes *you* one of the FBI's main suspects, along with Pavel, Hans-Peter, and the coaches. But I've read that the police consider opportunity first and motive last, so maybe we should take that approach. Then, there are all those other strange events, which don't seem to form a pattern. Vinnie's death—was it an accident or murder? And was it connected to Dima's? The icicle someone tried to drop on my head—was that meant for me or Kim? The notes and the snake—Zack passed them on to me, but who gave them to Kim?"

"That's easy, someone in PLAYFAIR who thought Red-loving should be discouraged."

"So that shows that they did have a definite grudge against Dima in particular. And was it a PLAYFAIR person or someone else who ransacked my room? I saw Kim outside just before. Maybe it was random vandalism, but I think some codeine tablets were taken. Strong ones, but the dose in the borscht wasn't lethal. Was Fyodor poisoned so Dima would be unguarded? Or was it meant for Dima himself, to disqualify him on doping? Or maybe the whole thing was just a coincidence."

"We'd better go back to the concrete evidence." He shuffled his papers. "Now then: Bruno Novak, the anti-Communist patriot. In spite of what Josh found out last night about his sabotage, I don't really think it was Bruno who killed Dima—I think he's all bluster."

"That wire gimmick could've hurt someone seriously."

"Not a skier on flat ground who'd just fall on the snow—he probably wouldn't be going fast enough. A skater, yes. That stunt was pretty amateurish. Anyway, the whole team including Bruno was at hockey practice till right before the Opening Ceremony—they didn't even have time for lunch. I've definitely confirmed that he was there the entire time. And he was the American flagbearer, so he couldn't have skipped the parade. But he did come right out and admit that he'd been in the hospital clinic and looked in the refrigerator."

"Really?"

"He said he was looking for evidence that the Russians were illegally doping, but couldn't read the medicine labels," Matt said. "And it was only yesterday, when the blood was gone."

"*If* he—or anyone—killed Dima in revenge for Vinnie's death, then they couldn't have had anything to do with Dima's fall because Vinnie died three days after that. But Bruno might have done it out of general Red-hating. I don't think we should tick him off the list yet. Well. Who else?"

"Next suspect: Dim, I mean Kim, Cranford. She was suspiciously unwilling to answer my questions, but she's pretty well-alibied. I talked to her roommate Elinor Rhodes too, after I saw her."

"Kim's staying outside the Village now."

"Yeah, and I had a helluva time finding out where. She and her mother and boyfriend are in a condo at King's Beach, top secret. But she didn't move in there till after the school figures on Monday, when she decided the Village was too noisy and distracting. She couldn't concentrate on the self-hypnosis tapes that Higgins made for her, poor thing. And she didn't want to risk any more snakes or icicles. Kim and Elinor had lunch together in the cafeteria on Opening Day, then went up to change into the team uniform, and Kim rehearsed her Athletes' Oath a few times. Then they lined up and marched in—they were together the whole time."

That gave me an idea. "I say, would it be any use to talk to the guard at the gate? Anyone going out to the practice rink from the Village would have to pass through it, and the rink is within sight of the gate."

"I doubt it," he objected, "especially after ten days. I bet lots of people were going in and out that morning, to and from practice or to the facilities in the Reception building: the bank, interpreters' bureau, overseas telephones, and so on."

"But from noon on most athletes, anyway, would be coming in to get ready for the ceremonies. I'll ask Dima's roommate what time he went to practice, and I'll have a go at the guard. I suppose I'd better get a notebook too." He gave me a sheet of paper and I jotted it down. "I'll see if the guard can pin down what time Dima went out to the rink, anyway. More coffee?"

"Sure. Now, Zack Higgins. He and Mrs. Cranford ate lunch at Le Petit Pier in Tahoe Vista, then drove to Squaw and didn't come in till the middle of the ceremony, because they had to park so far away."

"That sounds fishy. Anyway, it's impossible to prove the timing if they're in league. They'd alibi each other."

"I guess we could inquire at the restaurant; they probably had a reservation. But I'm afraid everyone's memory is going to be fuzzy, what with the mass confusion of the last week. And I frankly don't think anyone in the Cranford entourage had a strong enough motive. Higgins tried to laugh off the anonymous notes, by the way—said he thought he might as well get the maximum amount of mileage from them."

"You don't think he or Kim's mother might kill to protect their baby from evil influences?" I said jokingly. "But seriously, how about the boyfriend? He had a better motive: jealousy."

"He didn't even arrive here till yesterday. He's a law student from Chicago. Anyway, neither he nor Mrs. Cranford are supposed to have heard about Kim's little escapade with Dima, and she's terrified they'll find out."

"Which might be a rather strong motive for Kim to put Dima out of the way."

"Do you really think she could have planned and executed a murder?" he objected. "She's far too dumb."

"Nobody could truly be that stupid. I think she's putting it on."

"They all denied ever being inside the hospital," he continued, "except Kim for doping and femininity testing, and she says she used the main bathroom for doping control both times. She didn't seem to know where the Russian clinic is. As for what she was doing *this* Wednesday, the day Dima was killed, how's this for a humdinger of an alibi? She volunteered the information that she was visiting the pediatric ward of the hospital here in Truckee, and autographing casts on kids with broken legs! This gal is all heart. Of course, a photographer and reporter just happened to be there with her."

"Excuse me—" We looked up. A fat woman in a parka was standing by our table. "Aren't you both skaters? I think I've seen you on TV. I can't remember your names, but could you autograph this menu?"

183

"*Nein,*" Matt said in a gutteral German accent. "We are lugers from Deutsche Demokratische Republik. We are not allowed to give autographs to capitalists."

"Well, pardon me." She sniffed and walked away.

I stifled a giggle. "I used not to care for your sense of humor, but it seems to be growing on me. Well, next suspect?"

"Zoe McDonnell. She feels pretty bad about your walking in on her and Dima, by the way."

"I should think so, too!" I said with venom. "Some 'sister' she turned out to be."

"She begged me, with tears in her eyes, to apologize to you. She says she can't face you."

"She sent me the biggest floral arrangement I've ever seen—it arrived this morning. I suppose she wanted to make amends. The ironic thing is, all my flowers from last night froze, because I put them out on the balcony to keep them fresh. Each petal was encased in ice this morning. So hers are the only ones I'd have now, except that I told the messenger to take them to a hospital."

"That sounds pretty unforgiving," he warned. "Don't let Oglethorpe hear you talking that way. From the FBI viewpoint, your primary motive for killing Dima would be his unfaithfulness with Zoe."

I ignored this. "How's her alibi for Opening Day?"

"Airtight. She gave a big brunch for USOC officials, and then they all walked over to the Opening Ceremony together. She was in the VIP box with them the whole time. Anyhow, I just remembered that she didn't meet Kuznetsov till Saturday night. And there hadn't been time for her to be scorned yet." He smiled wryly. "I'm not seeing the forest for the trees."

"Was she going to organize his defection?"

"She says they talked about it on Tuesday, but nothing was arranged yet. He was afraid the team officials were going to yank him from the competition any moment on some flimsy excuse after he placed 3rd in the figures, so as to give Pavel a better chance. And he was absolutely determined to win the gold medal, because he thought he'd have more hope of being accepted here. Zoe told me that wouldn't have affected things one way or the other. The US grants asylum almost automatically to any refugee from a Communist country, though the INS talks a lot about defectors having to prove persecution."

"It's only automatic if it's not too awkward for them, and this defection would have been a bit sticky. What about Pavel's whereabouts?"

"Let's see." He shuffled through his papers. "He and Hans-Peter both have the same story as Kim—lunch, change, line up for the ceremonies. Their roommates back them up."

"Hmm. Suspicious? Everyone with the same alibi."

"What did you do that day?"

I laughed. "Lunch, change, line up. You too? I've just thought, though," I said, excited. "Naturally, Pavel would know the Russian team clinic, have free access to it, *and* be able to read the labels on the bags!"

"And you could say he has one of the best motives. With Dima gone, he's king of Russian skating."

"Oh, my God, I forgot to tell you." I recounted Pavel's boast at the disco that Dima was meant to lose the competition. "Pavel would have known that Dima could still win from 3rd in the figures, and maybe he thought he was going back on the supposed deal—which I don't believe for a moment that he really intended to carry out. There's your motive! And as for means of doing the murder, reading the labels was crucial. They were written completely in Russian; the murderer would have to be able to pick the right ones."

"Can you read it yourself?" he asked.

"I only know some of the Cyrillic letters—there are thirty-two! About all I can read is 'Dmitri Kuznetsov' and the first three letters of some Moscow Metro stops—that's how you identify them as a tourist."

"Don't tell Oglethorpe that. All you *would* have to read is 'Dmitri Kuznetsov' and 'A, B, and O.'"

"Oh God, that's true. Whoops!" I gulped.

"Would Pavel have gone in for blood doping himself?"

"I doubt it, he's not even twenty years old yet. By the way, Josh said he's the one who leaked the news that Dima was dead, when the officials were just going to pretend they'd sent him home."

"I don't know if that fits or not," Matt said, "but all the indications seem to be that the Russians did it, either Pavel or the KGB. Means, opportunity, and motive. Jolly good show! Well done, Holmes."

"You know my methods, Watson. Well, I'll have a go at the other Russians today, I suppose."

"Okay, kid. Try to get hold of Nina; I couldn't even find out where they've stashed her. We'll have to get our asses in gear—only three more days. We'd better quit drinking coffee now, or I'll flunk the doping test tonight."

"On the grounds of caffeine?"

He groaned. "That's worse than one of my puns. I can't have you taking over my quicksilver repartee. Okay if we split the tab?"

"Of course, what else?"

A Dutch speed skater at the TART stop told us the bus had just gone, and the next one wasn't due for 45 minutes. We browsed through a few boutiques and the Truckee River Book and Tea Company, then ambled around the little town. When we came to a snow-covered field, Matt let me walk ahead, then fired a snowball squarely into the middle of my back.

"Why, you rotter! I'll do you for that!" I grabbed some snow and began pelting him. We circled and dodged through the meadow, till Matt tripped and I threw myself on top of him and washed his face with snow.

"Uncle!" he cried. "Quit it, it's all going down my neck!"

We lay panting, laughing at each other. Suddenly Matt's grin faded and he stared intently at me. A strong pulse was beating in the hollow of his throat. "You have the most extraordinary eyes, Lesley. I think . . . never mind."

"What?"

"I'd rather not say. Get up, will you?"

As I did, puzzled, I saw a man in a tan overcoat and hat standing across the street. He turned and began to study a pine tree, not very convincingly.

"Matt, look! I think that man is watching us."

"Yes, I just noticed him too. Come to think of it, I believe he's been following us all morning."

"Do you think he's KGB?" I asked fearfully.

"Nope, he must be a G-man."

"FBI? But why?"

"I guess it would be strange if they weren't 'surveilling' us, to use their awful jargon. Their top two suspects leave the Valley, put their heads together over suspicious documents, then show evidence of intimacy. Very incriminating. They've probably tapped our phones too, so be careful."

"What do you mean? I've nothing to hide."

"Just don't call Oglethorpe an incompetent oaf on the telephone, or give away any of our hard-won information, that's all. As bad as the Soviet Union, isn't it? Here comes the bus."

We dashed across the street. The man in the overcoat joined the queue after us. As Matt was about to board, he stepped aside and said, "After you, sir." The agent made no response, and walked back to the last seat.

We watched the Christmas-card scenery stream past the window in companionable silence. Then Matt asked, "Have you seen Josh's column today?"

"No, I haven't had a chance yet."

He pulled a folded newspaper section out of his pocket, disentangling it from his notes, and handed it to me. The front page read: FBI TO PROBE MYSTERY DEATH; RUSS SKATER'S ACCUSATION OF CHEATING, MURDER. I read the story, which contained very little real information and didn't mention me by name, then turned to the sports page.

Grace under Pressure
By Josh McDonnell

Squaw Valley, CA, Feb. 20——Fortunately, the days are past when commentators were forced to say "You had to be there" about a magnificent skating exhibition. Thanks to worldwide TV coverage and videotaping of international competitions, millions of people now can watch worldclass skaters. That one-in-a-thousand performance isn't restricted to a handful of live spectators, as were those of the great artists of the recent past like Tenley Albright, Hayes Jenkins, and Laurence Owen—the latter's career cut short before many had seen her by the tragic 1961 Brussels plane crash.

Few compared to today's audiences watched Belousova and Protopopov, Peggy Fleming, and Janet Lynn at their competitive peaks. Athletic feats like the first triple jump (Dick Button's 1952 triple loop) and the first triple lutz (performed by Don Jackson in 1962) passed largely unseen in television's infancy. Not till 1976 did the Winter Olympics attract a huge prime time TV audience; thus the grace, élan, and athletic virtuosity of that era's champions (Curry, Cranston, Cousins, Babilonia and Gardner, Pakhomova and Gorschkov, Rodnina and Zaitsev) won deserved acclaim.

So if there's anyone out there who missed Lesley Grey's triumphal claiming of the Olympic gold medal last night, you'll have a chance to see it in the future. It will be rebroadcast as long as people want to witness an artist's transcending of technique to forge a thing of rapturous beauty from her own creativity and musicality, and from the relentless pressure of world competition, under the scorching magnifying lens of the media.

Grey has at last risen to the potential some of us always knew was there, and has leaped across the chasm from good to great skater. And she has demonstrated Hemingway's definition of courage: grace under pressure.

She gave the lie to skeptics who said she had peaked at the European Championships, where she took the silver. Coming back from a recent personal loss and an uninspired short program which left her lying 4th, she showed what she is made of. Only true champions can do that sort of thing; her unassuming manner masks her iron discipline and tenacity.

In a sense, however, you did have to be there. An upset in figure skating is rare, and creates an electric atmosphere. As well as television does its job in presenting to the millions a skater's every move from its best angle, it's only a pale shadow of the compelling experience of watching a great skater in person, preferably from the level of the ice.

Somehow, TV can't convey the speed, the shimmer and flash, the ear-filling music, the soaring height of the jumps. Your emotions aren't affected when you watch from your living room.

As in drama, music, and dance, it's the difference between a live and a canned performance: an artist in the process of creating something in your presence. Last night, the audience was almost too stunned to applaud. It was an experience no one who was there will ever forget.

Look elsewhere on this page for a list of Grey's jumps and spins, her costume and music, and how many 6.0s she received. They seem as inappropriate to this observer as an account of the choreographic steps in *Swan Lake* or the names on the paint tubes Monet used to paint his water lilies. For, make no mistake, what happened last night in Blyth Arena was the creation of a masterpiece.

Those who are the poorer for never having seen Curry or Lynn or Torvill and Dean will be able to say they have seen Lesley Grey.

Tomorrow: Downhill racers

"Oh, my God," I said, my face hot. "That's a bit much."

"It's well-deserved," said Matt. "I saw you skate, and it was a historic performance. Did you notice me jumping up and down and yelling? I'm still hoarse."

"Thanks very much, but I'm not sure that skating *is* art, even at its best. It's really sport, and it's the competitive aspect that makes it exciting. Don't you think exhibition skating is comparatively dull? Artistic elements are always there, certainly, but it's the gamble whether the risky athletic feats will work that gives it its spark."

"But you're leaving out the emotional communication that a great artist has with the audience," he argued. "I do see what you mean: skating has internal contradictions that make it never completely one thing or the other. But don't you think the Protopopovs and the others he mentioned transcended the gap? And so have you."

"If so, that goes for you, too. I suppose I could really debate either point of view. I'm just a bit uneasy about being compared with *Swan Lake* and Monet's water lilies."

"Where's your gold medal, by the way? I haven't seen one close up," he said wistfully.

"They took it away after the press conference to have it engraved—I was going to sleep with it under my pillow. Did you know it's not really gold at all? It's called silvergilt."

"What's it look like?"

"It has an engraving of the two Olympic flames. And it's heavier than you'd think."

I was overwhelmingly conscious of his physical presence, his arm and shoulder only centimeters away from mine. Each time the bus rounded a curve, we swayed together. I felt a growing warmth; no, a definite attraction to him that I tried to deny. How could I feel this way, when only two days ago I was crying my eyes out over Dima? The fact that he betrayed me doesn't mean that I should let myself fall for the next man who comes along. But this one obviously respects women and treats me as an equal, I argued with myself, not as someone to be seduced and then dominated. He's not afraid to be vulnerable and expose his emotions. And there's a mental companionship I never felt with Dima. He only wanted my adoration; I think Matt would want my friendship as much as my love. I believe he does fancy me. Back in the meadow, he was about to speak, but wouldn't let himself. He's considerate enough not to pressure me—he sees that I need emotional breathing space, and time to come to terms with myself. He probably won't say anything unless I encourage him, and I'm going to try not to, not yet. I just hope I can keep from falling into bed with him.

The bus stopped at Christy Inn in Squaw Valley. We got off and walked toward the Village, trailed at a distance by the agent. Near Blyth Arena, I stopped suddenly.

"Look at that!" I said, disgusted.

"What?"

I indicated the sketch artist, who was now offering "Your portrait, Vinnie Luciano's, or Dima Kuznetsov's" for $4. Saccharine pastel renditions of Dima's face, clothes-pinned to a rope, flapped in the breeze.

"Notice the halo?" Matt said with a grimace. "He's raised his prices, too."

As we showed our IDs to the Pinkerton guard at the glass gatehouse, I asked him, "Were you on duty a week ago Wednesday, just before the Opening Ceremony?"

"No, ma'am." He consulted a roster. "That was Flanagan. He got off an hour ago."

"When could I speak to him?"

"Let's see . . . he's on again here tomorrow, from three P.M. till eleven."

"Where is he now, do you know?"

The guard flipped through the pages. "He's on duty at the Nordic ski area, over at Big Chief."

"I'll wait till tomorrow, then. Thanks."

"Have a nice day, folks."

At the door to Matt's dorm, he said, "I've got practice now in the outdoor rink. What's on your agenda?"

"Questioning Bogachev and Pavel, I suppose. And Nina, if possible."

"Be careful. Try to talk to them in public."

"If you don't hear from me by tonight, send out the FBI."

"Oglethorpe to the rescue! That turkey couldn't find his ass with both hands. Are you coming to the men's final tonight?"

"I wouldn't miss it for anything. Do you think you can win from 3rd place? The others are pretty consistent, unfortunately."

"It'll be a cliff-hanger. It is in my favor that Kim lost. The judges never like to award gold book-ends to the US, though they don't seem to mind when it's the USSR. Of course, I'm glad you beat her for other reasons: (A) she sucks, and (B) you're dynamite! Well, take care."

As I walked into my room, the phone rang. It was Aunt Mavis and Uncle Harry calling from the UK to congratulate me. Everyone who worked at their ice rink had come to their tiny semi-detached house at 4 A.M. to watch the Olympic final, huddled in blankets and drinking cocoa. Taunton was already planning a "Lesley Grey Day" on my return, with a motorcade and public ceremonies.

Touched and warmed by their love, I had to steer my mind back to

190

the task at hand. I checked the practice schedule and found that one of Bogachev's pupils, the third-ranked Russian man, was in the group currently practicing at Blyth.

Kolya Skachko was watching from the stands, and I remembered I'd wanted to check what time Dima had left for practice on Opening Day.

"It was noon, I remember we are leaving our room together, and I am going to lunch. Dima did not, he thought the food here tastes terrible."

"Oh, that reminds me," I said. "Did you eat dinner with Dima and Fyodor on Tuesday? They called it 'Russian Night' and served borscht and stroganoff, didn't they?"

"*Da.* It was not bad, but Dima did not like that any better. He took one taste of the borscht and said it was bitter, not like his mother's. He made a face. Fyodor Viktorovich finished it for him, then went back for more. Of course, Fyodor will eat anything, I think he has no tasting buds left in his mouth after all he is smoking and drinking."

"Do you remember who else was sitting at your table?"

He wrinkled his forehead in concentration. "It was mostly skaters, but many were coming and going all the time. It was a long table, for fourteen. I think Pavel and Nina were there for a while with me and Katya, and Nokitov was keeping his eye on us all as usual. I'm remembering them talking about Russian food and longing for the real thing. Some others were there part of the time: I think some hockey players, Hans-Peter and the German pair, Jean-Marc, Hiroshi. Maybe more."

"Thanks, you've been a help. I must talk to Dima's coach now."

I found Bogachev more forthcoming than I'd expected, but I couldn't decide whether to believe him. In fractured English with tears in his eyes, he assured me that he'd loved Dima like a son, and had vetoed the plan to pull him from the competition or make them throw the race. He had wanted to send him immediately to hospital when he collapsed, but had been overruled by Nokitov and the others.

"The FBI think it was a KGB operation," I lied.

"Those shits!"

"Which?"

"Both of them, all policemen in big boots. Bah, all the same all over the world. I don't think it was KGB, though. Fyodor Viktorovich in big trouble with—how you say?—the brass, for not take better care of Dmitri Pyotrovich."

"Where is Fyodor now? I'd like to talk to him," I said, emboldened by my success with the coach.

"Sent home. So is Dr. Sologubova—and the judge who gave you two 6.0s."

"Is Nina Aleksandrova still here?"

"Yes, they want her to skate exhibition on Sunday. But she is—what?—incommunicated. They won't let her talk to nobody."

"Do you think Pavel's coach would speak with me?"

"Maybe tomorrow, I fix up for you. He's too busy today. Why you ask so much questions?"

"I want to find out what happened to Dima."

"Don't meddle. Very dangerous for you. You can't bring him back, and you must be careful for yourself," he said ominously. "You are *mezh dvukh ognei.*"

"What does that mean?"

"Between two fires."

*. . . nobody ever remembers who finished second in
an Olympic race.*
—Rex Cawley, track, gold medal at Tokyo, 1964

*I'm happiest when I skate for myself. But this year I
feel I had to skate for the press. To hell with you guys.*
—Beth Heiden, speed skating, bronze medal at
  Lake Placid, 1980

Friday, February 21, 9:10 P.M.

The last six men to skate in the Olympic final took to the ice to
warm up with a ruthless assurance that erased the memory of all previous competitors. The audience vented the rising excitement in na-
tionalistic yelling and frantic flag and sign-waving.

The Toronto Curling, Skating, and Cricket Club had come en
masse to support Canada's champion with placards and organized
cheers, and they sounded off every two minutes. On the ice, crimson-
clad Pavel Marchevsky slashed backward in rapid strokes, then completed his triple lutz just short of the barrier as the spectators cringed.
Hans-Peter, in electric blue, landed a triple combination in a spray of

ice. Matt threw himself into his inimitable death drop. For an instant his open axel hung in the air, parallel to the ice five feet below it, before he dropped into a sitspin. I wondered why I'd never noticed his extraordinary style or looks before the last few days. He was strikingly handsome, like an autumn leaf in the brown velvet costume with his auburn hair and beard.

Wholeheartedly, I wanted him to win. I marvelled that I could ever have found his skating effete. His natural grace only accentuated his strength and power. And there was no doubt that height was an asset to the line of any skater, man or woman. Matt's ideas on choreography and style were like mine: neither of us crammed our programs full of tricks and triple jumps, but considered the performance as a whole. The linking steps, spins, and holding of positions were equally important. Each musical line ought to be fluidly fulfilled, rather than abruptly punctuated. Nor did either of us believe in cutting and pasting four or five unrelated musical pieces, but used excerpts from one composition, further unifying the program. The skating thus became tangible and visible music.

He could just win tonight, going into the final in 3rd place, if the other placements fell the right way. I calculated in the margin of my program. If Matt won the long with Hans-Peter 2nd and Pavel 3rd, Matt would win the gold. But if Pavel beat Hans-Peter tonight even though Matt came 1st, the Russian would win—assuming no dark horses upset the three leaders. I wished ardently for Hans-Peter to be a tiny bit better than usual, and for Pavel to be much worse.

"Please clear the ice." I squeezed Matt's hand as he passed me on his way back downstairs. "Representing the German Democratic Republic, Hans-Peter Koenig."

Skating to a motley medley of Broadway show tunes, Hans-Peter seemed to perform precisely as instructed by his coach; no hint of his affable personality broke through his stiff and uninspired routine. Like far too many skaters, he didn't seem to understand that the body was the true instrument, the skates only a tool. As I watched his hunchbacked sitspins and powerful but wobbly jumps, I wondered how such a nice chap could be such a robot when on skates. His marks ranged from 5.4 to 5.8—probably not high enough for 2nd place.

An elegant Canadian and a fiery Japanese followed, each marked 5.3 to 5.7. When Hiroshi collected flowers from his fans, he didn't see a solemn little Japanese-American girl, her hair in two ponytails, shyly holding a single carnation toward him at the barrier. She'd tried to offer her flower to an earlier Japanese competitor, but he had also overlooked her. The nearby spectators screamed "Hiroshi!" "Over here!", finally attracting his attention to the small girl, and he gave her a kiss, to everyone's satisfaction.

Now Matt was next to me but a million miles away, as he shook out his arms and legs and did a few deep knee bends while his coach whispered last-minute advice. When he skated out, the introduction was drowned in a cacophony of screams and air horns usually heard only at hockey matches. Matt stood poised at the center of the ice as *Appalachian Spring* began.

I dug my nails into my palms and held my breath for the opening jump, his quadruple toe loop. It was flawless—he was really on form tonight! An explosion of applause, more for a high delay axel and a triple lutz, then such a spellbound hush that the only sounds were the wistful melody "The Gift to be Simple" and the whisper of his skates as he leapt into a flying camel, a spin in arabesque position. His back arched, one arm extended to lengthen the line and the other upraised at a right angle, he seemed to revolve around the central point of his upstretched hand. He showed his virtuosity by following it with another in the opposite direction. With every movement, he conveyed emotion like an actor.

A rousing finale with a tuck axel, high speed triple jump combinations, and a split lutz. A spread eagle into three Russian splits and then the final death drop. Cheers, flowers, lengthy applause, and high-pitched screams of "USA! USA!" Polaroids thrust into his face, sticking out their tongues. Several 6.0s. It seemed that Matt would decisively win the long program, but would it be enough?

A lackluster Austrian was quickly dispatched with 5.2s and 5.3s, in spite of his supporters' yells of "Sechs!" Now it all rested on Pavel and the judges, five of them from the Soviet bloc. Oh, please let them split between the Russian and the East German! Pavel put on a flashy show to *Sabre Dance:* a changefoot sitspin with innumerable rapid changes, six splits in a row, eight triple jumps, knee slides, and a sideways Bobrinski. I reluctantly had to admire his talent, though his performance seemed slick and superficial, more acrobatic than athletic. He received 5.8s and 5.9s and beat Hans-Peter. Though he'd lost the battle to Matt, he'd won the war.

I ran to the dressing room and scrambled into my costume; I'd forgotten that the women medalists were to give an exhibition. While belatedly changing, I missed my chance to speak to Nina.

My heart was sore for Matt as I swooped and glided to a Rachmaninoff piano concerto. But he showed no regret or animosity when he bent his head, smiling, for the silver medal, and shook hands with his rivals as the others received tepid applause from the disappointed audience. The three stood at attention while the red flag rose to the haunting strains of "Gimn Sovietskogo Soyuza." (Dima'd told me it was never sung now, because the lyrics praised Stalin.)

I squeezed into the back of the press room just as Josh stood to ask the first question: "Matt, I've been talking with members of the audience who don't understand why you didn't win the gold tonight. Both your long and short program were stunning, you won them by wide margins, yet you still placed 2nd over-all. Why?"

"Only judges and skaters really understand the marking system, unfortunately," Matt replied ruefully. "It's a lot of mumbo-jumbo to the public."

"If injustice is to be done, it ought to be seen to be done?" Josh asked with a grin.

"No comment. No, just kidding. My 4th in the figures wasn't quite high enough because Pavel was more consistent than I over both the compulsories and the freeskating. He placed 1st, 2nd, and 2nd."

"Is the marking system fair?" asked *Corriere della Sera.* This question seemed to be asked at every press conference.

"I think so," Matt said. "Any judging system without absolutes of time or distance has to be arbitrary and fallible. No one would argue with that, so I hope it doesn't sound like sour grapes. I think the best man won tonight, and usually does, the one who wants it the most. . . . Sometimes in sports," he went on thoughtfully, "desire seems to be the overwhelming factor, though talent and hard work have to be there too; I'm thinking of Franz Klammer at Innsbruck and the US hockey team at Lake Placid."

"Didn't you want to win?"

"Yes, of course, but maybe not quite as much as he did."

"What effect did the absence of Dmitri Kuznetsov have on the final placings?" asked *Newsday.*

"Impossible to say, except that it would've been a real horse race because of his great freeskating. I'm sad that we'll never compete again."

"Why wasn't your 4th place in the compulsory figures moved up to 3rd after Dima's withdrawal?" *Paris Match* asked.

"I don't know."

"That's not allowed," put in the official. "It's clearly stated in the rulebook."

"If you *had* been moved into 3rd, you would have won," the reporter persisted. "The multiplying factor of thirty percent of your score would have been three instead of four, which would have given you the winning margin over Marchevsky."

"Well . . . yes," Matt said, looking uneasy at the journalist's public presentation of a viable motive for murder. I glanced around the room to see if any of the reporters had grasped the point, and spotted the back of a pudgy head, unmistakably Oglethorpe's.

"Or Dima could have won, with 1sts in the short and the long," the reporter said.

"Yes, it's like the decathlon in a way. You can lose some of the events and still win the whole thing as long as someone else doesn't place consistently high. Back in 1978, for instance, Charlie Tickner placed 3rd, 3rd, and 2nd, and still won the world championship."

Skating away from the dangerous topic of Dima's death, *Sovietski Sport* asked Hans-Peter technical questions about his training, and *The Guardian* asked Pavel about his jumps. Though both spoke adequate English, they preferred to answer journalists' queries through interpreters, and long conferences usually produced one-word answers. Each said he didn't intend to retire from competition for many years, and there were a few stifled groans.

When the reporter from *The Guardian* asked Pavel his feelings about his victory, his coach Kisov replied for him. Neither seemed to understand the laughter, or the reporter's comment that it was Pavel's feelings she wanted to know, not Kisov's.

"Mr. Galbraith, will you compete in the world championships next month at Geneva?" asked *der Spiegel.*

"Sure, I'd like one more crack at these two. Then I'm definitely retiring and going back to my long-neglected studies."

"Thank you, members of the press," said the moderator. "Let's allow these gentlemen to get on with their medical tests."

A persistent local-TV newsman pounced on Matt as he was leaving the arena, and thrust a mike in his face as the cameraman turned on his lights and zoomed in for a close-up. "Matt, tell our live audience how you feel about losing."

"Fucking awful," snapped Matt, and walked out the door as the frustrated newsman screamed, "Cut!"

Matt saw me outside and took my arm. "I've always wanted to do that, and tonight I was just fed up enough with their hounding to do it."

"Yes, they're bloody ghouls sometimes," I sympathized. "I don't blame you."

He had to write autographs all the way back to the Village. At the gate, he was attacked by an impetuous middle-aged woman who told him he was a champion in her book, and smeared his face with lipstick. After he'd signed the back of the guard's duty roster—"It's for my sister, Matt, if you don't mind"—and passed through the gate, we were finally able to walk undisturbed. I noticed that his normal cocky swagger was subdued. I took his hand.

"It's jolly unfair, Matt. I got 3rd, 5th, and 1st, and finished 1st. You got 4th, 1st, and 1st, and finished 2nd. You should have won a gold medal, not me."

"Life's unfair, as many people have noticed. But you did deserve to win, even if you were a bit lucky that the others weren't terribly consistent throughout. Your free program will go down in skating history. What really did *me* in was probably my diatribe against the IOC at Zoe's party."

"Yes, I don't suppose that went down too well. I thought so at the time."

"The brass were there, including the ISU president, and I'm sure it got around. I imagine those judges thought a 4th in the compulsories would put me in my place. And this contest was won and lost in the figures, as they so often are. But you wanted the gold more than me— you were hungrier for it. I was ambivalent, you know. The Olympic gods are jealous; they won't give the gold to unbelievers."

"Yes, I did want it badly, not just for financial reasons. I suppose, in a way I felt that it was a . . . a tangible symbol of self-respect."

"Now that the chance is gone, I'm surprised how much I did want it. I really do feel fucking awful." I squeezed his hand, longing to comfort him somehow. "Always the bridesmaid, that's me, first to Kuznetsov and now to Marchevsky. But my life isn't going to change because of losing. I'll go on doing the same things I would've done if I'd won. It would have made a bigger difference to you to get only the silver."

We walked on in silence to the medical building and paused at the door. "*Only* the silver," he mused. "That's what they always say, isn't it? I used to think that was absurd, that second best in the world was pretty damned good. Now I know how bittersweet it is."

198

"So near and yet so far?"

"Yeah. Well, I'm off to pee if I can," he said, a little more cheerfully. "I think it's going to take about ten Perriers. I'll see if I can manage to sneak into the Russian clinic and get caught doing something incriminating."

"When'll I see you? I'm going to have a long lie-in tomorrow morning."

"Exhibition practice is—what? One o'clock. We'll talk then. So long."

He turned to go, but I grasped his arm and looked up into his downcast face. It was paler than usual, and the lipstick smears showed up lividly. "Remember what you said to me? I hope you'll consider me a friend—I do care. And, by the way, *I* think you're pure gold."

He grabbed my shoulders and kissed me suddenly on the mouth. "Bless you." He disappeared through the door.

I walked slowly back toward St. Moritz, still tingling from his brief but violent kiss. Too late, I saw a shadow detach itself from the bushes and follow.

*[International sport] is bound up with hatred,
jealousy, boastfulness, disregard for all rules and
sadistic pleasure in witnessing violence—in other
words, it is war minus the shooting.*
—George Orwell

*They shouldn't call this the Olympic Games. It's
not a game out there.*
—Bill Toomey, decathlon, gold medal at Mexico
    City, 1968

I didn't get my long lie-in. At 8:00 the phone rang, waking me from a confused dream of giant snails sliding across an ice rink while Dima did quadruple toe loops over them.

"This is Duane Oglethorpe, FBI. We'd like to talk to you this morning. Would you please be at Security Headquarters at ten thirty?" It was definitely an order, not a request. After that, I'd been unable to get back to sleep, my mind buzzing with uneasy speculation. At least I knew a solicitor's name, if worse came to worst.

I picked up the newspaper at breakfast and turned automatically to the sports page: 'Unofficial' Team Scores Led by Russ, E. Germany. The story on Pavel's victory was headlined THREE OF FOUR SKATING TITLES CHANGE HANDS. I turned back to the front page and did a double take.

TALES OF NOVAK'S SECRET SABOTAGE
Hockey Captain on Whitman Payroll
By Josh McDonnell

Squaw Valley, CA, Feb. 21——Captain of the US hockey team Bruno Novak may face multiple criminal charges which include computer vandalism and assault. The athlete, held Friday at Olympic Security Headquarters, has been barred from competition by the USOC in tonight's final with the Soviet Union.

Sources within the multi-billion dollar empire of Ulysees S. Whitman, 81 years old, claim that Mr. Novak was on the payroll, and was "assigned to undermine Soviet bloc competitors" by a variety of clandestine and extra-legal methods.

The FBI is investigating the alleged involvement of the hockey star, 23, in criminal activities ranging from intent to inflict bodily harm to malicious deletion of computer data.

The former accusation was the first to be brought, and led to the investigation. Thursday night, a security guard at Big Chief Ski Area caught Mr. Novak stringing a thin white wire at ankle level across a Nordic ski trail. That particular lane was to be used by the USSR men's ski team at the start of Friday's 4 × 10-kilometer relay.

The New York Times has learned that Mr. Novak is now additionally under suspicion of attempting to sabotage an East German bobsled by loosening bolts. In another assault incident, an athlete narrowly missed injury by a falling icicle which Mr. Novak and an unknown confederate had allegedly dislodged from a dormitory roof.

The FBI is also conducting a preliminary investigation into the tangled business and political affairs of Mr. Whitman, a Nevada millionaire. The Internal Revenue Service is co-operating in the inquiry. Several upper-echelon members of PLAYFAIR, his national sports lobbying group, are undergoing questioning today.

"Novak's advance payment from the slush fund was $50,000," a disgruntled former member of PLAYFAIR told a reporter, "with a bonus for each Communist bloc athlete he could screw up." His sabotage of the Olympic competition was supposedly to have begun last week with tampering of interim scores in luge, figure and speed skating, biathlon, and Nordic combined.

Using sophisticated computer programming knowledge, Mr. Novak, a computer hobbyist or "hacker," allegedly patched into the scoring system with a fraudulently obtained user's code to delete data and replace it with false information. He was believed to have left the leaders' scores untouched, but to have altered slightly those of less conspicuous Eastern bloc competitors who were farther down in the standings.

Over-all rankings would have been affected, as well as crucial competition order in some sports, and next year's team selections in those which use the Olympics as world championships. Data processing officials are working overtime to doublecheck all official results by hand, and state that any erroneous standings will be rectified today.

Mr. Novak is also alleged to have written threatening anonymous notes to several Western athletes he suspected of pro-Soviet sympathies, and to have frightened and harassed one such competitor further with a realistic rubber snake and the falling icicle. Investigation continues into these episodes, in which the competitor's coach may have used some of these bizarre weapons against still another athlete.

The FBI spokesman revealed that the preliminary inquiry has cleared Mr. Novak of any complicity in the mysterious death of USSR skater Dmitri Kuznetsov. "He has well-established alibis for certain important time periods," explained the spokesman.

See related story, page 10, on U. S. Whitman's Olympic lobbying activities and business empire.

I shook my head in amazement. It boggled my mind that Novak would be capable of such encyclopedic sports knowledge and complicated manipulation, considering his primitive political views and redneck grammar. The biathlon's interface of time and marksmanship; luge and speed skating's multiple heats; the Nordic's combination of time, distance, and style; figure skating's translation of numerical scores into ordinals by judges' majorities, then back to numericals—it made my head ache to think about it all.

Reading between the lines, I suspected that the police wouldn't have discovered any more than the wire-stringing episode if Josh hadn't ferreted out the rest from his confidential sources (and extrapolated from the incidents I'd told him about). He had undoubtedly dumped the whole unsavory mess in front of the FBI's noses and insisted on action.

The weather had finally changed, and the sky was filled with ominous slate-gray clouds when I presented myself at the windowless Security Headquarters. Highway Patrolmen, Pinkertons, forest rangers, and local police bustled in and out. The building's austerity was relieved only by portraits of the US president and the FBI director, and by maps bristling with colored pins to mark security placements.

Matt was there too, to my surprise; he didn't know the purpose of the interview either. While we waited, we hashed over the startling revelations of the extent of Bruno's illegal activities.

We finally were shown into a small office with Oglethorpe at the desk, another agent he introduced as Ward Buggins, and a stenographer behind them. On the desk lay a file folder whose label I read upside down. I couldn't help smiling; it actually said ICEKILL.

"Y'all have been going around asking questions," Oglethorpe began. "Why?"

"Have there been complaints of harassment?" Matt asked smoothly.

Buggins said, reading from a list, "Just tell us why you've been questioning Kim Cranford, Elizabeth Cranford, Zachary Higgins, Elinor Rhodes, Zoe McDonnell, Hans-Peter Koenig, Pavel Marchevsky, Mikhail Bogachev, Nikolai Skachko, and others too numerous to enumerate."

"The answer's obvious," I said. "We're trying to find out who killed Dima."

"Do y'all really think amateurs have a better chance than trained investigators?" His tone was patronizing.

"Yes," Matt answered flatly. "And you're the one who implied that some of these people are suspects."

Oglethorpe popped his Juicy Fruit. "If so, a couple of meddlers are likely to tip 'em off and mess up the investigation. Crimes get solved by police routine and tips from informants. Miss Grey, you were publicly accused of cheating and murder on Thursday night."

"Oh, did she mean me?" I asked innocently.

"Miss Aleksandrova states that you were jealous of Kuznetsov's ability," Buggins said, "and that the only way you could have won the gold medal was to make secret deals with the judges. She claims your jealousy led to murder."

Matt let out a short bark of laughter. "Don't tell me you believe this fantasy! It's just sour grapes from an old girlfriend—Lesley wasn't the jealous one. How's she supposed to have offed Dima?"

"If she'd persuaded *you* to do it, y'all both would have come out ahead," said Oglethorpe, with a hard stare at Matt.

"Wasn't Kuznetsov ahead of you in the standings?" put in Buggins. "He'd beaten you consistently over the last several years."

"Very good," said Matt. "I see you've finally done your homework."

"He was a place ahead of you in the compulsories; didn't you think the only way to win was to get rid of him?"

"I won't bother to answer that," said Matt in a bored voice. "How did Lesley manage to persuade me to become a murderer?"

"Y'all have been observed in public displays of affection," said Oglethorpe with a smirk.

"Oh, I *see!* She granted me her favors, which she'd previously reserved for Kuznetsov before he began to play around?" he said tightly.

"That's the truth, isn't it?"

"Oh, for God's sake!" he said in disgust.

"What were you doing this last Wednesday morning, Galbraith?"

"I told you, I was watching the women's giant slalom."

"But no one saw you there; very peculiar. Miss Grey, where were you?"

"I've already told you."

"Just tell us again."

They went on shooting questions alternately for another hour, following no logical sequence, interrupting, going back over and over the same ground. The stenographer stolidly wrote everything down.

At one point, Oglethorpe took me into another room and grilled me about my relationship with Matt. "Come on, you've slept with him, haven't you? It'll make everything a lot clearer if you just admit it." When we came out, Matt's face was flushed and angry; apparently Buggins had been questioning him along the same lines. I was finding it difficult to keep my own temper in check.

"Y'all aren't being very cooperative. We'd like you to take a lie detector test or a sodium pentathol test, Miss Grey. You too, Galbraith."

"What, now? It's noon—we've got practice in an hour, and we've had no lunch."

"No, probably Monday or Tuesday. We've got to bring the equipment and a technician here from Sacramento."

"We're leaving on Monday," I said.

"Don't count on that. It'll take Washington at least a week to analyze the tests."

"But we both have the world championships coming up in just a couple of weeks," I protested. "We must go home with our coaches, or we'll get badly out of shape for competition."

"This is absurd. I want a lawyer," Matt said angrily. "Who's the head honcho here?"

"I am," Oglethorpe said. "Y'all aren't being arrested or charged yet."

"My rights are being violated!"

"That is incorrect."

"Look here," I tried to reason with him. "What about the story the doctor told me? Doesn't that point to the KGB's involvement?"

"Unfortunately, we've been unable to find any evidence to back up that story." He didn't sound very concerned.

"But I told you, my roommate saw the Russians burst into the clinic and take the doctor away!"

"That don't prove a thing."

"There must be a record of the Aeroflot jet leaving Reno Wednesday afternoon."

"It doesn't tell us how he died. The Soviets now claim it was the old head injury that killed him, a—let's see—a subdural hematoma. Not that we necessarily believe them," he added.

"I see," Matt said, biting off his words. "You can't find out anything from the Russians, so you take it out on us. I warn you, push us too hard and we'll take a walk. I still say you're playing fast and loose with our rights. You interrogate us, tail us—"

"That might be for your protection," put in Buggins.

"You've probably tapped our phones and searched our rooms and mail, you've made crude and insulting suggestions about our private lives, and all without a scrap of evidence. I think you're going to have to show cause to a judge."

"Are y'all going to bring charges?" Oglethorpe asked impassively.

"Possibly. Right now, I'm going to have lunch. Coming, Lesley?" The FBI men made no move to stop us.

"Putzi really shouldn't wear French-cut skating pants, with an ass as big as hers," Matt muttered to me. We were sitting in the judges' box at the arena awaiting our turns to practice for the exhibition that would precede the Closing Ceremony the next day. The winners, 4th through 1st place, were to skate in reverse order of finishing, with the gold pairs medalists Katya and Kolya last as always.

I grinned as the hefty German yanked down the brief highcut pants under her skating dress for the third time during her routine. "I think the idea's to make her legs look longer."

"How come you don't have linebacker legs and a big bottom like so many women skaters?" Matt asked. "Some of them have thighs like Eric Heiden. I'm not being sexist, I'm just curious."

"That comes from overpracticing jumps. Some skaters are just un-lucky—they're constantly slimming, but everything they eat turns to muscle and hardens, particularly on their thighs and bums."

"I guess that can happen to men too, but ours don't show. But you've got the best legs here. In fact, the best since—let's see, Tai Babilonia, or Irina Moiseeva of 'Min and Mo.'"

"Oh, you're a non-sexist connoisseur, are you?" I teased.

"I must admit I've always been a leg man." The 4th place pair took over from Putzi and their Streisand ballad began. "Look, there's Mar-chevsky's coach over there, and Pavel isn't around. Let's go talk to him."

We threaded our way through the half-empty house to a group of skaters and coaches on the opposite side near the barrier gate. "Pardon me, Mr. Kisov. Could we speak with you a moment?" I asked.

"*Da*, Bogachev said you wanted ask me questions."

"We're just trying to clear up a few things." Matt lowered his voice. "Would you mind telling us what you were doing on the morning of the Opening Ceremony?"

The coach scratched his head, puzzled. "Why you want to know?"

I missed Matt's excuse because Dany Caron came over and chirped, "*Bonjour*, Lesley. *Félicitations* for your gold medal." She kissed me on each cheek and Jean-Marc did the same, saying, "*Mes compliments.*" It was evidently one of their Be Kind to the British days. They nattered away while I strained to hear Pavel's coach.

I caught: ". . . had a team meeting, I think maybe at ten thirty for an hour or so, then I go to arena to get good seat for ceremony."

"Where was Pavel at that time?"

His answer was drowned out by the Carons' enthusiastic greetings to Katya and Kolya Skachko. For my taste, the twins fawned rather too obviously over the celebrated pair. What arse-kissers they are, I thought, disgusted, and edged a few steps away from the group to re-join Matt. He was saying, "Did you actually see Pavel marching in with the team?"

"I think so. Hard to tell, with all athletes wearing *shapkas* and same coats." We all stepped back to let the bronze medal Russian dancers squeeze by. "Are you working for FBI, you two?" he asked with a laugh.

On the ice, Hans-Peter Koenig had just finished his program. More skaters arrived; some warmed up and others gossiped in the stands.

The boards were draped with their jackets and sweaters. Several had caught the Olympic flu, and kept returning to handkerchiefs in jacket pockets.

"Did you or Pavel ever visit the clinic in the medical building where Dr. Sologubova worked?" I asked Kisov.

"Sure, why not? I went there often, to get ice packs, flu medicine, cortisone, DMSO for muscle pulls. It was for all the Soviet team. Pavel used the jacuzzi in the bathroom for his knee, too."

Matt and I exchanged quizzical glances. We weren't going to find out anything this way; the clinic was too accessible, and the team had used it freely. And asking him directly about the blood would only make him clam up.

"Why did Pavel leak the news about Dima's death?" I asked.

"He didn't know it was secret. He saw all the fuss in the clinic, and told a friend of his, a Hungarian journalist."

We asked him a few more questions, for form's sake, while we watched the Russian dancers' melodramatic tango. Pavel was stroking around the ice to warm up now. I tried to decide what sort of questions might trap him into an admission of knowledge or guilt. Kim Cranford was next to skate her program, and Zack Higgins was standing by the barrier with his usual stone face. She handed him her sweater in a regal manner, like a queen to a lady in waiting.

After Kim finished her routine to "Singin' in the Rain," complete with umbrella, the Carons stepped through the barrier gate onto the ice. The bronze medal-winning dance pair, who had stayed to work out a rough spot in their tango, stopped at the boards to put on skate guards and collect belongings. The man slung a red team jacket over his shoulder and waited for his partner to precede him from the ice.

"I think you have the wrong jacket, Ilya," said Dany helpfully, peering up at him meltingly from under her eyelashes. She never missed a chance to curry favor with famous skaters. "Isn't that Pavel's?"

He gave her a dazzling grin. "You're right, thanks. Oh, there's mine over there."

Matt's hand clutched my shoulder, and my treacherous pulse leapt. Why did he have to be so attractive? "Our shadows are back," he said, nodding across the ice. Two overcoated men stared back at us from the stands. "Do they really think they're inconspicuous in those hats and sunglasses?"

"You know," I said, "they might be some use, on the off-chance that we do learn something valuable, and the real murderer gets the wind up."

"Save us in a blazing gun battle, you mean? If they're anything like Oglethorpe, they'd be more likely to catch us in the crossfire. What really pisses me off," he went on, "is that I thought if we answered their questions honestly, they'd realize we had nothing to hide, and would stop wasting their time on us. But our openness only seems to have made them more suspicious."

"That, as well as neither of us having an airtight alibi for the morning Dima died, even though that's not the time we know the murder was actually done. Probably Bruno's alibi for that day got *him* off the hook. What annoys me is that they won't use our expert knowledge to help sort this thing out. Why must they treat us as enemies?"

"Because they think we did it. We'd better count on those lie detector tests to get us out of this, or our ass is grass." We sat down in the front row and glumly watched the Caron's mirrorskating to the tinkling harp of Debussy's *Danse Sacrée et Danse Profane*.

"I wonder why the FBI's so keen on finding Dima's murderer all of a sudden."

"Pressure from above, I bet—probably from the State Department," said Matt. "And now that Bruno's no longer a murder suspect, the two of us must seem that much more prominent. Say, did you hear who won the fifty-kilometer cross-country skiing Thursday?"

"Yes, some unpronounceable Finn. Anatoli Ivanov was 8th. Missing his extra blood, I expect." I chuckled.

"By the way," Matt said as Dany and Jean-Marc finished with a catch-waist camel spin, "you'll have to do an encore, you know—all the gold medalists do. Have you got something prepared?"

"Thanks to Paula; she remembered to bring along the second tape. It's an exhibition program from last season to 'Dreams,' the old Fleetwood Mac song, for a change from my usual style."

"Speaking of tapes, would you mind keeping this for me while I skate?" He pulled his mini-recorder from his pocket. "I'm next, and I don't like to leave it lying around."

I put it in my handbag. "Taped any good confessions lately?" I teased.

"Jeer at me, Holmes, I expect it." He draped his jacket over the barrier and skated away into an insouciant routine to "Staying Alive."

I wasn't going to tell him how good he was—he already knew it.

When he returned and sprawled next to me, I said, "John Travolta or Robin Cousins?"

"A bit of both. Did you catch my David Santee shimmy?"

"Very sexy. You'll probably inherit Dima's teeny-bopper groupies."

Hans-Peter leaned over my shoulder. "Some of us are going up to the Gold Coast for a drink. You two want to come?"

"Lesley won't be finished for a while yet," said Matt.

"You go ahead with them—I'll catch you up later," I said. "That's the bar up the top of the gondola, isn't it?"

"Yeah. Okay, see you." The two men went off, along with Putzi, Kim, Hiroshi, and both pairs of Russian ice dancers. One of the FBI men followed. I wondered if he'd get right in the gondola with Matt or follow in the next car, in a vain attempt to keep the shadowing surreptitious.

I pulled a paperback out of my bag and started to read while the ice was being resurfaced, then noticed Pavel leaning on the barrier nearby.

"Well, Pavel," I said coolly, "everything turned out as you predicted."

"What you mean?"

"You won the gold. Dima didn't. It's your turn, you're the king now."

"So? I won it square and fair." He gave me a frigid look.

"But Dima would never really have agreed to step aside and let you have it," I pressed him.

"What if he didn't? I would have won anyway."

"So maybe you thought you'd take matters into your own hands. Did you ever look in the refrigerator in the hospital clinic?"

"*Nyet*," he said in a surly voice.

"Did you know about the transfusion Dima was to have?"

"I know nothing! Let me alone!"

"Why'd you tell the journalist he was dead?"

"He is my friend, he's done interviews of me. I wanted to give him exclusive story. Why would I tell him if I had something to hide?" He skated rapidly away, his blades throwing back ice chips.

Why, indeed? I couldn't answer that one. As a sleuth, I made a good skater. Trying to puzzle it out, I watched Nina skate to "Kalinka." She and her coach left immediately afterward, before I could manufacture an excuse to speak to her—apparently she was still "incommunicated." The East German silver medal pair took her place.

I couldn't concentrate on my book and my thoughts kept chasing each other around in the same confused circles. A copy of the new *Paris Match* lay on the bench where the Carons had been sitting, with a cover picture of Dany and Jean-Marc on the podium receiving their bronze medals. I flipped through it idly. There was a feature story on the twins, with photos taken in action on the ice, along with other informal shots.

Something familiar caught my eye and I looked more closely. One flash picture showed Dany chattering vivaciously, sitting on a floral print sofa I recognized. Of course, it had been taken here, in the lounge of the women's dormitory—I remembered the crew of reporters. I saw myself in the picture, a blur in the background crossing the room. There was a gap next to Dany on the sofa, but in another picture Jean-Marc was sitting there beside her. I spotted Angela behind them, out of focus, beading her dress and chatting to the Hungarian dancer.

Pavel, first of the gold medalists, skated his program and began the encore. I tried to remember that evening. It had been the first Wednesday, day of the Opening Ceremony. I'd just visited Dima in hospital and was on my way to my room to change for practice. I had thought I'd seen Dany upstairs in the hall just before finding my room vandalized, but here was proof positive I was mistaken. She had been in the lounge with the journalists the whole time; they'd been leaving when I ran downstairs to call Angela.

It was almost my turn to skate. I crammed the magazine into my overstuffed bag, and went on the ice to warm up with a few laps during Elinor and Brent's jitterbug to "In the Mood." Angela had once explained why so many ice dancers picked forties-era big band music for their free dances: "Great rhythm, and it reminds the judges of their lost youth."

Paula was sitting in the stands, surrounded by young skaters and their parents; evidently business was good. With a gold medal-winning pupil, she was now one of the hottest coaches in the country. Last night an American skater she'd once briefly coached had asked her to stand beside him before his performance, to lend him prestige by association in the judge's eyes. She had it made for the next four years.

My Rachmaninoff exhibition number and the "Dreams" encore went without a hitch. As I skated to Stevie Nicks's plaintive ballad I seemed to hear the lyrics for the first time:

But listen carefully to the sound of your loneliness
Like a heartbeat . . . drives you mad
In the stillness of remembering what you had
And what you lost . . . And what you had . . . And what you lost.

A sudden sharp wave of longing for Dima washed over me. He was gone; when would I get used to it? I would have lost him anyhow, but it shouldn't have been this way. I owed it to him, to what we had, to bring to justice whoever had so wantonly extinguished his life.

I left as Katya and Kolya took the ice and Vivaldi's "Winter" began. The wind was moaning through the pine trees and clouds were piling up, so I went back to my room and changed from my skating dress into jeans. A light snow began to fall, and snowflakes landed on my parka sleeve like miniature lace doilies for an instant before disappearing.

I walked along, deep in thought. The germ of an idea about Dima's death was beginning to form in my mind, made up of unlikely elements. Two team uniforms. A recipe. A skatebag. A bit of history. A medicine. A family joke. A person who should have been somewhere, but wasn't. An object that shouldn't have been somewhere else, but was.

When I reached the gate again, I remembered the Pinkerton guard I'd wanted to question came on duty at 3:00. I looked at my watch: 3:30.

"Excuse me, are you Mr. Flanagan? Weren't you on duty here a week ago Wednesday, the morning of the Opening Ceremony?"

"Yes, Miss Grey. Congratulations on your gold medal. I watched you skate Thursday night. I'm a figure skating fan, and I was really rooting for you."

"Thanks very much. I'd like to ask you some questions. Can you remember anyone you recognized leaving the Village between say, eleven thirty and one that day before the parade? I imagine most of the traffic would have been coming in, to have lunch and get ready for the ceremony."

"Hmm." He rubbed his chin. "Yeah, Dima Kuznetsov, he came out about noon. Looked really pissed off too, didn't say 'hi' as usual. He went into the practice rink over there. That big guy that was always with him, his bodyguard or something, went too, but he came out after a while and went off toward the main arena. Say, was that the day Dima got hurt? I didn't think of it till now."

"Yes, that was the day. Now, did you see anyone else go into the rink after him? His coach or any other Russian officials or skaters?"

"No one like that. Just the French twins."

"Oh, yes? The Carons? Funny, they didn't mention seeing him earlier. They were with me when I found him. What time did they go in?"

"Maybe thirty minutes after Dima. They were dressed for skating."

"And how long did they stay?" I asked.

"I didn't see them come out, but I noticed them in the parade later."

"Are you sure no one else went into the rink?"

"I couldn't really say. I wasn't looking in that direction much of the time. Plenty of people were coming into the Village, and I had to check all their IDs and watch the Friskem—that's the metal detector here. It goes off pretty easy, so then I have to get the people to empty their pockets and go through again."

"I suppose the FBI has asked you all this."

"They didn't ask me anything about Opening Day, just about last Wednesday, the day Dima died. I had to look through stacks of mug shots, Arab-terrorist types."

"Well, I'll talk to the Carons. They might have seen something. Thank you very much indeed."

"Sure thing. Say, could I have your autograph?"

I walked toward the gondola terminus at Olympic House, absently whistling "Dreams" while I had a good think. I had to lower my head against the rising wind. Surely the Carons couldn't be involved. What motive could they possibly have to kill Dima? No, it was ridiculous. Still, it would be a good idea to ask them some questions. Maybe the murderer had come in before they left.

For once, only a few people were waiting in line for the gondola. When I reached the head of the queue, there was no one behind me; I'd have to go alone in the light little four-passenger car, which frightened me even more than the larger tram. The wind gauge on the wall was swinging violently, with gusts pushing it up to 35 and 40 miles per hour. Reluctantly, I looked around for my FBI tail, now lingering back in the doorway, to ask him to keep me company, then caught sight of two familiar faces behind him.

"Hey—Dany, Jean-Marc! Are you going up to the Gold Coast? Come in this car with me." This was my chance to pin them down.

"D'accord," Dany said. We climbed in, the attendant slammed the door, and the gondola jerked into its swaying ascent.

"What a funny coincidence," I said. "I was just thinking I wanted to talk to you."

"And we want to talk to you," said Dany, her smile gone. "We followed you here, in fact. Are you and Matt working for the FBI?"

"Good heavens, no," I said, glancing down and seeing the FBI man get into the next car. "Why do you ask?"

"We heard Kisov mention it," said Jean-Marc.

"We're just asking people the odd question, since the FBI seem to think Matt and I were in some sort of conspiracy to kill Dima. We're trying to find the murderer, because we don't think they ever will."

"And what have you found?"

"Not a great deal. But the guard at the Village gate just told me he saw you two go into the practice rink after Dima on Opening Day," I riposted.

"Is that a crime?"

"Why didn't you tell me that later, when we found him on the ice?"

"Too much confusion," said Jean-Marc.

"We were just there a minute," added Dany. "I was looking for my gloves I'd lost the day before."

"Did anyone else come in?"

"No, I told you we weren't there long enough to see anyone. *Eh bien*, what does it matter?"

"It matters," I said, "because whoever killed him a week later made the first attempt that day."

"*C'est ridicule!*" said Jean-Marc, looking down his long nose.

Suddenly, I remembered Dany saying at the late-night pairs practice that they never wore gloves for skating. A wild surmise entered my mind. Suppose they *had* done it? It seemed that they had had the opportunity for the first attempt, anyway.

I reached into my handbag and pretended to grope for a handkerchief. Matt's mini-recorder was under the magazine; I pushed the red RECORD button, covering the click with a cough. If only the tape didn't need rewinding and the batteries were working, I might be able to trap them in some inconsistency and record something important. I pulled out my handkerchief and wiped my nose, leaving the bag unzipped. The gondola bumped as the cable traveled over a pylon, and Lake Tahoe gradually appeared below on the horizon. Lights winked in the gathering twilight.

I took out the copy of *Paris Match* and found the picture of Dany in the lounge. "Why wasn't Jean-Marc in this picture?" I asked.

"How should I know? I suppose he joined us later."

"No, he must have been there *earlier*. Look here, in this picture with Jean-Marc, there's Angela sewing. In the next one, with you alone, I'm on my way upstairs. About two minutes later I was back, telling Angie our room had been vandalized. You were standing and saying good-bye then. Why did you leave, Jean-Marc, and what did you do?"

"I really don't remember. Do I have to account to you for all my movements?"

I decided to change the subject. "So you didn't go to the rink to practice before the Opening Ceremony?"

"My sister has already said that we did not," said Jean-Marc icily.

I thought back to the appearance of the ice that day. Besides the marks left by Dima's figures and freestyle practice, there had been another kind of tracing, right in the center of the ice. All of a sudden I could see it; it had been stored away in the back of my mind, waiting for me to recognize it. It was a tracing Dima couldn't have made by himself, a wide spiralling circle like the center of a seashell, that could be made only by two pairs of skates. A seashell or a snail's shell—my dream that morning! The clue was there in my subconscious all along. I opened my mouth to speak and found my throat tight with nervousness.

"If you two didn't practice then," I asked, clearing my throat, "why was there a death spiral tracing in the center of the ice?"

"Who says there was?" said Jean-Marc in a belligerent tone.

"I saw it myself, I just didn't remember it till now. But you must know that it's an unmistakable tracing to a skater."

"It was probably put there earlier by some other pair."

"No, Dima called in the Zamboni for layout ice for his patch. Why haven't you told me the truth?" This was my chance to ensnare them in the coils of the listening tape.

"We owe you nothing," said Jean-Marc coldly. "Anyway, why would we want to harm Dima? We admired him very much—he was in the tradition of great Russian skaters."

Russian! Another picture flashed into my mind: Dany batting her eyelashes at Ilya and telling him he had picked up the wrong jacket. She read the Russian name—she could have read the Cyrillic letters on the label of the bag of blood! A violent gust of wind buffeted the gondola. I grabbed the cold plastic seat uneasily. My heart pounded faster.

"Yes, Dima was a great Russian skater," I said, scanning each of their faces in turn. "But he planned to defect to the United States."

"So?" Dany shrugged.

"Did you know that?"

"None of our business," Jean-Marc said. "If he wanted to be so stupid, that was his problem."

"Why is that stupid?"

"He had everything, didn't he? Athletes are privileged in the Soviet Union. He would have been a nobody in this country."

"But he would have been free."

"Free!" Jean-Marc snarled, pushing away Dany's restraining hand on his arm. "Free to join the ice show and make a million dollars. Mountains of gold and oceans of whiskey, *that's* what motivates defectors."

"Why not, if that's what he wanted? As you said, it was his business."

"How did he get to be a world champion? Not by himself!" he said angrily. "His parents are factory workers; could they have paid for his training? If he were born in the West, he never could have become an elite athlete. The State supported him, nurtured him, made him what he was. Was that any way to repay what had been done for him? His skills were the property of the State, and his ambition should have served his community's interests, not propelled him to stardom." His voice rang and echoed in the tiny cabin.

"Jean-Marc, *attention!*" Dany warned him.

"Anyway, he wanted to compete for America, not turn professional," I said, moistening my dry lips. The blood pounding in my ears drowned out the whistling wind.

"That's even worse!" he spat. "Why should the decadent capitalists reap the propaganda benefits of what the Soviet Union had made of him? He was a traitor and a disgrace, all that drinking and sleeping around."

Another piece of the puzzle slid into place: Dany was a medical student. She'd know all about blood-group incompatibility and codeine overdose. My mouth was dry, and my limbs curiously numb. I'd better shut up, I thought; if they've done one murder, they might do another. Nevertheless, with a compelling sense of inevitability, I said, "So you couldn't allow it. So you killed him."

"Don't be absurd," Dany said scornfully. "What possible reason would we have to kill him?"

"I haven't worked it all out yet. But the facts all fit. You were there at the rink and covered it up with a clumsy lie. You must know about transfusion reactions, as a medical student. And earlier today, you gave it away that you can read Russian—you could have read the names and blood groups on the labels. In fact, you're the *only* ones who could have done it! You had the means and the opportunity for both the first attempt and for the murder."

"None of that is evidence you can show to the police."

"I think they'll listen to me. You know, if you were really innocent, you would have asked what blood groups and transfusions I was talking about—that's been kept secret. But why did you do it?"

"What do you care?" Jean-Marc snapped. "He betrayed you as well as his country."

"Jean-Marc! *Silence!* Do not say more," cried Dany. "Of course we didn't do it."

"*Non, chérie,* what does it matter if she knows? She must be on our side. We did her a favor. He'd only have brought her more ridicule and heartbreak."

"You did it for me?" I asked incredulously.

"Certainly not. What does your silly love affair matter to us? We did it for Communism, for the solidarity of the Left," said Jean-Marc complacently.

"Of course. You're Communists," I said flatly. Why hadn't I seen it before? The French Communist Party is the largest and most established in Europe. I didn't even feel surprised; it all made sense.

"*Bien sûr,*" said Dany, resigned. "We always have been. We were sympathizers since childhood, though never Party members. Our family is Communist on both sides, ever since all four of our grandparents were in the Resistance network during the Second World War. Their partisan groups were Communist-led. Their families were killed by the Boche—or by British and American bombings of the factories where they were forced to work. Our parents met and fell in love on the barricades in Paris during the great General Strike of 1968."

Dany went on, the light of fanaticism gleaming in her eyes. "We believe the Soviet Union is France's only true friend, the sole barrier to America or Germany—or both together—taking over the world. Fascist imperialism did not die with Hitler! We have to keep our sympathies hidden from the athletic officials, of course, because they have these silly prejudices. We might not even have been allowed into this country by the FBI. But we don't mind if you know. You're working class, you can understand. And we did hear at one time that you were thinking of defecting to the Soviet Union. You still can, you know, they'd be glad to have you."

"Oh yes, I'm still considering it," I prevaricated hastily. They had to think I was on their side.

"So you understand our reasons?"

"Yes, it would have been such bad publicity for Communism for one of their showcase athletes to repudiate the system so publicly. I do see that."

One of Oglethorpe's questions from our first interview suddenly came back to me: 'Were you ever approached by the Soviet delegation about doing intelligence work for them?' I asked now, "Was this all your own idea, or did the Russians know you were on their side?"

"*Certainement*," said Jean-Marc smugly. "Nokitov suggested our working for them during the tour last year. So we went to Dzerzhinsky Square—that's KGB headquarters—during Moscow Skate, and told them we'd be honored to aid the struggle for socialism in any way we could."

"Then they ordered you to kill Dima?"

"*Mais non*, that was our idea. All we'd done till now was to report who was pro-Soviet in the skating community, which judges could be influenced, who had sexual weaknesses that could be exploited for blackmail, and that sort of thing. Quite a few skaters want to stay in the closet, you know. But what a great blow we've struck for them now! I expect we will be even more well-rewarded when they know the truth." He lolled back in his seat with a grin.

It struck me that they might be in for a surprise. The Canadian in Moscow had told me that everyone there sneered at the naïve European comrades for their idealism. And in killing Dima, they had rather exceeded their brief. No doubt, they'd burned for years to equal the exploits of their grandparents in the Resistance and their parents on the barricades. "But tell me, how did you actually kill him?" I tried to sound admiring, aware that I was skating on very thin ice.

"It was easy," Jean-Marc boasted. "Even before the Olympics began, we heard rumors he was going to defect. He wasn't very discreet, was he? Hopping from bed to bed, and asking each woman to help him. He even tried it with Dany."

"I tried to reason with him afterward, but he wouldn't listen," Dany

218

said. (Afterward? Then he'd betrayed me even more often than I'd known.) "But he guessed from what I said that we were Communists, and I felt sure he would have exposed us. With the neo-Gaullists in power now in France, we'd certainly be barred from competition. He knew too much. And then, another reason for getting rid of him was that Pavel would have a better chance without Dima splitting the pro-Russian vote. We didn't really think Dima could win, and Pavel is a credit to the system. Anyway, the day of the Opening Ceremony, we overheard Bogachev telling Dima he had to practice his figures and quadruple toe loop instead of marching."

"You do speak Russian?" I interrupted.

"*Naturellement*," said Jean-Marc impatiently, "we studied it for years in the *lycée*. We thought it was a perfect chance to give him a warning that day. We went to the rink and practiced for a while to make our being there seem genuine. I did not realize we had left such a distinctive tracing. Dima was doing his patch. Dany started talking to him, flirting a little. He was a pushover for anything in a skirt!"

"What if Fyodor had been there?"

"He was even more of a pushover. While Dima's attention was on Dany, all I had to do was get his right freestyle skate out of his bag and loosen the screws with the screwdriver I always carry in my own bag. I was bent over, behind the barrier, *entendu*. From the ice, it would have looked like I was lacing up my own skates. I had watched him in practice, and I noticed the right was his take-off and landing foot for the quad. And I knew the terrific torque and force of that jump would strain the loose blade to the utmost. The rest was simple—we'd brought our parade uniforms in our skatebags so we could change there and join the parade just outside the Village gate."

"We didn't mean to kill him then," Dany interjected, "just put him out of the running and teach him a lesson. We had to make him stop and think."

"But he didn't even remember your being there," I said. "He thought it was an accident."

"Concussion, of course," said Dany. "We were a little worried about being there when he regained consciousness, but I expected some memory loss. We thought he'd realize later, though, that it was a warning. We learned at the dinner party last Saturday night that he hadn't changed his mind about defecting—Jean-Marc heard him whispering to Zoe McDonnell. And Fyodor was babbling about it; he probably had his suspicions. So we knew then we'd have to kill him.

How else could he be prevented from dealing such a blow to the Soviet Union?"

"*Non*," Jean-Marc said, "first we tried to get him to take that nasal spray with ephedrine—that would have disqualified him for doping. But you stopped that," he said resentfully to me. "If it weren't for you, he'd still be alive. Then we tried to slip codeine into his soup, for the same purpose."

"You did steal it from my room?" I broke in.

"I knew either you or Angie were bound to have it," Dany said with a shrug. "All you British swear by it. And with any luck, it would be traced to you."

"But Angela had only left our room about ten minutes before I arrived that night. And you were downstairs the whole time."

"Use your brain," snapped Jean-Marc. "You're not unintelligent."

I stared at him, then it clicked. "*You* were in my room! But how?"

"Bravo!" he said condescendingly. "That silly guard didn't look twice. She had mixed us up before, so I thought it would work. Rather useful, being twins. Dany had a perfect alibi—and so had I. Nobody expected to see a man upstairs, so nobody saw one. Kim Cranford walked past me in the nude without a second glance. But you came back too soon—you nearly caught me in your room."

I almost had to admire his coolness. "And how did you put the codeine in the borscht?"

"Dany dissolved the tablets in water and put the solution in a little vial I kept ready in my pocket. I sat next to Dima at dinner, he turned to gawk at a pretty girl, and I poured it into his soup. *Et voilà!*"

"But you forgot it would taste bitter," I said. "Dima said it wasn't like his mother's. And Fyodor ended up with an overdose of codeine."

"It didn't matter. If the codeine didn't disqualify Dima, the blood would—permanently. So there was really no alternative to killing him. Anyway, death is the only punishment for treason," Jean-Marc concluded in an eerily matter-of-fact voice.

This can't be happening, I thought. They're mad. They act like murder's perfectly natural and logical. And why are they admitting all this? I suppose they want praise for their brilliant plan, but how can they let me go free? Are they going to kill me too? I pushed the thought to the back of my mind and decided to stall for time. I tried to match Jean-Marc's calmness. "How'd you find out about Dima's blood transfusion?"

"While we were waiting to go through doping control Sunday night after the pairs final, Dany thought of it," he said proudly, encircling his sister with his arm. "There had been no chance to use the codeine yet, and we were getting worried. She remembered passing through the hospital earlier in the week, Tuesday I think, and seeing through an open door Dima having a unit of blood drawn. We were waiting for our doping tests in that little room next to the bathroom where they put the—flow-overs?"

"Overflow," Dany corrected. "I remembered that I had seen Dima in that very room. I looked in the refrigerator—it wasn't even locked —and there they were: all the bags of blood, with Dima's right on top. I would have expected their endurance athletes to have transfusions, of course. Why shouldn't they have every advantage over the capitalists? But it surprised me that Dima did it; he must have felt he was getting too old, or maybe his hemoglobin was low. It was so simple—all I had to do was find a type A, B, or AB. The next bag was Anatoli Ivanov's; he was type A. I merely switched the labels."

"Didn't you care if you killed him too?"

"Don't be ridiculous! Why should I kill Ivanov? Type O wouldn't hurt him at all—Dima was a universal donor. You're a real *bourgeoise*, aren't you?" she giggled, shooting me a look of malice. "Well, it did occur to us that we could kill two birds with one stone. We assumed he'd have the transfusion right before his short program, the day before the women's final. We hoped you would be temporarily deranged by his death—at least until you realized that it was in your best interest—so that you would drop out, or do badly."

"Me? Why did you want me to lose?"

"Nothing personal," she said. "We wanted Aleksandrova to win, of course. If she and Pavel both won, a Soviet sweep of all the gold medals would have been almost a certainty. What marvelous publicity for Communism! Unfortunately, those damned American dancers somehow fooled the judges into giving them the gold."

I looked out the window to see if the nightmare ride would be over soon. But as far as I could tell, we had traveled less than two-thirds of the distance to the top. Far below us, skiers swooped obliviously down the mountain on the day's last run. The holiday atmosphere outside was a surreal contrast to the air of ugly menace and twisted reasoning inside the gondola.

"So that's why you didn't mind not winning the pairs," I said, "since

Kolya and Katya did. Did you tell Nina that I killed Dima?"

"We dropped a hint, yes," said Jean-Marc. "She seems to have done well with it."

"She repeated it to the FBI, with embellishments, after she first brought it up at the press conference, and now they suspect me."

"Don't worry, they will let you go. There's no evidence against you, is there? It will all be forgotten in a few days. Who cares if the traitor's dead?"

His callousness made tears sting my eyes, and I forgot to be careful. "Anyone interested in justice," I said hotly, "and everyone who loved him! A man and woman and little boy in Moscow. His coach, his friends. Everyone he's ever loved, no matter how—temporarily."

"But you—we thought you wouldn't care. You *are* grateful to us for getting revenge, aren't you?" asked Jean-Marc, studying my face closely. Suddenly, I remembered that if they believed I'd turn them in to the FBI, even if it were only my unsupported word against theirs, I was in grave danger. I opened my mouth to assure the twisted pair that I was grateful to them for killing my lover. A loud click punctuated the silence.

"What was that?" Dany grabbed my handbag. The tape recorder was damningly evident under the handkerchief on top of my other paraphernalia. I was well and truly for it now.

"*Merde!* She has taped everything we said! She is an agent of the police!"

"Nonsense!" I cried. "It's not mine, I'm just keeping it for a friend. It's not even running."

Dany turned the little machine over. "I see which friend—your fellow agent!" As a precaution against burglary, Matt had unfortunately engraved his name and address on the back. "I know it was taping, I heard it go off."

"*Tiens*, erase it," said Jean-Marc.

"There isn't time, we'll be at the top soon. I'll just keep the tape and get rid of it later."

"She will call *les flics*, the cops, as soon as she gets out," Jean-Marc argued, "and Galbraith is waiting for her there. We must make it vanish so she has no evidence for her story. There is no other, now that Dima is dead and Fyodor and the blood are gone. I'll throw it out, it'll be smashed on the rocks."

He took the recorder from Dany and pushed at the plexiglass window of the gondola, then at the handle-less door. "*Merde*, the window's jammed. How do you get this door open?"

I told myself to stay calm, against a rising tide of panic. There was no way out, nothing they could do. He couldn't get rid of the tape, and guards or police would surely be at the top.

"Hold her," he snapped. Dany moved across and sat next to me, grabbing my wrists. Jean-Marc slid as far back from the door as he could and began to kick it.

At the third blow, the door flew open. Icy air poured in. The little car twisted and swayed, high above the barren peaks and snowfields. Jean-Marc stood in the doorway and held the recorder outside the car, waiting to pass over the next jagged outcropping of boulders to the place where a chasm yawned.

"No!" I cried. "You won't get away with it! An FBI man's in the next car down, he's seen everything." I lunged for the recorder.

Dany, still holding my wrists, was thrown off balance by the sudden movement. Her full weight caromed into her brother just as a violent gust of wind tilted the car.

Jean-Marc fell out of the open door. I was frozen, too terrified to look. Dany screamed in despair. Then we saw his hands grasping the bottom of the doorframe. He had dropped the recorder and saved himself with a desperate grab.

I dropped to the floor and clutched his wrists, bracing my feet against the wall. "Just pull yourself up, Jean-Marc," I yelled into the howling wind. I saw his terrified face and his legs kicking helplessly in the air, a hundred feet above the rocks. "Come on, it's easy, just like a pull-up," I encouraged him.

He began carefully to hoist himself up. Then Dany shoved me violently. "*Non!*" she screamed to her brother. "She'll push you out, she'll betray you! *I* will save you." She pounded my shoulders and clawed at my face.

"Stop it, you idiot!" I cried. "I won't let him fall. You're smaller than me, you're not strong enough to hold him."

Dany stamped on my hands and strained, squashing me, to grab Jean-Marc's wrists. The gondola swayed with the struggle.

"Please don't, we'll do it together," I panted, trying to hang on. A vicious kick in the ribs sent me sprawling to the other side of the car and banged my head against the seat.

Dany knelt in the doorway and wriggled her hands into

223

Jean-Marc's. "*Viens, mon frère,*" she crooned. "You've always lifted me, *chéri,* now I lift you." I watched, dazed from the blow. My head was ringing, and black spots chased each other in front of my eyes.

Jean-Marc's hands grasped Dany's, as the wind again tossed the car and slammed the door repeatedly against him. She strained to hold him, as his weight slowly pulled her down till she lay full-length on the floor with her arms dangling outside. The wind tilted the gondola at an acute angle. Dany slid forward. In an instant she was gone.

I hung onto the doorframe, transfixed in horror. Down they fell, clasping one another in a deadly embrace. Their shrieks of terror were cut off as the rocks a hundred feet below received their last death spiral.

L'important aux Jeux Olympiques n'est pas gagner,
mais y prendre part. L'essential n'est pas conquerir,
mais bien lutter.

(The important thing in the Olympic Games is not the
winning, but the taking part. Life is not the triumph,
but the struggle.)
—attributed to Baron Pierre de Coubertin

"In the name of the International Olympic Committee, I offer to the
people of the United States and to the Organizing Committee of
Squaw Valley our deepest gratitude. I thank the competitors, officials,
spectators, the media and all those who have contributed to the success of these Games. . . ."

Mutzenbecher stood on the arena's rostrum, the flagbearers before
him in a semicircle. The skating champions had performed our exhibition. The Greek, American, and Italian flags had been raised and their
anthems played. All the other flags hung at half-staff on their poles.
Once again the athletes were lined up, but this time we were intermin-

gled "without distinction of nationality, united only by the friendly bonds of Olympic sport." Many of them now wore uniforms of countries not their own, because of the traditional trading on the last day of the Olympics. Suitcases were half-packed, and Eastern Europeans had filled bags with California fruit unobtainable at home.

My hand gripped Matt's. I was remembering how I'd searched for Dima only 12 days ago in this very place, unaware that he was lying in a pool of his own blood in the skating rink, the victim of fanaticism. I'd already lost him, but I hadn't known it yet. I lost myself for a while, too.

A shudder shook me, and Matt put a comforting arm around my shoulders. I still had icy chills every time I recalled the horrifying events in the gondola car. The ski patrol had recovered Jean-Marc's and Dany's broken bodies and brought them down in the tram. Thank God, they found the tape recorder intact in the snow. It verified my story, as did the FBI agent who had witnessed the struggle through binoculars from the next car.

"It was the sister who accidently knocked Caron out the door in the scuffle," the agent reported to Oglethorpe. "Miss Grey did everything she could to pull him back in, but that crazy Frenchwoman fought like a wildcat. You can see the bruises and scratches." He indicated my battered face.

"I've listened to the tape, and I want to commend your courage and resourcefulness, Miss Grey," said Oglethorpe pompously. "You really kept your head and played it just right, the way you led them into that confession."

"And are you satisfied that the murder is solved?" I asked.

"The case is closed. I always thought there was something suspicious about those froggies. Say, you must have been scared to death alone with those two. You're a brave little girl." He clumsily patted my shoulder.

"If only I'd been there with you!" Matt lamented, later on Saturday evening. He was missing the US-USSR hockey final to be with me, and we were in his room. "I'm sick when I think of the danger you were in."

"If you had been there, probably nothing would have happened and we'd still be under suspicion," I pointed out. "The Carons never would have confessed in front of a witness. They were crazy enough to think I'd be on their side, but they didn't trust you. And without the tape, it would have been only my unsupported word against theirs."

"That's so, we still wouldn't be any the wiser. At least now the truth is out. But it must have been such a nightmare for you."

"But I survived, more or less unscathed. If only I hadn't tried to grab the tape recorder. . . ."

"You should *not* feel any guilt over their deaths," he said emphatically.

"It's hard not to feel a bit responsible. But it was so flukey and accidental—it all happened so fast. I was afraid the police would think I'd pushed Jean-Marc, or both of them. If only Dany had been reasonable! She went absolutely berserk. There's no way she could have held him; she was eight inches shorter than me, and at least two stone lighter. He could have pulled himself up if she hadn't grabbed his hands."

"I don't think Dany could have survived without Jean-Marc. They were almost like one person with a split personality."

"Fanatics in that, as in everything else," I said, shaking my still-aching head. "I should have guessed long ago that they were Communists."

"How?"

"There were a lot of clues, if I'd only put them together earlier. The way they always favored the Russian athletes and ran down all the others. Their family background they mentioned at the dinner party; not all the rebellious students in the sixties dropped back into the *bourgeoisie.* I should have remembered Dany was a medical student as soon as I learned about the transfusion and the codeine. I was there when Jean-Marc offered Dima the medicine that would have disqualified him on doping. And that first day, when they left the practice rink after the doctor took Dima away, they were carrying their skatebags, which they'd hidden there earlier with their skating clothes inside. That should have been a red flag."

"Neither of us noticed that," he said, "though there would have been no reason to carry them in the parade, and in fact they didn't have them earlier."

"At La Vieille Maison, Jean-Marc was so busy eavesdropping on Dima and Zoe talking about defection that he ignored everyone else. I just thought he had bad manners. And when Dany slipped up at practice today and showed she could read that Russian name, I should never have got in that gondola with them."

"All those millions of dollars the organizing committee spent on security," Matt said ironically, "—the SWAT team, the nuclear detection device—and the terrorists were inside the whole time. What I can't figure out is why Jean-Marc didn't stomp on the tape recorder; that would have ruined it just as effectively."

"He said he wanted to get rid of any tangible evidence. I suppose he thought it would never be recovered at the bottom of that crevasse he was aiming for. Or maybe he was just given to flamboyant gestures. Perhaps he was going to throw me out next." I shuddered.

"Thank God you're all right. The thought of losing you like that—!" He jumped up and began to pace around the room. "I wasn't going to say anything yet but I can't help it, I have to. I'm in love with you." He sat down by me and took my hands, gazing longingly into my eyes. "I love you very much."

"Why weren't you going to tell me?" Here it was, and I wasn't ready for it.

"Because Kuznetsov's only been dead a few days, and you've been through a hell of an ordeal. How can you possibly know how you feel? I don't want to put any pressure on you." He kissed my hand gently.

"That's what I thought, and I'm grateful."

He lay back again and stared at the ceiling, his arms folded across his chest as if to keep them from embracing me.

"You're right," I went on. "I don't know how I feel yet, though I'm sure you can tell I like you a lot, and I'm very attracted to you. I value your respect for my independence, too. . . . I made a fool of myself over Dima, and I still have a strange mixture of feelings for him: bitterness, pity—and still some love, I suppose. He *was* my first love, after all. I need time to get over him and regain my self-respect. Can you give me a while to sort things out?"

"All the time you need. Will I see you at Worlds in Geneva?" he asked hopefully.

"Of course. It would be rather letting the side down not to compete, wouldn't it? Since the winners determine how big the team is next year, I mean. Anyway, I want to trounce Kim and Nina again."

"And after that?"

"Paula's already got some offers from shows for me, and she's found an agent to negotiate them. Whichever show I sign with after Worlds, I'll be based in New York City for over a year, then up at Oxford, I hope. Will you be back at Columbia next autumn?"

"You bet. Maybe I can even get a Rhodes scholarship to Oxford the year after. So we might have lots of time together. I won't rush you, but just keep in mind that I want you. Almost as much as I love you."

"I don't think you'll have to wait too long, you know." I smiled at him and tenderly touched his cheek. "I think we can be comrades as well as lovers. We'll have good times. . . ."

"The IOC would like to call for a moment of silence," Mutzen-becher was saying, "out of respect for those athletes who tragically lost their lives during these Games. We remember now: Vincent Luciano . . . Dmitri Kuznetsov . . . Danièle Caron . . . Jean-Marc Caron."

In the cold stillness, the only sound was flags flapping in the wind. I gazed up at the Olympic flag with its black mourning band. The five rings blurred. "Good-bye, Dima," I whispered.

"And now I declare the XVIth Olympic Winter Games closed, and in accordance with tradition, I call upon the youth of all countries to assemble four years from now at Cortina d'Ampezzo, Italy, there to celebrate with us the XVIIth Olympic Winter Games."

The scoreboard lit up: WE'LL MEET AGAIN IN CORTINA. The twin Olympic flames, which would be forever linked in my mind with the Caron twins, began slowly to die.

"*The fire returns to the sun* . . ." Matt murmured.

"What?" I whispered.

"It's that poem from the end of the *Tokyo Olympiad* movie we saw the other night. It goes on something like: *For mankind dreams thus only once every four years / Is it then enough for us / This infrequent, created peace?*"

"That's lovely, but unreal. These Olympics weren't very peaceful, were they?"

A five-gun salute boomed across the valley, as if ironically to underscore my words. The honor guard, members of the gold medal-winning US hockey team, lowered the Olympic flag and carried it away. Even without Vinnie and Bruno, they had come from behind to beat the Russians 5–4 last night.

The Marine Band played the Olympic Anthem for the last time, then segued into the Rolling Stones as fireworks and laser beams lit the darkening sky. Some of the athletes started dancing. Rhythmic gymnasts in the center of the oval swirled ribbons, banners, and hoops.

"Oh look, Matt—how beautiful!" I exclaimed. The audience were all lighting matches, and the arena seemed full of fireflies, flickering in the dusk.

Reluctantly, the athletes finally began to disband. A few die-hards kept a snake dance going, with shouts of "USA!" and "We beat the Russians!"

"I suppose these Games were as peaceful as most," said Matt. "Remember? We decided the Olympics wouldn't happen at all without nationalism, so political dissension seems to be inevitable. Murder just carries it to its logical extreme."

"Dissension's not always inevitable. Just look around." I gestured toward the boogieing, back-slapping, hugging army of athletes. "I see plenty of international good will and understanding here. It *is* possible —just look at the two of us."

"Jim McKay said it best," said Matt. "'The Olympics are more hope than history.'"